Evelyn Waugh was born in Hampstead in 1903, second son of Arthur Waugh, publisher and literary critic, and brother of Alec Waugh, the popular novelist. He was educated at Lancing and Hertford College, Oxford, where he read Modern History. In 1928 he published his first work, a life of Dante Gabriel Rossetti, and his first novel, *Decline and Fall*, which was soon followed by *Vile Bodies* (1930), *Black Mischief* (1932), *A Handful of Dust* (1934) and *Scoop* (1938). During these years he travelled extensively in most parts of Europe, the Near East, Africa and tropical America, and published a number of travel books, including *Labels* (1930), *Remote People* (1931), *Ninety-Two Days* (1934) and *Waugh in Abyssinia* (1936). In 1939 he was commissioned in the Royal Marines and later transferred to the Royal Horse Guards, serving in the Middle East and in Yugoslavia. In 1942 he published *Put Out More Flags* and then in 1945 *Brideshead Revisited*. *When the Going was Good* and *The Loved One* preceded *Men at Arms*, which came out in 1952, the first volume of 'The Sword of Honour' trilogy, and won the James Tait Black Memorial Prize. The other volumes, *Officers and Gentlemen* and *Unconditional Surrender*, followed in 1955 and 1961. *The Ordeal of Gilbert Pinfold* appeared in 1957, the *Life of Ronald Knox* in 1959 and *A Little Learning*, Waugh's last book and the first volume of a projected autobiography, in 1964. Evelyn Waugh was received into the Roman Catholic Church in 1930 and his biography of the Elizabethan Jesuit martyr, *Edmund Campion*, was awarded the Hawthornden Prize in 1936. For many years he lived with his wife and six children in the West Country. He died in 1966.

Waugh said of his work: 'I regard writing not as investigation of character but as an exercise in the use of language, and with this I am obsessed. I have no technical psychological interest. It is drama, speech and events that interest me.' Mark Amory called Evelyn Waugh 'one of the five best novelists in the English language this century', while Harold Acton described him as having 'the sharp eye of a Hogarth alternating with that of the Ancient Mariner'.

Richard Jacobs was brought up in north London and read English at Oxford University, where he gained First Class Honours and studied Waugh's satire in postgraduate research. He subsequently taught for many years in secondary and tertiary education, including six years as Head of English at the College of Richard Collyer in Horsham. He has contributed articles and reviews to many periodicals, is the author of 'The Novel in the 1930s and 1940s' in Volume 7 of *The Penguin History of Literature: The Twentieth Century*, and has also edited Waugh's *Vile Bodies* for Penguin. He now divides his time between writing and lecturing.

EVELYN WAUGH

The Ordeal of Gilbert Pinfold

A CONVERSATION PIECE

Edited with an introduction by
RICHARD JACOBS

PENGUIN BOOKS

PENGUIN BOOKS

Published by the Penguin Group
Penguin Books Ltd, 27 Wrights Lane, London w8 5TZ, England
Penguin Putnam Inc., 375 Hudson Street, New York, New York 10014, USA
Penguin Books Australia Ltd, Ringwood, Victoria, Australia
Penguin Books Canada Ltd, 10 Alcorn Avenue, Toronto, Ontario, Canada M4V 3B2
Penguin Books (NZ) Ltd, Private Bag 102902, NSMC, Auckland, New Zealand

Penguin Books Ltd, Registered Offices: Harmondsworth, Middlesex, England

First published by Chapman & Hall 1957
This edition published in Penguin Books 1998
2

Text copyright © Evelyn Waugh, 1957
Introduction and Appendix copyright © Richard Jacobs, 1998
All rights reserved

The moral right of the editor has been asserted

Set in 10.5/12.5pt Postscript Baskerville
Typeset by Rowland Phototypesetting Ltd, Bury St Edmunds, Suffolk
Printed in Great Britain by Antony Rowe Ltd, Chippenham, Wiltshire

CONTENTS

INTRODUCTION

The Ordeal of Gilbert Pinfold is Evelyn Waugh's last comic novel. He might have suspected and even, perhaps, intended that; but he would not have intended it to have been his last, discrete novel of any kind, which is what it turned out to be, nine years later when Waugh died at the early age of sixty-three.

Pinfold arrived at a difficult and intriguing time in Waugh's career – and time, career and intrigue are anxious issues in the novel. As intimated both at its outset and its close, it was written during the composition of an apparently more significant, major project (the *Sword of Honour* trilogy): interrupting the rather lack-lustre work on the latter also helped to hasten its completion. In nice coincidence, a few years earlier, a very different writer had negotiated an equivalent process with a trilogy of novels (*Molloy, Malone Dies, The Unnameable*) that, also at the two-thirds point, was proving difficult. *Waiting for Godot* was written as a relaxation during Beckett's painful progress with his masterwork. *Pinfold* is subtitled, as if equivalently, a 'conversation piece', the suggestion being that serious critical scrutiny would be wasted on it. After *Pinfold*, and the third volume of the trilogy (*Unconditional Surrender*), Waugh wrote nothing of substance – apart from the first volume of a projected autobiography and a dutiful biography of Ronald Knox. But *Pinfold*, as is designedly obvious to all readers, is autobiographical in a much more anxious way. Indeed, the issue of autobiography in *Pinfold* is so vexed – at once transparent and opaque – that it might be better to return to it after considering the novel itself.

Gilbert Pinfold, a Catholic novelist of fifty, enjoying both critical and popular esteem, living in some comfort but not much affluence with his large family in quiet rural surroundings, undergoes an 'ordeal'. Worried by ill-health, insomnia and increasingly frequent signs of instability of mind (only some of which he recognizes himself), Pinfold, armed only with sleeping-draughts and writing-materials, joins a cruise to the tropics. On board the *Caliban* he is tormented by what seem to be a number of practical jokers manipulating what, at first, Pinfold supposes are the ship's communications systems and what he later 'discovers' to be a fearsome implement designed to effect psychological damage. He manages to trace the source of torment to a fellow-passenger called Angel (who works for the BBC and who, Pinfold has reason to believe, holds him a grudge), his odious wife (whom Pinfold calls Goneril) and his sister Margaret (reluctantly in the 'game', as she calls it: reluctant because amorously attached to its victim). Unable to get help from the *Caliban*'s Captain Steerforth, Pinfold abandons his voyage, fights back against his tormentors with threats of disclosure and recrimination and, when Angel, rattled, apologizes and proposes a deal, Pinfold bravely (his wife's word) refuses it and proceeds towards home. Only at the reunion with his wife does he realize, as the reader has realized more or less from the start (for the novel makes no attempt at deception of that kind – quite the opposite in fact) that the voices had been self-generated, the ordeal internal, the journey to the tropics of his own interior life. At that point the voices cease and Pinfold is left to enjoy the 'victory' and 'triumph' (his words) which are confirmed in the act of writing it all up – as a 'conversation piece', with the title the reader has begun with.

Put like that, we might be struck by how very literary this all seems. (A foreign lady on board the *Caliban* announces to other travellers her belief that Pinfold will 'make notes of us. You see, we shall all be in a humorous book'.) And that assessment would be right ('seems' is a word that will repay examining later). The critical notion of intertextuality (whereby texts are recognized as circulating fragments or versions of other texts through their own signifying systems, usually in the colder currents below their conscious purposes) appears to have been turned blandly upside down, ('blandly' is one of a number of harmless adverbs marvellously detonated during the course of the novel), for the innards of this novel, the references to and points of contact with literary antecedents, lie open for inspection.

From the outset the reader is confronted with two evidently literary features: the novel's title and its chapter headings. This title is chosen to evoke Meredith's *The Ordeal of Richard Feverel* – a mid-Victorian novel, the first of many written more or less 100 years before *Pinfold* to be evoked in the course of the text – whose opening gesture is a betrayal (of a husband by his wife) and which then concerns itself with the need of a son to come to terms with an oppressively interfering father. (Meredith worked as a reader for Chapman & Hall, Waugh's father's firm and Waugh's own publishers.) The chapter headings, prominently displayed in a determinedly pre-modern way on a Contents Page (omitted from the previous Penguin edition), lead the reader in variously high/lowbrow fictive directions – from Joyce to Milton via *Punch* and the *Boy's Own Paper* – and their cumulative effect is to suggest a kind of literary maze, in which readers might be teased into taking the misleading turn, thereby to misassess the book's purposes.

There is also the notion of the allegorical journey, to the extreme or the edge in search of self-knowledge, a familiar enough high-literary formula, from Bunyan (and Everyman before him), through *King Lear*, to Defoe and Swift, and on to Conrad, Mann and beyond – to, for instance, Waugh's own *A Handful of Dust*. The uses of Shakespeare need little labouring. 'Caliban' and 'Goneril' push the reader in clear enough directions, and Margaret is a 'sort of Cordelia' (Cordelia is also the charming younger sister in Waugh's *Brideshead Revisited*). Pinfold is the magician trapped inside his own monster (*The Tempest*), and/or he is the king/parent/earl driven mad/blind by his own offspring/guest (*King Lear*). Just as well signposted are 'let me not be mad, sweet heavens', 'then he saw light' and less elaborate examples like Pinfold being described (twice) as 'baffled'. Malvolio, a very relevant antecedent, is baffled ('alas, poor fool! How have they baffled thee!') by the practical joking in *Twelfth Night*; Goneril is christened by Pinfold when he hears her say 'tie him to the chair' ('Mr Pinfold at once thought of *King Lear*') and there she is referred to as the Captain's 'leman', an almost grotesquely literary word, used by Shakespeare only three times, once in *Twelfth Night*.

Angel directs the reader in two directions: towards Hardy (Tess's Angel drives her to abandonment and despair) and towards the angels at the heavenly gates inquiring of the state of the dead man's soul (the Angels interrogate Pinfold equivalently). With bright young things (apparently) on board along with the Angels, a sly look towards Waugh's own *Vile Bodies* (which opens with young things and a troupe of angels together on board ship) seems intended. The joke about Margaret's portability ('was she portable? he wished he knew her dimensions') may also evoke the often-derided passage in *Brideshead* where Charles, on board a ship (and shortly after comparing himself to King Lear), 'took formal possession of her as her lover . . . as I was made free of her narrow loins (that is, he sleeps with Julia Flyte for the first time). The portable joke may also pay a debt to Wodehouse, who'd used it twenty years earlier ('one of the things I like about you is that you are so slim, so slight, so slender, so – in a word – portable').[1] Dickens and Conrad are together implicated: the novel must have *Heart of Darkness* in its ancestry, if only via another H of D, Waugh's *A Handful of Dust* where the hero, wounded by betrayal, journeys into the darkness only to find himself condemned to read Dickens to a madman. Steerforth is the Dickens idol who painfully betrays the hero. At one point Steerforth doubles, in Pinfold's troupe of performers, as Hamlet's 'treacherous' uncle and at another Pinfold notes that the hooligan Fosker has 'something in him of the dissolute law students and government clerks of mid-Victorian fiction'.

T. S. Eliot is, as often in Waugh, a shadowy presence. *A Handful of Dust* borrows its title from *The Waste Land* and Eliot's 'The Hollow Men' has Conrad's 'Mr Kurtz, he dead' as epitaph. Waugh's Dickens-obsessed Todd (=death) is a Kurtz (=brevity) figure. Another Eliot epigraph cites a Dickensian ventriloquist from *Our Mutual Friend* (who did the Police 'in different voices'); the mad Todd can't read and has to hear the Dickens voices read to him; Kurtz is, above all (perhaps only), a powerful voice; Pinfold's madness is having to hear an orchestrated ventriloquism of voices (but he gets some revenge by monotonously reading mid-Victorian fiction – Kingsley's *Westward Ho!*, a tale of derring-do on the seas, which takes its title from Malvolio's play – back at them).

Eliot is also one of a number of sources evoked when a pseudo-elegiac/epic note is struck, the literary reference as much in the generalized rhythmic suggestiveness as in the wording. (Before his ordeal the sleepless Pinfold would routinely 'lie in the dark dazzled by the pattern of vocables'.) 'But all was not well with him' strikes echoes from the 'all shall be well' refrains in the *Four Quartets*; 'and now his mind became much overcast' deploys the archaic phraseology that might belong to a Victorian plot-summary of *King Lear*; 'there were no funeral obsequies, no panegyric; no dirge on board the *Caliban* that night' is sonorously consoling in the tradition of that most unmemorable of imperial poems *The Burial of Sir John Moore*, dinned into schoolboys of Pinfold's (and later) generations ('not a drum was heard, not a funeral note . . .'). More distantly echoed in the passage are the deaths of Little Nell (that paradigmatically mid-Victorian demise) and (another wistfully unavailable daughter) of Ophelia.

If *Pinfold* evokes a tissue of texts, Pinfold himself is most signally like another voyager into the dark from a very different text, one that appeared in paperback translation two years before the novel (and a few months after the experiences the novel deals with): von Aschenbach, in Mann's *Death in Venice*. Aschenbach, too, is the artist famed for cool craftsmanship, driven by forces and into extremities both hitherto repressed. The baiting voices on board the *Caliban* accuse Pinfold of being homosexual and of wearing make-up: they tempt him with the idea of sexual desirability to visit the barber and then they mock the result. It's remarkable how this evokes Aschenbach, whose doomed quest for his boy-love leads him to a barber who temptingly makes him up. There is a sense in which Aschenbach and Malvolio are the presiding absences in the novel (as Lear is its presiding presence: Pinfold's name, after all, features in an unexplained moment of abuse in *King Lear*).[2] Malvolio is tormented, in his dark house, by voices taunting him with the notion that he is mad: he thinks there are many voices but it's Feste, a resourceful impersonator, like Angel. Frustrated and ill-recognized status, unexplored desire and delusions of vanity, the unexpected vulnerabilities and terrors of middle-age – they shadow the novel with these defensively literary versions of recognition.

Why so extensive and overt this deployment of other texts? The effect is of daring the reader to refuse belief, to conclude that the very literariness of this text-saturated text must, indeed, be a matter of make-up, a parodic recycling of elements in a formulaic allegorical design. Just a text, a fiction – a 'game' as Margaret insists. The use of words like 'triumph' at the novel's close dares the same scepticism: how can it be a triumph over the torments of madness merely to refuse to do deals with them? Madness can't be routed like Alice scattering the playing cards at the end of *Wonderland* and waking up (Pinfold's voices disappearing is phrased in such a way – 'the thin grating of a slate-pencil . . . a whisper, a sigh, the rustle of a pillow' – as to evoke the end of the Alice books, as it is earlier when Pinfold refers to the 'half world into which he had stumbled'; the books were long favourites of Waugh's), and nor can we really be expected to think so – though that seems to be the intention when Pinfold blurs into Waugh at the end.

The unstated challenge is this: this is what happened to me, I don't care if you don't believe me, so I'll make it seem as fictive and unbelievable as I like. The suggestion is that this need to test our belief, as somehow the novel's function (something for us to make a 'conversation' of), is a symptom of a crisis of more fundamental belief elsewhere – in the author's roles as writer, citizen, family-figure, Catholic. The text supplies evidence (without our needing recourse to Waugh's biography) of a character beset by a sense of roles having solidified over the unitary self, masks grown into the features, fictiveness literalized. The 'ordeal' takes the literalizing process one stage further: Pinfold will be literally tormented by literariness. It will be the revenge of the craft on the craftsman, which, of course, is another literary story, that of Pygmalion or Frankenstein.

Two pages from the end is a passage that is symptomatic of this challenge. Pinfold wonders why the tormenting voices attacked him with 'such a lot of rot' and the narrator comments: 'Mr Pinfold has never understood this; nor has anyone been able to suggest a satisfactory explanation.' This awkward, troubled moment at once insists that this stuff is just fiction and there's no point pursuing the matter any further (haven't I given you enough intrusive stuff anyway?); suggests that for Pinfold, if not necessarily his readers, there may be good reason not to find satisfactory explanations; and, in closing off further investigation, is evasive just at the point where the issue of autobiography is explicitly breached. The phrasing (not 'Pinfold never did . . . nor was anyone able . . .') breaks the fictive illusion (the change of tense suddenly foreshortens the distance between narrator and narratee), at the moment where it's also refusing to admit the possibility of non-fictive explanation. The ending works in the same way.

2

Nothing in the above can yet account for *Pinfold* being such an oddly compelling text, the most sheerly interesting of Waugh's later novels. To turn to that is to return to its fictive surface. For *Pinfold* is a dazzling verbal construct. If its intertextual energies serve ambiguous purposes, as suggested above, its wordplay counterpoints the novel's linear unfolding of narrative detection and discovery. The wordplay unfolds a double narrative of knowing and unknowing that teases both at the illusions of the narratee's fantasies and at the narrator's acquiescences in the process of illusion.

Enormously elaborate wordplay on notions of seeming and conceit is one way of describing the novel. Phrases like 'it seemed', 'it appeared', 'presumably', 'he supposed/surmised', 'it occurred to him' and 'not/scarcely/just conceivable' are, at once, the balanced, equable, judicious, even orotund tricks of style of a writer in a silver-age, craftsman tradition ('notable for elegance and variety of contrivance') as ruefully attested to on the first page (the novel's opening gesture is a fastidiously qualified 'it may happen . . .'), and, through a muted re-energizing of those dead clichés, a way of nudging the reader towards the notion that Pinfold's mind is quietly but feverishly working away to bemadden him.

'It' (indeed) does, or should, only 'seem', 'or appear'; the presumptions, surmises and suppositions are precisely, and only, just those; ideas have the habit of occurring, because the brain, and not events, run on. And there is bewilderingly inventive potential in what the brain can conceive, in its conceits. At its simplest, the paranoia-symptom of hearing oneself endlessly discussed (especially in the figments of love) is a product of uncertain self-conceit, but lurking also in the notion of what is 'conceivable' is conceit in its seventeenth-century poetry sense: the freeplay of figuration in bringing unlikenesses (like Pinfold and his inventions) together. It's as if clues are being dropped (as in the best signposted of reader-friendly mysteries, from Agatha Christie – Waugh's favourite for light reading at this time – to *Emma*) but in the form, not of incriminating objects, but of misleadingly appropriate or illuminatingly inappropriate phrases ('this . . . recalled him to strict reason'; 'then he saw light') or single words – often adverbs, where Waugh was always lethal (Pinfold asks about an 'accident' he 'heard' the night before which, he thinks, incriminates Steerforth: ' "No one told me of one," said Captain Steerforth blandly') – and the effect is of muted detonations in the creamy, unruffled surface of the prose.

Shortly after joining the cruise, Pinfold thinks he overhears a 'very curious scene being played near him'; a sermon, evangelical 'it seemed', was being 'addressed presumably to members of the crew', one of whom is then quizzed about girlie pictures by his bunk. His name is Billy; given the nature of the charge – 'have you been impure, Billy?' – the literary joke is presumably at the expense of *Billy Budd, Sailor*, another allegorical journey. 'Mr Pinfold was horror-struck. He was being drawn into participation in a scene of gruesome indecency.' Trying to account for the incident, Pinfold reasons the presence of 'religious mania perhaps on the part of one of the officers'; and 'the *Caliban*, plainly, was equipped' to transmit accidentally into his cabin.

Words like 'seemed', 'presumably' and 'perhaps' chip away a little at the fictionalizing, over-worked mind; 'scene' and 'part' suggest its play-writing inclinations; 'plainly' is poignant because, like 'knew instinctively' later, it's plain enough that this comes all too instinctively. When Pinfold's cabin is then invaded by the noise of jazz – appropriately enough, even predictably, given the novel's opening gesture of listing Pinfold's abhorrences, jazz being among them: the music apparently relayed by the on-board bright young things (the revenge of or on *Vile Bodies*?) – he suggests to himself that their rhythms were perhaps derived from some primitive tribe. 'This guess was confirmed.' The confirmation takes the form of hearing the 'young man who acted, without any great air of authority, as leader' asking the others to try the 'Pocoputa one'. Without any great air of authority – and where, and yet where else, would the author[iz]-ing come from?

This fictionalizing habit might be illustrated in another inventive bit of authoring where Pinfold's mind elaborates on, and he goes in literal search of, the military gentlemen he thinks he has been hearing. 'He had formed a clear idea of their appearance' and a whole paragraph of summary biography ('they had served loyally in offices, done their turn at fire-watching, gone short of whisky and razor-blades') is then confidently supplied, doubly fictional histories (they might have done, might indeed have already been done, for use in Waugh's war trilogy). The pathos is sharp when the paragraph punctures itself with this last sentence: 'he did not find them on deck or in any of the public rooms.' Formed a clear idea – that carries the sting, but the pathos is additionally in the frustrated search for confirmation, not only of a sanity but of a mere companionability, even if only among perceived enemies. It's the need for the friendliness of fiction – and it's poignantly sensed as a chance to demonstrate 'his duty', for the duty of a novelist, but not of a soldier, is, after all, to invent.

A series of clues about the improbabilities of bad fictions tease at the improbability of the reader (but not Pinfold) failing to notice their suggestiveness. Pinfold has to witness a 'scene which might have come straight from the kind of pseudo-American thriller he most abhorred' (thus, like jazz, an appropriate torment) and to be the 'solitary audience' of a scene which 'had it appeared behind footlights on a real stage, [he] would have condemned . . . as grossly overplayed' (an almost exact version of Fabian's 'if this were played upon a stage now, I could condemn it as an improbable fiction' in *Twelfth Night*); later the general's diction became 'strangely Celtic as sentiment overpowered' him into mouthing the vacuities of sentimentalized deep-country-speak.[3]

Another series of clues derive from Pinfold's own biographical data, wittingly scrambled into the conspiracy. Margaret's mother spoke in 'yearning tones that reminded Mr Pinfold of his deceased Anglican aunts' and Margaret herself, in her 'fervent' love, 'reminded him of the letters which used to come two a day' from besotted fans of his novels; Pinfold, in a scene already mentioned, tries to torment the tormentors by relentless readings of *Westward Ho!*: this revisits an early, casual observation that his 'most disagreeable' dream was of 'reading a tedious book aloud to his family' (the clue being the dream connection).

But most dazzling are clues/jokes of this kind: 'as though in response to these thoughts the device overhead clicked into life'; or 'it was the general who voiced the thought uppermost in Mr Pinfold's mind'. During a particularly ill-tempered onslaught from his tormentors, he learns that 'he was a reincarnation (Mr Pinfold, not they, drew the analogy) of the "new men" of the Tudor period who had despoiled the Church and the peasantry'. That's a neatly (un)disguised parenthesis. For the author is, after all, likely to be a better historian, to have the analogy quicker to hand (or mind), than the hooligan.

The 'elegance and variety of contrivance' in this deployment of clues call modest attention to themselves in the craftsmanship tradition and seem part of a process whereby issues which might be thought more pressing, like the manipulation of sympathy, call for less or no attention. But the novel has been deft in the elliciting of sympathies and the source of such pathos is the way the narrative calmly, blandly agrees with, colludes with the fantasy and unstable comedy in Pinfold's version of events.

Early in his career Waugh had seen the comic potential in the omniscience of classic realism's narrative-voice. In *Decline and Fall* Dr Fagan tells Paul, on sports day, that they might encounter his daughter in the marquee, 'that is Diana's province. I expect we shall find her at work' and then we have 'sure enough, there was Dingy helping two servants . . .'. The note of mild surprise in the understating 'sure enough' parodies the omniscient narrator's usually futile attempts to pretend that he isn't pulling the strings. In *Pinfold* this is given a further twist, as if in parody of parody. Within a couple of pages of each other, the narrating-voice has two particularly nice interventions. Angel calls off one operation in the torment – a series of conversations designed for Pinfold to 'hear' – with the words 'he's not sleeping enough' and the narrator comments 'this was indeed true'; later Pinfold goes on the offensive with Angel: 'I know exactly what you are doing for the BBC' and, delicately positioned between dashes, the narrative has 'this was bluff'.

Other versions of this parodic intervention might include the way the narrator stoutly defends Pinfold against his tormentors, as when two hooligans approach his cabin: 'you're going to cop it. Now he's locked the door'. The narrator: 'Mr Pinfold had done no such thing.' The scrupulously observed narrative appellation 'Mr Pinfold' is an equivalently ironic defence, absurd as it relentlessly accumulates. (And the more it accumulates, the more the reader may think of the psychoanalytic recourse of third-personing, whereby patients refuse their own histories.) And there's the way the usual relationship between narrative and thought-processes can be neatly reversed, as when Pinfold searches his cabin for the supposed love-token left by Margaret: 'he opened the cupboard over the wash-hand-basin. There was nothing there./"There's nothing there," said Margaret.' The

narrative can collude so seamlessly with Pinfold's version that
it almost looks like cheating the reader. The morning after the
hooligans fail to beat up Pinfold, vomiting up their drunkenness
on deck instead, Pinfold rises early. 'He went on deck, where
seamen were at work swabbing. They had already cleaned up
all traces of the night's disgusting climax' (the seamen/climax
wordplay is stylish).

It's symptomatically difficult to assess Waugh's intention here:
it's as if the coolly achieved prose is both a mask for real feeling
and its only chance of evocation. In the same way, the comedy
is unstable because it depends (more edgily, more ambivalently,
than most texts) on the reader reconstructing the potential for
pathos in or behind the joke. Thus the question posed to Pinfold's
heated imaginings – 'what was the proper procedure, if any
existed, for putting a Captain in irons in his own ship?' – is
shadowed, behind its earnest absurdity, by the notion of Pinfold
sitting down to think through this absurd question – as is the
idea of Pinfold having 'devoted some thought' to the wholly
fantasy-derived topic of burial at sea: and there the silver-age
understatement suggests the terror of long, lonely imaginings.
Most poignant of all is the pathos all too recoverable behind
the scene, when Pinfold fights back 'with the enemy's weapons',
reading *Westward Ho!* 'very slowly hour by hour . . . to wear
them down with sheer boredom . . . Then Mr Pinfold tormented
them in his turn by making gibberish of the text, reading
alternate lines, alternate words, reading backwards, until they
pleaded for a respite. Hour after hour Mr Pinfold remorselessly
read on.'

For that matter, the most harmless, neutral words can carry
the sharp pathos. After Pinfold's comic-grotesque attempt to
talk to the hooligans through what he supposes is their temporary
transmission-device, the tablelamp in front of him at breakfast,
we are told: 'the lamp was not designed to be moved. His pull
disconnected it in some way. The bulb went out and the voices
abruptly ceased.' The emptiness of that 'and' (drained of all
but its syntactical value) is its pathos; classic realism would have

the 'and' that is so blankly vacant here replete with consequentiality. 'Said' is the very smallest small-change of the traditional novelist's currency; invariably used in the pseudo-dialogues Pinfold conducts with his tormentors, it carries the ghost of pathos in the possibility that Pinfold is, indeed, giving bodily voice to his side of the exchanges. The saddest example of the pathos of apparently harmless words[4] also contains the novel's most moving use of 'seem'. Goneril responds to Margaret's explanation for the failure of her tryst with Pinfold – 'when I got there he was lying in the dark snoring' – with bitter scorn: ' "Snoring? Shamming. Gilbert knew he wasn't up to it. He's impotent, aren't you, Gilbert? Aren't you?"/"It was Glover snoring," said Mr Pinfold, but nobody seemed to hear him.'

3

The impression is that Waugh had a thick skin, a shell that (in Pinfold's words) 'seemed impervious'. So the bare admission 'it hurts' surprises: this comes from a letter written ten years before the publication of *The Ordeal of Gilbert Pinfold*.

There are, for no obvious reasons, no diary entries between October 1948 and September 1952, so the letters are the main primary source of biographical information.[5] In a letter to Nancy Mitford, Waugh writes 'Would you say I was a very ill-tempered & self-infatuated man? It hurts'.[6] 'It' is the literary establishment's reception of an admittedly disappointing novella (*Scott-King's Modern Europe*) and it's a painful moment at the start of an extended, painful period during which, in Martin Stannard's words, Waugh 'became an old man . . . every year, it seemed, he aged by a decade'.[7]

The Labour Party were in power; what Waugh took to be civilization was, or so he thought, in retreat – and the literary effort was proving harder to summon or sustain. *Brideshead Revisited* had brought wide popularity and fan-mail, neither of which was relished; but Waugh's next project, *Helena*, which he considered his most important to date, was a punishing five years' work (only relieved by the composition and success of *The Loved One*), and even a piece of journalism, undertaken largely for financial relief, an essay on 'The American Epoch in the Catholic Church', took him almost three months' hard effort. Jaunts to London began to be the opposite of restorative. 'I get so painfully drunk whenever I go there ... complete collapse, with some clear indications of incipient lunacy. I think I am jolly near being mad.'[8] He's only forty-six. 'Two suicides among my friends last year. How many to come?'[9] And by the turn of the decade the supply of friends among whom Waugh could stir and circulate gossip was dwindling for another reason – because he had managed, usually wilfully and self-punishingly, to alienate them out of his life altogether.

In the new decade, serious financial embarrassment, caused by a mix of profligacy, generosity (particularly to Catholic causes) and financial insouciance, all three on the grand scale, was a more or less permanent threat (not lifted even by the combination of the patient wiliness of Waugh's agent A. D. Peters and the prospect of a million Penguin paperbacks).[10] One particularized sense of persecution, by the Inland Revenue, was sharpened when the Revenue got its hands on Waugh just after the election of a Conservative government in October 1951 – as if even that lot had betrayed him to the taxman. The first attacks of a rheumatic condition that afflicted him till the end compounded his embattled melancholy – the kind that Waugh claimed a doctor pleasantly consigned him to in January 1951 when pronouncing that his blood-pressure was 'the lowest ever recorded ... In an access of sudden hope I said: "Does this mean I shall die quite soon." "No. It means you will live absolutely for ever in deeper & deeper melancholy"'.[11]

His diary resumes in the autumn of 1952 with muted satisfaction at the publication and reception of *Men at Arms*, the first volume of the war trilogy, *Sword of Honour*. But 1953 'started badly ... and ended worse: trouble with his children, more trouble with the Inland Revenue and his agents, the next novel[12] dragging to a dead stop, quarrels, persecution mania'.[13] Massive over-reaction to a presumed snub by Diana and Duff Cooper when Waugh visited them in France at Easter marked the 'first symptoms of mental breakdown'[14] and he equivalently over-reacted to the reviews of his very thin *Love Among the Ruins*.[15]

There is another shorter interruption in the diary between June 1953 and New Year's Day 1954. This is the period that saw Waugh's increasingly severe sense of being harried, particularly by the Beaverbrook press and the BBC. 'Everyone eagerly on the watch for failing powers,' ends in 1953 entries;[16] the first eleven days of 1954 are recorded – 'clocks barely moving. Has half an hour past? no five minutes'[17] – and then there is another, longer interruption, till June 1955. After it resumes: 'very soon, perhaps the next time I write a book, I shall be humiliated by the lack of interest shown and shall look back on these as years of plenty'.[18] The next book was *Pinfold*. Christmas 1953 had found Waugh 'thunderously depressed'.[19] So at the end of January 1954, two weeks after visiting his very sick mother, Waugh went on a cruise to Ceylon, and mad. 'My late lunacy' was his way of describing afterwards the acute and terrifying hallucinations that he now endured.

The letters to his wife Laura from the journey survive. Waugh left the ship at Port Said within a week of departure and travelled to Cairo and then Columbo. These letters (five are here abridged) say this:

> *Darling, I wish you were with me . . . My nut is clearing but feeble. It is plain that I had been accumulatively poisoning myself with chloral in the last six months . . . When I wake up which I do 20 or 30 times a night I always turn to the other bed and am wretched you aren't there & puzzled that you are not – odd since we usually have different rooms . . . To add to my barminess there are intermittent bits of 3rd Programme talks played in private cabin and two mentioned me very faintly and my p.m. took it for other passengers whispering about me [3 February] . . . Then when I was beginning to rally I found myself the victim of an experiment in telepathy which made me think I really was going crazy . . . I know it sounds like acute p.m. but it is real & true. A trick the existentialists invented – half mesmerism – which is most*

*alarming when applied without warning or explanation to a sick man [8
February] . . . It is rather difficult to write to you because everything I say or
think or read is read aloud by the group of psychologists whom I met in the
ship . . . the artful creatures can communicate from many hundreds of miles
away. Please don't think this is barmy. I should certainly have thought so three
weeks ago, but it is a fact . . . it is a huge relief to realize that I am merely
the victim of the malice of others, not mad myself as I really feared for a few
days [12 February] . . . As I write this I hear the odious voices of the
psychologists repeating every word in my ear . . . It is most putting off [16
February] . . . I am still grossly afflicted by the psychologists. I think they can
be better dealt with from England* [18 February].[20]

Presumably 'p.m.' means persecution mania. The casual abbrevi-
ation suggests that it was frequently mentioned between Waugh
and his wife. It has a long history. The signs of a persecution
complex are detected by Waugh's biographer as early as his post-
university days, certainly in his behaviour at the break-up of his
first marriage.[21] Then they re-emerge with noticeable sharpness
in, for instance, Waugh's responses to what he took to be unfavour-
able or hurtful reviews of his work – to *Scott-King*, as seen above,
and more emphatically to *Helena* in November 1950: this was a
novel that Waugh took very elaborate pains over and thought very
highly of. The press notices were by and large warm and supportive
but Waugh found them 'peculiarly offensive' and (in a phrase that
has relevance to *Pinfold*) a 'kind of chastisement'.[22]

In the months leading up to the experiences dealt with in *Pinfold*,
the letters admit evidence of memory breakdown: 'my memory is
not at all hazy – just sharp, detailed and dead wrong',[23] and the
wash-hand stand incident, rehearsed exactly in *Pinfold*, follows
in December; there is, again as in *Pinfold*, the growing sense of
persecution: BBC broadcasters 'tried to make a fool of me and I
don't believe they entirely succeeded';[24] there is something that
seems more pathological than professional writer's block: 'I am
stuck in my book from sheer boredom';[25] he is voraciously reading
an 'enormous life of Dickens';[26] and he is troubled by a source of
surprising desire: 'my sexual passion for my ten year old daughter
[Margaret] is obsessive . . . I can't keep my hands off her'.[27] Virtually

the first letter after Waugh's recovery has this: 'my unhealthy affection for my second daughter has waned'.[28]

The letters and diaries in the period between Waugh's 'sharp but brief attack of insanity' and the publication of *Pinfold* in July 1957 are very suggestive.[29] His mother's death six months after his recovery 'fills me with regret for a lifetime of failure in affection and attention'.[30] It is then that *Pinfold* is begun, during a two-month trip to Jamaica. In the following year, after the publication of its second volume (*Officers and Gentlemen*), he suddenly seems to have planned out the rest of the trilogy and wants to move 'anywhere . . . I would like to sell out'.[31] Two days after this unexpected instruction to his estate agent the diary has the first mention of *Pinfold*: 'I am planning to stay at the hotel near her [Ann Fleming] in August to write the account of my late lunacy'.[32] But August in Folkestone proved fruitless – 'doing no work, not even feeling very well'; 'I shall slink home with much money squandered and no work done'[33] – and within a few weeks the 'prospect of starting a new life' makes him feel 'dismayed rather than stimulated'.[34]

In October 1955 he is working on the trilogy and 'neat little literary jobs', not apparently on *Pinfold*.[35] In the new year he sees a 'play about Burgess and Maclean' in Worthing; makes 'no sense of the last act of *Godot*' (having turned up late for it); rereads his schoolboy diaries and is 'appalled' by them; spends 'the first February . . . in England since 1944. Never again. I meant to write a great work of literary art but I am numb'; and finds himself stirred by a poor production to read *Lear*: 'King Lear's sufferings seemed no sharper than mine . . . Most of the time I keep reading *Lear* and thinking what a good film it would make'.[36]

At the end of February 'my fingers and brain begin to thaw and I can get to work' – but on what?[37] As yet there's no evidence from these sources of any further progress with *Pinfold* – although the rueful self-comparison with Lear is suggestive. 'Failing powers'? *King Lear*, after all, opens with an attempt to make 'potency . . . good'. Also suggestive is the strange, muted wording of this diary entry in May: 'there is no reason for me not to work. I will try one day soon. I did a little work'.[38]

In the summer of 1956 Waugh's oldest daughter Teresa has her coming-out ball. It is a measure of the difficulties of this period that the diary and the letters represent it so contrastingly. 'I spent most of the evening in the house, fairly cheerful at first but with deepening boredom. By 3.30 it was plain that the party was a great success . . . so I slunk away'.[39] Compare this:

> *Your mother insisted on bringing all 14 cows and they took up most of the ball room . . . A lot of criminals came uninvited and began robbing everyone so the police charged with truncheons and, I am sorry to say, arrested Alec Waugh and Alick Dru by mistake . . . To make things difficult Alick Dru had five watches, six diamond rings and some silver spoons in his pocket when arrested so he may get sent to prison for a year or two. / One of the cows escaped from the ball room into the Kensington Square Convent. The nuns have been milking her ever since & feeding her on sun-flower seeds. / Polly Grant was murdered by a black man whom your uncle Auberon brought. / Otherwise the ball was a great success.[40]*

The roots of that kind of extravagant comic inventiveness go right back to *Decline and Fall*. But they were not so easy to tap into at this stage, amidst the recurrent, crippling boredom and the melancholy which are so manifestly the enemies as Waugh tried to negotiate his early fifties. The overriding impression of Waugh, from the diaries and letters of this period, is of a brave man constantly striving to take the fight out beyond the embattled self, to sustain the varying demands of a self-made high-pressure, often contradictory, literary, social, traveller's, family and Catholic life. The letters, particularly, suggest a daily determination to keep entertaining, goading, admonishing his friends, agents, sparring-partners – and performing comedy, as in the bizarre domestic routines in which visitors were bemused to find themselves inveigled, as in the touching letters to Margaret and his other children. But it wasn't easy. Warmth of affection with Laura, for example, seemed to depend on separations not only of the three-day drinking variety in London but also of protracted travel every winter. The repeated refusals to have anything to do with the births of their successive children (staying put in London, more or less eschewing all contact with his wife) strike a worrying note now and doubtless did then too. And long-lasting friendships were stretched and broken, as if those friends were being dared or goaded into betraying all their care for him, as if thus to confirm him in his worst self-image.

It is not till September that the composition of *Pinfold* is, as it were, formally acknowledged. On the same day that the diary records the acceptance of Waugh's offer for their new home, we have this, nestling among bits of family and social gossip: 'I have resumed work on *Pinfold*'.[41] Two weeks later a letter refers to 'several days hard work in the last few weeks. The mad book is going to be very funny, I believe'.[42] On 2 October Waugh seeks formal permission from Daphne Fielding to dedicate the novel to her – and chooses the same moment to tell her that he has been spellbound by the beauty of her son Alexander (then about twenty-three), 'the most enchanting creature of either sex I have met for twenty years . . . goodness I fell in love . . . goodness he is a beauty. I say, talking of mad, I am full in the middle of writing an account of my going off my rocker. It seems funny to me'.[43] Correspondence with friendly and sophisticated women about the beauty of their own sons, or about the sexual attractiveness of his own pubescent daughter (Waugh enjoyed the then notorious *Lolita*, but only as 'smut'),[44] takes, presumably, the danger out of the idea-cluster (beauty–enchantment–love–madness), allows it to be fantasized into the uneasy fictiveness that's at issue with *Pinfold*.

The three last relevant diary entries or letters (as the family finally move house in October) are these: 'I have worked hard and easily, seldom writing less than a thousand words a day. The book is too personal for me to judge it';[45] 'the last day in the old home . . . My only sorrow that I shant quite finish the barmy book, which is going to be quite long but I believe funny';[46] 'my "novel" has progressed well but is not finished'.[47] The diary then breaks off again for four years.

A review of the evidence suggests that Waugh was uncertain about what was emergent or imminent with *Pinfold*: there's a not-quite jokey uncertainty over how to refer to it, an odd, even superstitious reluctance to refer to work on it at all until, thirty or so months after the ordeal itself, it was well underway – and yet, then, once it has emerged, there is a repeated confidence in its comic success, a confidence rather different from Waugh's muted assessments of both the early volumes of the trilogy (he would tell some friends not to bother with reading them). And it's notable that the one literary production from the period before *Pinfold* which caused him 'more pleasure than anything I have written for a long time' was a rather elaborately vengeful, not especially funny article in the *Spectator* about an attempt by Nancy Spain, an *Express* journalist, and a titled friend of hers, to invade his country privacy.[48] When the magazine arrives the 'article gives me keen pleasure still'[49] – and the lurking suggestion is that this kind of comic performance on the instrument of his persona is all that he can now manage ('keen pleasure' is an oddly suggestive way of putting it; the 'failing powers' he earlier assumed everyone was on the watch for could equivalently be read in more than the literary sense). Waugh's article is included in the Appendix to this edition.

Anxieties about personal material in relation to comic performance, as well as uncertainty over *Pinfold*'s textual status, were brought into question by one of Waugh's earliest critics, his friend Christopher Hollis, in his British Council pamphlet.[50] Declining to refer to *Pinfold* as a novel in his bibliography (calling it instead a 'narrative'), he commented: 'some have professed to find the chapters of near-madness amusing ... but a reader has to be hard-boiled indeed who finds madness funny ... What remains odd is that one who has been through such experiences should be willing to tell the world of them in such a comparatively casual fashion, and, as it were, to lunch out on them'.[51] This focuses a number of anxious issues. But who has to be hard-boiled? The novel was itself a way of hard-boiling material that was otherwise inaccessibly vulnerable and slippery. *Decline and Fall* is again pertinent: Grimes's mock-suicide in that novel revisits in comic detail Waugh's own suicide attempt, as recounted in *A Little Learning*, the surviving one volume of autobiography.

4

What exactly *Pinfold* takes, and how exactly it takes it, from Waugh's own experience is uncertain, if only because no diary entries exist for the relevant period (either because Waugh destroyed them, as he certainly did with much earlier material, or because he didn't write any).[52] Waugh encouraged the uncertainty in the structure and texture of this apparently sealed-tight text. The manifestly autobiographical opening material and the circular ending invite a non-fictional reading precisely as the novel repels any attempt to read through to transparent, unmediated biography. Its craft, artfulness, and high comedy (above all its brilliance of wordplay, deployed exactly and cagily between notions of knowing and unknowing) are so obviously too literary, too contrived and writerly for that.

In a letter of August 1957 to Robert Henriques (who Waugh first wrote to for help in writing the Wandering Jew material of *Helena*: 'you are the only religious Jew of my acquaintance'),[53] Waugh seems to face the question directly:

> *Mr Pinfold's experiences were almost exactly my own. In turning them into a novel I had to summarize them. I heard 'voices' such as I describe almost continuously night and day for three weeks. They were tediously repetitive and sometimes obscene and blasphemous. I have given the gist of them . . . My voices ceased as soon as I was intellectually convinced that they were imaginary. I do not absolutely exclude the possibility of diabolic possession as the source of them.*[54]

'Intellectually convinced' is intriguing. Martin d'Arcy, who received Waugh into the Catholic Church in 1930, was forcibly struck by how Waugh treated his conversion as a matter of intellectual conviction, basing it 'primarily on reason. I have never myself met a convert who so strongly based his assents on truth . . . Hard, clear thinking had . . . given him the answer.'[55] A battle won against irrational feelings, surprisingly coolly won, in both these cases? This assertion to Henriques about the novel's quasi-transcriptive accuracy remained Waugh's consistent response to the question.

There's also the evidence of Frances Donaldson, who, with her husband Jack, was present at a meeting on Waugh's immediate return from his experiences, as well as Waugh's fellow passengers on the ship. One of these tells of Waugh knocking relentlessly on her cabin-door in search of 'Margaret Black' (Black from the BBC was the origin of Angel), and throwing articles of furniture at illusionary enemies.[56] These incidents have left no trace in the novel. Like Christopher Hollis, Frances Donaldson was a close friend to whom the book came as a disappointment, mixed with a sense of puzzled, bemused relief at the way Waugh himself was treating it as a hilarious episode that had happened to somebody else. (A letter of August 1957, refusing his publisher's attempt to persuade him on to television, has this strange, cryptic paragraph: 'Pinfolds the friend, not Waugh'.)[57] The suggestion is that these friends were disappointed because Waugh's own version retailed to them, privately, was both more terrifying and more comic. And there's also the sense in which they felt the novel was a betrayal of their protectiveness towards him. We've seen already Waugh's self-punishing habit of antagonizing his friends into betraying their friendship. *Pinfold* seemed to some of them like a public sharing of stuff that was too raw. That's the (rather pained) word used by Waugh's first biographer: 'In the main plot of *Pinfold* Evelyn seems to have not only drawn heavily on his raw material but to have left it raw.'[58]

Donaldson's testimony is an invaluable first-hand account of what Waugh said had happened to him. This chapter in her illuminating study, *A Portrait of a Country Neighbour*, is supported in its evidence by the accounts of other friends, like Tom Driberg and Christopher Sykes; it is included in the Appendix. Driberg quotes Waugh admitting to at least some significant compressions – 'there must have been half a dozen times . . . when I rushed out with a stick, convinced that they were waiting for me' and Stannard notes that the ending is both more complete and up-beat than was the case with Waugh himself.[59] Pinfold gets to work on his new material and is confident about resuming work on his larger novel-in-waiting; we have seen that Waugh managed neither.

A glance at the letters to Laura during Waugh's ordeal suggests at least something of the transmuting process that came, as one might have expected, between the experience and the novel. 'There are intermittent bits of 3rd Programme talks played in private cabin and two mentioned me very faintly and my p.m. took it for other passengers whispering about me.' The difference in the novel's treatment is not only that 'very faintly' becomes two broadcasts of all too audible and crudely defamatory comments (lifting the original into higher absurdity) but, crucially, altering the story so that the 'p.m.' is manifested, not in misinterpreting the 'broadcasts' as passengers whispering, but in the sharp comedy of ensuing scenes in which Pinfold assumes that passengers have heard those broadcasts, the full-blown p.m. being reserved for separate, extended incidents later in the novel. Rather than summarizing and giving the gist, this example suggests the opposite, a crafty realignment and dramatic elaboration of original experience.

To look again at the evidence from the diaries and letters, before and after the experiences, suggests ways by which material might have found its way into the novel. We've noticed Waugh's retrospective recognition, in 1961 when he was reading about its trial, that a passage from *Lady Chatterley* had directly formed the sentimentally Celtic scene between Margaret and her father: an acknowledged example of recycled fiction as hallucination. And in the diaries before the ordeal, apart from the documentarily exact treatment of discrete material (the wash-hand stand incident, for instance), the reading of the Dickens biography and the sexual obsessiveness about his daughter Margaret are suggestive details. That Margaret was the name of the actually hallucinated daughter/lover-figure is certainly striking (the revelation as evasion).

Dickens, in Waugh's unconscious mythology, evokes the father-figure. In the thirties Waugh was surprised to find himself enjoying the Dickens novels: the idea is that he avoided Dickens because it was his father's territory (Arthur had written a biography; his publishing firm Chapman & Hall had the Dickens copyright, and they were Evelyn's publishers too: there is tangled literary-filial Oedipal stuff here), and also because the Dickens novel suggested pre-modern, unworldly sentiment (which is what Waugh found exasperating in his father).[60] And Dickens was, as the Edgar Johnson biography Waugh was then reading would have made clear enough,[61] a charismatic performer – as well as, like Ruskin, a determined devotee of worryingly young women (whom he liked to think he could mesmerize: in which case Margaret mesmerizing Pinfold may be a transferred, wish-fulfilling version).[62] Margaret suggests some intriguing transference if only because the father-figure says to her in his lecture about the 'art of love' (an 'old man can show you better than a young one') that he'd 'like dearly to be the one myself to teach you'.

One event the diaries and letters are understandably muted about, after the ordeal Waugh went through, is the death of his mother. The charges levelled against Pinfold by his tormentors are detailed below; the one that evidently (self-)inflicts real bitterness is that Pinfold treated his mother badly (letting her 'die in destitution'). Waugh didn't; but after his ordeal his guilt about her is painful and clear (that 'failure in affection and attention'). The mother-of-Margaret-figure in the novel is evoked as a lingering, imprecisely persistent presence, different from the broad, military strokes by which the father-figure is drawn: she is muted, not all together present, given to gnomic remarks like 'all loving is suffering' – but also, crucially, it's she who voices the most acute of the analyses of Pinfold: 'you just pretend to be hard and worldly, don't you? . . . But I know better'. (When Pinfold suddenly turns on her and calls her an 'old bitch', it is, after that charge, not entirely unaccountable.) As a matter of crude chronology the hooligans' charge about Pinfold's mother indicates that, as already suggested, at least some very guilty material circulating through the novel's processes derives from experiences later than Waugh's ordeal. Another suggestive example includes the way Waugh's sudden plan to move house is phrased as his wanting to 'sell out', particularly in the light of the play about Burgess and Maclean that he later saw ('gossips' that Pinfold 'overhears' have it that the 'missing diplomats' were 'friends of his').[63]

Betrayal is a crucial notion in the novel's unconscious. Steerforth's betrayal of David Copperfield's idealizing love is the most painful thing of its kind in Dickens; betrayal is also dominant in *King Lear* which Waugh was insistently 'rereading'. Lear and Steerforth are blandly obvious in the novel at the level of allusion and reference; but their penetration in the shared matter of betrayal cuts further. 'King Lear's sufferings seemed no sharper than mine' is the wry disappointment in the diary. And sharpness is the physical sensation Lear associates particularly ('sharp-toothed unkindness'; 'sharper than a serpent's tooth') with the charge of ingratitude, the betrayal of love. Betrayal runs through the charges levelled at Pinfold. In one sense this is not surprising, given that this is the period of those two painfully symbolic betrayals, losses of collective face: Suez, and the Burgess/Maclean/Third Man débâcle. But the charges of betrayal are also displaced versions of an edgy, generalized sense of betrayal felt by Waugh himself. 'Everything . . . that had happened in his own lifetime' Pinfold abhorred: behind the joke is the perception that the years of Waugh's maturity had only brought the sense of not belonging (as for instance in the Second World War, in which he felt sharply under-appreciated), of having missed out or been missed out – without mission. (More than twenty-five years earlier Waugh had to negotiate both a sharp personal betrayal and an anxiety about only part-belonging to a younger generation that itself felt missed out after the First World War; the result was the shiftily, edgily personalized *Vile Bodies*.)[64] The available response is 'disgust', tempered only to boredom, and strenuous performance of a 'character of burlesque'.

Pinfold 'typifies all that is decadent in contemporary literature' according to one Third Programme broadcast and is a 'dreadfully dim little man' according to the other, a contradiction neatly suggesting a more or less comprehensive betrayal of the literary vocation – and, for that matter, of the national psyche as well, for he also typifies 'the decline of England'. ('Typify' has a suppressed force, for Waugh would hardly have wanted to typify anything.) He is a communist and/or a fascist. Either way he is an ineffectual coward. He treated his mother disgracefully and shirked during the war. His religion is 'humbug'. He betrays his manhood, being both impotent and a sodomite. (That rather self-consciously literary word was, of course, the trigger to the Oscar Wilde scandal.) He drinks far too much, thinks of death rather too much, stole a moonstone – another mid-Victorian novel read too far: Wilkie Collins's moonstone was stolen under the influence of opiates – and 'looks down on all of us' from his lord-of-Lychpole eminence. Oh, yes, and he's a Jew.

The notion of Pinfold as a supercilious lord of the manor, and a figure of 'decadence' in modern literature because of it, can be pieced together. As it happens, Waugh's country lifestyle was far removed from luxury; he chose to live there rather than in 'literary' London because (in his friends' belief at least) more time spent in London would have meant alcoholic burnout and no writing. The country may have meant cold discomfort (as it often did for the Waughs) but at least it allowed the conditions for writing. But there was a certain predictability, in the light of those charges, in what became a notorious *New Statesman* review of the novel by J. B. Priestley, headed 'What was Wrong with Pinfold', in which he claimed that Waugh went off his head because of the irreconcilable tensions between his roles as writer and country-squire. The charge carried enough to hurt, despite its shaky biographical grasp and its hectoring over-assertiveness, and Waugh felt stirred enough to answer it, in the form of an article (just a little too edgily sarcastic) headed 'Anything Wrong with Priestley?' (and published in the *Spectator*, the *New Statesman*'s political opposite). The exchange is included in the Appendix.

The charges ('self-infatuated and ill-tempered' were the ones that 'hurt' in the diary entry cited above) have varyingly intensive personal force, whether unmediated (being homosexual) or displaced (being Jewish, as opposed to a hater of Jews).[65] It's clear that they're mixed in such a way that the ones with stings are deliberately disguised among the absurdities – and not just because that's the way hallucinations work. But Waugh would hardly have expected the reader not to suspect that the most 'ill-tempered' of them were precisely what he himself routinely drew on, in his daily performance of the combative English novelist in his fastness. The world out there provided a ceaseless supply of necessary others.

Enemy is not quite the word; the diaries suggest a more bemused and genial attitude towards these fictions, the unknowingly supporting actors in his play: the pansies, the Jews, the shirkers, the decadents, the betrayers of the cause, whatever that might have been – true Catholicism, literary standards, landed conservatism. It was play; it was more or less playful; but it was also more. Friends were genuinely lost. The Angels claim towards the end that 'you did need help', and there's perhaps not entirely examined self-criticism there. Waugh's self-beliefs were never easy; the fierce defensiveness of the role in conscious life and the Pinfold accusations share some uneasy sources. The mother's charge is the crucial one: 'You just pretend to be hard and worldly . . . But I know better.' This is the performance betrayed. It's also the little boy found out; and relieved to be found out.

5

What was wrong with Waugh? He insisted on the physiological explanation for his temporary madness: in his increasingly desperate and prolonged attempts to fight insomnia he'd poisoned his brain with bromide and chloral, washed down with excessive alcohol; the hallucinations were consequently drug-induced. His doctors supported him in this view and changed his prescription. And there's the bizarre coincidence (as if Waugh had masochistically wish-fulfilled, into his suffering, material from his own much earlier biographical labours) that Rossetti, whose life Waugh wrote as a young man, suffered (like Waugh, at fifty) from bromide-induced hallucinations. Recent research has shed more light on the diagnosis and its socio-literary antecedents.[66] Alternatively, Waugh was suffering from an over-abrupt withdrawal from the cocktail of drugs: this phenomenon subjects the addict to delirium and hallucinations often more terrifying than those induced by the drugs themselves.[67]

Or there's the more prosaic, more worrying diagnosis. This is that Waugh was suffering from a short, sharp attack of schizophrenia, an extension of the 'p.m.' which he and his wife Laura familiarly recognized. Two factors suggest that this explanation may be as telling as the physiological one (but no doubt the latter would have been an exacerbating factor).[68] First, drug-induced hallucinations tend to be visual rather than auditory. Secondly, Waugh received an embarrassingly large postbag of letters from fellow-sufferers who recognized Pinfold's symptoms in their own; it's rather unlikely that all these were voracious ingesters of bromide, chloral and Crème de Menthe. An estimated one per cent of the population, after all, suffer from schizophrenia.

The symptoms specific to the disability include these: the subject suspects that he is being hypnotized (as in the letters to Laura), he hears voices telling him what to do, commenting on or repeating his thoughts, discussing him between themselves or threatening to kill him. Although intelligence remains relatively intact, the whole personality is affected. Single attacks, from which patients then recover, are not the norm but are well-known to psychiatry.[69] Waugh himself told Graham Greene that the second volume of the trilogy might well be the last because he feared a more violent recurrence of his attack. 'I may go off my head again, and this time permanently'.[70] Hence, perhaps, the wound inflicted by Priestley when he blithely warned Waugh/Pinfold that any more of this incompatible role-playing business would send him properly off his rocker. (Waugh did suffer recurrences, though minor.)

If one incident, or group of incidents, can be said to have contributed most to persecution mania tipping into schizophrenia (if that was what happened), then it was Waugh's dealings with the BBC and the press in the summer and autumn of 1953. Waugh believed that the Beaverbrook press were actively persecuting him and that Lord Beaverbrook was involved in the conspiracy to do so. There is some, but only rather tenuous, support for this idea.[71] But it is the case that Waugh was sufficiently stung by what he saw as orchestrated character assassination to take the uncharacteristic step of replying to the Beaverbrook press notices of what was, after all, his least consequential novella, *Love Among the Ruins*, in an article in the *Spectator* in July 1953: this, significantly, uses the phrase 'failing powers' that worries away in the diary at the same time.[72] (The Beaverbrook saga continued in 1955, as we've seen, when Nancy Spain and a Lord Noel-Buxton tried to visit Waugh in search of journalistic copy. Waugh's reaction was rage on an epic-comic scale. His revenge is printed in the Appendix.)

But more damaging to Waugh's self-image was his series of encounters with what he took to be inquisitorial BBC radio interviewers. There were three occasions, the first in September 1953 in Waugh's home, with Stephen Black (who became Angel; this corresponds to the scene in *Pinfold*), broadcast on 29 September in the *Personal Call* series for the Overseas Service only; and then two in London (September and October) which were edited together for a *Frankly Speaking* broadcast of 16 November, in which Black was one of three interviewers. (There were two versions taped because Waugh was dissatisfied with the first. It was increasing financial straits that led Waugh, again uncharacteristically, to participate at all in these broadcasts.) It was the first of these that, in his son Auberon's opinion, 'drove my Father mad'.[73] Extracts from these interviews are given in the Appendix.[74]

These were variously revealing, part genial, part prickly encounters; but Waugh was haunted by their memory. (Black does rather come across as a needling, slow-witted cross-examiner: it's easy to believe that this interview helped to form the interrogation scenes in *Pinfold*. And at least one question – 'does your wife fit in with [your] demand for interesting or beautiful people that you want to have around you?' – is more impertinent than pertinent.) The haunting idea seems to have been that the inquisitors' intentions were to puncture a façade, his dramatic performance. His later dealings with the *Express* he saw in the same light. These were not just intrusions on his privacy but (in Waugh's fevered reading of them) malicious attempts to deflate, tear off the stage-costumes, reveal the sham beneath. And the form they took was dramatic in their own right, as if answering theatre with theatre, putting the actor into another play, one where he'd have to answer to another's script and direction. The baffled, bear-bated Malvolio, again, seems the most relevant antecedent. (Auberon Waugh wrote of how his father was 'driven mad by the jackals snarling and whining around his ankles').[75] If Pinfold/Waugh's torments were the revenge of the fictions on their maker, the novel was, as in Malvolio's last cry, his counter-revenge on the whole pack of them.

This returns us to *Pinfold*'s highly fictive literariness with which we began (and which is in such edgy, productive tension with its autobiograhical status) – or, rather, its dramatic theatricality. There was, indeed, a well-received BBC radio dramatization – an appropriately ironic medium, given the above.[76] Film would also have been appropriate: Waugh had saturated himself indiscriminately in films for many years as a way of staving off debilitating boredom[77] and, as we've seen, thought that only film could do justice to *King Lear*. And here an image in Stannard's acute analysis is worth considering. He sees Waugh's hallucinations as 'cutting-room snippets edited out of the film of his life · . . . scene after scene of shameful embarrassment he thought he had destroyed'.[78] The novel may be read as the film of *Lear* as written/played by Keaton or Chaplin, or a composite Laurel/ Hardy; the kind of role that Waugh enjoyed assuming. A good Waugh anecdote is of a crowd of strangers at an auction loudly supporting his derisory bid for a huge and hideous piece of furniture which the auctioneer insisted was worth more as firewood: 'Oh, let the little chap have it!'

Waugh's performance of role at the Foyles luncheon to mark the publication of *Pinfold* had significantly hardened further into self-caricature. What became his notorious ear-trumpet had just been acquired and he wielded it for the cameras with élan, conspicuously not utilizing it during Malcolm Muggeridge's opening speech in Waugh's honour; he then claimed he hadn't heard a word of it.[79] He had agreed to appear partly to appease his publisher, with whom he had quarrelled over the book's shoddy appearance (they 'made such an ugly book of poor Pinfold'.)[80]

This leads us to the single most startling piece of evidence from the letters and diaries for the period covering *Pinfold*'s publication: Waugh wanted a Francis Bacon painting reproduced on the novel's dust-jacket. He wrote to his publisher, enclosing the 'new end'[81] and added: 'for wrapper, could we get permission to reproduce one of Francis Bacon's paintings? . . . he might let us have "serial rights" of an existing horror'.[82] As Waugh's attitude towards modern art can be more or less fully accounted for in his/Pinfold's abhorrence of Picasso and Charles Ryder's 'modern art is all bosh' (*Brideshead*), this comes as a shock. But then Bacon, though the opposite of the Victorians Waugh collected, was a figurative painter in the grand-master tradition. And the paintings Bacon was obsessively concerned with in the period leading up to *Pinfold*, his masterworks from the late forties to the mid-fifties, are some thirty paintings of tormented heads (mouths silenced, or screaming, or choking) in small, confined spaces (like Malvolio in his dark house) – the heads loosely referred to now as his 'screaming popes'. (Given Waugh's idiosyncratic sense of true Catholicism it may not be fanciful to suggest that these figures had an unintended piquancy.)

Bacon had two exhibitions in Britain, both at the Hanover Gallery, which Waugh might have attended.[83] The first was from November to December 1949 and it featured six of these heads (the most celebrated, *Head VI*, is in the Arts Council collection). The second was from March to April 1957 (more or less concurrent with one in Paris) and very largely consisted of variations on a van Gogh self-portrait. Davis's dating of the request to the publishers about the wrapper makes it likely that Waugh had one or more of the heads in mind when he referred to an 'existing horror'.[84]

If so, what message would he have wanted the dust-jacket to convey? The Bacon heads have been well described by art critic John Russell as 'statements about what it feels like to be alone in a room . . . the disintegration of the social being which takes place . . . and [the] person is suddenly adrift, fragmented, and subject to strange mutation'.[85] *Head VI*, in particular, is trapped, tormented, the head in some kind of inquisitorial box (Pinfold's Box?; radio interviews?), its upper part in such straits that it has mutated away. (Often suggested about the Bacon paintings is that they oddly predict Eichmann on trial in his glass box. Waugh attended the 1946 Nuremberg war crimes trials, intending to write what might have been, in Stannard's nice phrase, a 'post-war, melancholic tour of dead Europe' but nothing came of it.[86] Waugh considered the trials a 'surrealist spectacle' and compared Ribbentrop to a 'seedy schoolmaster being ragged', caught out by the class in his ignorance.[87] The inquisitorial scenes in *Pinfold* may well have a source in these trials as well as in the BBC interviews.) But *Head VI* is also a figure in grand ruins, Lear at Dover or Pozzo in Act 2 of *Godot* (the Act Waugh *did* see) – a figure 'reverted to infant-state . . . a grown man in swaddling clothes', the 'licensed dissembler'.[88] A more recent suggestion about the Bacon heads, made by Darian Leader in a BBC2 programme, not at all irrelevant to Waugh's biography, is that they have a derivation in the painter's suffocated anxiety about his own father.[89] The notion of man isolated and adrift; cabined, cribbed, confined, and tortured in his head (Macbeth's words have an eerie pertinence); grand authority (and author-ship) reduced to, caught out as, the dissemblings of the fool, the child in fancy-dress (and the son suffocated): these are the concerns of high modernism as they are of classic tragedy. A Francis Bacon on the dust-jacket would have made a bid for affiliation with such exemplary texts.

An ironic one? The ordeal was terrible. Madness is not trivial, even if it's comic. And yet *Pinfold* is subtitled 'A Conversation Piece'. As how serious, how momentous a novel did Waugh expect it to be read? Contemporary reviews were mixed, rather bemused;[90] but astute colleagues like Graham Greene and Anthony Powell thought Waugh had never written better fiction.[91] The lingering perception, which has persisted, that it was (merely) autobiography manqué (a view which, after all,

Waugh didn't exactly discourage) has not helped its reputation. As Greene and Powell realized, it deserves more.

The view advanced here is that it is Waugh's most brilliantly controlled and acutely styled post-war novel, its stylistic register tuned most efficiently and precisely to its complex comic-ironic purposes, the tone weighted exactly between comedy and pathos, the comedy functioning from an internally motored ironic drive not seen since *A Handful of Dust* – which is Waugh's most brilliantly controlled and acutely styled pre-war novel (where style functions as the most bitter of ironic weapons). The irony is self-punishing in both cases: and in an important sense it is equivalent to the terrible ironic charge carried by the calculatedly comic-sadistic design of *King Lear* – a reason, perhaps, for Waugh's concentrated attention on that play, its strange subtextual grip on *Pinfold*.

An affiliation between *Pinfold* and the lofty terrors of its cultural ancestors may seem preposterous. It must be too playful, too evasive for that. A voyage to self-discovery? The ending rather suggests an avoidance, a fear of self-knowledge. But here is an ordeal of a man adrift, confined and tortured; a text of dazzling craftiness; impossibly funny, and affecting in the least expected of ways.

The manuscript of *Pinfold* is kept at the University of Texas. Laid inside the handsomely bound volume is a printed leaf of Greek and Latin commentary on the Annunciation. The oddest thing about Waugh's going mad (the thing that made him so disconcertingly gleeful about it all afterwards) was that it presented him with what he thought he might never be visited with again – fresh novelistic material. It did this by reactivating what was looking like an impotent or even barren comic power. And so (the) Angel came with the special gift, the terrible appointment. After all, then, Waugh had been chosen to be different, found out – to be given the mission, at last. For here is the evidence. Urgent business: fresh, rich experience: perishable goods.

RICHARD JACOBS

Notes

1. *Summer Moonshine* (1937). The debt may go the other way; Wodehouse in 1937 shows the influence of early Waugh.

2. Act 2 Scene 4. A Gilbert Pinfold was a previous owner of Waugh's house in Gloucestershire. See Jolliffe, in Pryce-Jones, p. 232.

3. In 1961 Waugh noted in his diary that this episode had a specific, unconscious source: his earlier reading of Lawrence's *Lady Chatterley's Lover*. 'The ludicrous scene between Mellors and Lady C.'s father . . . This father of Lawrence's was the father I had heard urging his daughter to my cabin.' See *Diaries*, p. 781.

4. See Note on the Text; it was a later addition.

5. It goes without saying that the principal secondary source is Martin Stannard's excellent biography. This section draws gratefully on the relevant chapters in the second volume.

6. To Nancy Mitford, December 1947; *Letters*, p. 264.

7. Stannard, pp. 147, 212.

8. December 1949; *Letters*, p. 315.

9. January 1950; ibid., p. 318.

10. See Stannard, pp. 254–6.

11. *Letters*, pp. 343–4.

12. The second volume of the trilogy.

13. Stannard, p. 319.

14. Ibid., p. 328.

15. Ibid., pp. 329–31.

16. *Diaries*, p. 722.

17. Ibid.; this, perhaps the most expressive entry in the entire volume, appears exactly as printed here.

18. Ibid., p. 726.

19. Stannard, p. 343.

20. *Letters*, pp. 418–21.

21. See Stannard, p. 288.

22. See *Letters*, pp. 339–41 and Stannard, ibid.

23. September 1953; *Letters*, p. 410.

24. December 1953; ibid., p. 415.

25. Ibid.; the book is the second volume of the trilogy.

26. September 1953; ibid., p. 409.

27. September 1952; to Ann Fleming; ibid., p. 380.

28. May 1954; to Nancy Mitford; ibid., p. 432. The psychologist who examined Waugh on his return alerted him to the likelihood of this happening. See Stannard, p. 351.

29. March 1954; *Letters*, p. 421.

30. December 1954; ibid., pp. 434–5.

31. July 1955; ibid., pp. 443–4.

32. *Diaries*, p. 728.

33. August 1955; ibid., pp. 735–6.

34. September 1955; ibid., p. 741.

35. Ibid., pp. 743, 745.

36. *Diaries*, pp. 751–2, 754; *Letters*, p. 468.

37. *Diaries*, p. 754.

38. Ibid., p. 760. In Davie's edition this entry is oddly laid out: the last sentence may be a separate paragraph.

39. *Diaries*, p. 764.

40. To his younger daughters; *Letters*, p. 474.

41. *Diaries*, p. 768.

42. *Letters*, p. 475.

43. Ibid., p. 476.

44. See *Letters*, pp. 457, 516, 523; see also Donaldson, p. 92.

45. *Diaries*, p. 769.

46. *Letters*, p. 477.

47. *Diaries*, p. 770.

48. July 1955; *Diaries*, p. 728 – one day before the diary's first mention of *Pinfold*.

49. *Diaries*, p. 729.

50. First edition 1954.

51. 1971 ed., p. 38.

52. Davie inclines towards the former explanation. See *Diaries*, p. 724.

53. *Letters*, p. 220.

54. Ibid., pp. 493–4.

55. See d'Arcy, in Pryce-Jones, p. 64.

56. See Hastings, pp. 562–3.

57. *Letters*, p. 492.

58. Sykes, p. 367.

59. *Sunday Dispatch*, 14 July 1957; quoted in Stannard, p. 344. Donaldson describes one 'set-piece' to which this presumably corresponds: Waugh was perhaps editing as early as that first account.

60. See Stannard, vol. 1, p. 329.

61. *Charles Dickens*, 1953.

62. Stannard, pp. 338–41, has an illuminating discussion of the complementarily obsessive interest exercised over Waugh by Dickens and Ruskin.

63. 'Sell up' is the more usual phrase, used by Waugh when contemplating emigration to Ireland in 1946. See Stannard, pp. 179–80.

64. See the introduction to the Penguin Twentieth-Century Classics edition, *Vile Bodies*, 1996.

65. Stannard argues that Waugh's 'prejudice was anti-Zionist rather than anti-Semitic' (p. 285).

66. See *Evelyn Waugh Newsletter*, Autumn 1982; cited in Hastings, p. 565.

67. How much of his concocted prescriptions he took with him on board is not clear; compare Donaldson, p. 56 and Stannard, p. 343.

68. Compare Stannard: 'he was suffering from the classic symptoms of schizophrenia . . . the drugs released a barrage of self-hatred which, in his right mind, he suppressed' (p. 348).

69. The previous three sentences are adapted from the relevant entry by R. E. Kendall in the *Oxford Companion to the Mind*, p. 697.

70. Greene, writing in 1976; cited in Stannard, p. 348.

71. See Stannard, pp. 330–31.

72. *Essays*, pp. 440–43.

73. Letter to Martin Stannard; see Stannard, pp. 334–8.

74. Also extracted is the celebrated television interview of 1960 with John Freeman; this discusses *Pinfold*.

75. *Spectator*, 6 May 1966.

76. National Sound Archive ref. 42538.

77. See Donaldson, p. 23.

78. Stannard, p. 349.

79. See Stannard, p. 391.

80. *Letters*, p. 491.

81. See Note on the Text.

82. *Letters*, p. 482, undated; Davie places it in or before November 1956; R. M. Davis must be right in placing it in late January 1957 when Waugh rewrote the last two pages of the novel. See Davis, p. 281.

83. The Hanover Gallery no longer exists. Its archives are stored at the Tate. These do not, unfortunately, include visitors' books.

84. The exhibitions attracted considerable press coverage. Waugh, according to Frances Donaldson (p. 24), read *The Times* daily from cover to cover. At the least, he would have read about Bacon's progress. *The Sunday Times* review of the 1949 show speaks of how the paintings induce 'vague horror . . . typical of certain dreams' (13 November 1949).

85. Russell, *Francis Bacon*, p. 38.

86. Stannard, p. 163.

87. *Letters*, p. 226; *Diaries*, p. 646.

88. Russell on the Velazquez portrait behind the Bacon heads; Russell, p. 42.

89. *In the Name of the Father*, broadcast 7 May 1996.

90. See *Critical Heritage*, pp. 380–92 for a representative selection.

91. See Stannard, p. 396.

NOTE ON THE TEXT

The text of *Pinfold* here printed is (with a few misprints silently corrected) that of the 1973 volume published by Chapman & Hall as *The Ordeal of Gilbert Pinfold and Other Stories* (the others being 'Mr Loveday's Little Outing', 'Scott-King's Modern Europe' and 'Love Among the Ruins'); this is in the series of hardback reprints, the 'Uniform Edition' to which Waugh, when alive, contributed prefaces. This text has been collated with the first edition of 1957. The Penguin edition (1962) which this one replaces included the stories 'Tactical Exercise' and 'Love Among the Ruins'.

The manuscript and typescript material relating to *Pinfold* is stored at the University of Texas at Austin, along with the rest of the Waugh manuscripts apart from those for the novels *Put Out More Flags* (which no longer exists) and *Vile Bodies* (which quite recently resurfaced though now again in unknown hands: for more detail see the Penguin Twentieth-Century Classics edition). The material has been studied closely by Robert Murray Davis for the chapter in his book *Evelyn Waugh, Writer* (pp. 281–94); what follows is a brief summary of his findings. Grateful acknowledgement is offered to Professor Davis.

The last two pages of the novel were rewritten as late as January 1957 (see below);

the second paragraph of the manuscript shows Waugh toying with the idea of using present tense for the narrative (the manuscript of *Vile Bodies* shows the same verbal slippage between fiction and reportage, in an equivalently autobiographical uncertainty of purpose);

a passage in the original first chapter detailing Pinfold's regular searches of press cuttings in the hope of finding libellous material was deleted in March 1957, presumably because of Waugh's then current libel suit against the *Express* and others;

what are now the first two chapters were created 'with scissors, paste, and a clearer sense of purpose' [Davis, p. 286] when the typescript was being revised, out of what was one long chapter;

the last sentence of Chapter 6 (picked out for especial comment in the Introduction) was a later addition. Davis notes Waugh's fine ear for the anti-climactic effect [ibid., p. 287]

Margaret's role in the novel is much developed from the original manuscript stage, her intimacy with Pinfold being significantly highlighted. Her final 'I do love you, Gilbert' and his earlier 'he loved her a little' were revisions;

the 'Box' as the misleading explanation that deludes Pinfold made a relatively late appearance in the manuscript, and material preparing the ground for the idea was added to the novel later;

'Angel' was 'Andrews' throughout the manuscript. Davis proposes that the change may have been made when Waugh inserted, on the reverse of the manuscript page, Pinfold's second letter to his wife with its speculation that it may be 'literally the Devil who is molesting me' [ibid., p. 290]; see also Waugh's letter to Hendriques cited in the Introduction;

the role of Mr Murdoch is developed; in manuscript he disappears from the novel when Pinfold leaves the *Caliban*;

work on the ending went through three distinct stages:

The first draft has Pinfold reflecting on his courage in rejecting 'Andrews'' offer, Mrs Pinfold agreeing ('Heroic, darling') and then this final exchange: 'And what's more I shouldn't have been able to write a book about it.' 'That would have been a pity,' said Mrs Pinfold.

The second version, added to typescript, introduces the material about the odd 'rot' in the charges, brings in the Bruiser, has Pinfold turning from the unfinished work to the new 'load of experience' that needs to be 'deposited in its proper place', writing the title and chapter heading, then rejoining his wife (as the Bruiser leaves the house) to announce his embarking on 'an account of my barminess . . . it ought to amuse a certain number of people' – and that because 'nearly half the inhabitants' of the country are 'more or less barmy at one time or another.' 'Oh dear,' said Mrs Pinfold, 'Have you thought of the fan mail?'

The third and last stage was the rewriting of the last two pages in January 1957 – as late as the time when, Davis notes, serial rights to the novel were being offered. This rewriting is in effect a remarkable compression of the above [ibid., p. 294] – as well as the moment when the 'load of experience' becomes a 'hamper' of 'perishable goods' and the novel gains its 'conversation piece' subtitle. (The light comedy of both images gently disengages the seriousness.) The rather edgy, almost truculent claim Pinfold makes in the second version and the weak joke that follows it (though it turned out to be prophetic: the volume of fan-mail was indeed disconcerting [see Introduction]) are replaced by the calmly, as if not quite bodily voiced, as if studiously neutral, 'neat, steady' (and, of course, circular) return to the novel's opening gesture.

FURTHER READING

This list restricts itself to material (books but not articles) relatively easily available. Place of publication is, unless stated otherwise, London.

(i)

Amory, Mark (ed.), *The Letters of Evelyn Waugh* (1980). This and the below are the crucial evidence for the years up to, during and after the *Pinfold* experience.

Davie, Michael (ed.), *The Diaries of Evelyn Waugh* (1976).

Donaldson, Frances, *Evelyn Waugh, Portrait of a Country Neighbour* (1967; edition with new preface 1985). The chapter on the 'real' Pinfold is in the Appendix.

Gallagher, Donat (ed.), *The Essays, Articles and Reviews of Evelyn Waugh* (1983). Two articles are featured in the Appendix to this edition.

Hastings, Selina, *Evelyn Waugh* (1994; references are to the Minerva paperback, 1995). The most recent biography.

Pryce-Jones, David (ed.), *Evelyn Waugh and his World* (1973). Useful collection of memoirs and essays.

Stannard, Martin, *Evelyn Waugh, The Critical Heritage* (1984). Important collection of contemporaneous articles and reviews.

Stannard, Martin (ed.), *No Abiding City* (1992). The second volume of his magnificent biography, drawn on extensively in the Introduction to this edition. (References to the first volume, *The Early Years*, are to the Flamingo paperback ed., 1993.)

Sykes, Christopher, *Evelyn Waugh* (1975). The superseded biography, by a friend and contemporary. His reaction to *Pinfold* is referred to in the Introduction.

Waugh, E., *A Little Learning* (1964). The first and only volume of autobiography, covering only the first twenty or so years.

(ii)

Bradbury, Malcolm, *Evelyn Waugh* (1964).

Carens, James F., *The Satiric Art of Evelyn Waugh* (Seattle, 1966).

Davis, Robert Murray, *Evelyn Waugh, Writer* (Oklahoma, 1981). An illuminating study of the manuscripts and typescripts held at the University of Austin, Texas. Davis's findings form the basis of the Note on the Text in this edition.

Eagleton, Terry, *Exiles and Emigrés* (1970).

Greenblatt, Stephen J., *Three Modern Satirists* (Yale, 1965).

Heath, Jeffrey, *The Picturesque Prison* (1982).

Littlewood, Ian, *The Writings of Evelyn Waugh* (Oxford, 1983). This is a notable literary-critical study. The section on *Pinfold* is typically balanced. The novel 'is at once a demonstration of artistic mastery and a revelation of how precarious that mastery is' (p. 230).

Lodge, David, *Evelyn Waugh* (Columbia, 1971).

Myers, William, *Evelyn Waugh and the Problem of Evil* (1991). A fine, if uneven book; the *Pinfold* pages contain an astute and closely reasoned assessment of the novel's strategically limited self-disclosure. 'What we are invited to "see" is that the self-constructions, self-bifurcations, self-disclosures and, above all, the knowingness of the text about its own paradoxes, do not set up a vicious regress but constitute a style, a fist, a way of willing which is one with a way of telling . . . *Pinfold* is sealed in on itself' (pp. 103, 105).

Stopp, Frederick J., *Evelyn Waugh, Portrait of the Artist* (1958). The first substantial critical study, undertaken with Waugh's consent and assistance. The title of *Pinfold*'s first chapter may be seen as something between an endorsement and a preemptive strike.

ACKNOWLEDGEMENTS

The editor gratefully acknowledges the permission kindly granted by Professor R. M. Davis to summarize his findings in the Note on the Text to this edition.

The publishers gratefully acknowledge permission to reprint the following copyright material in this book:

Extracts from *Face to Face*, *Personal Call* and *Frankly Speaking*, reproduced by kind permission of the BBC, the Estate of Jack Davies, and Dr Stephen Black; '*The Real Mr Pinfold*' from *Evelyn Waugh: Portrait of a Country Neighbour* by Frances Donaldson (Weidenfeld & Nicolson, 1967), reprinted by permission of the publisher; 'Awake My Soul! It is a Lord' by Evelyn Waugh (*Spectator*, 8 July 1955), 'Anything Wrong with Priestley?' by Evelyn Waugh (*Spectator*, 13 September 1957), and 'What Was Wrong with Pinfold' by J. B. Priestley (*New Statesman*, 31 August 1957), reprinted by permission of The Peters Fraser and Dunlop Group Ltd.

The publishers also wish to thank any copyright holders who are included without acknowledgement. Penguin UK apologizes for any omissions in the above list and would be grateful to be notified of any corrections that should be incorporated in the next edition of this book.

The Ordeal of Gilbert Pinfold

A CONVERSATION PIECE

Chapter One

It may happen in the next hundred years that the English novelists of the present day will come to be valued as we now value the artists and craftsmen of the late eighteenth century. The originators, the exuberant men, are extinct and in their place subsists and modestly flourishes a generation notable for elegance and variety of contrivance. It may well happen that there are lean years ahead in which our posterity will look back hungrily to this period, when there was so much will and so much ability to please.

Among these novelists Mr Gilbert Pinfold stood quite high. At the time of his adventure, at the age of fifty, he had written a dozen books all of which were still bought and read. They were translated into most languages and in the United States of America enjoyed intermittent but lucrative seasons of favour. Foreign students often chose them as the subject for theses, but those who sought to detect cosmic significance in Mr Pinfold's work, to relate it to fashions in philosophy, social predicaments or psychological tensions, were baffled by his frank, curt replies to their questionnaires; their fellows in the English Literature School, who chose more egotistical writers, often found their theses more than half composed for them. Mr Pinfold gave nothing away. Not that he was secretive or grudging by nature; he had nothing to give these students. He regarded his books as objects which he had made, things quite external to himself to be used and judged by others. He thought them well made, better than many reputed works of genius, but he was not vain of his accomplishment, still less of his reputation. He had no wish to obliterate anything he had written, but he would dearly have liked to revise it, envying painters, who are allowed to return to the same theme time and time again, clarifying and enriching until they have done all they can with it. A novelist is condemned

5

to produce a succession of novelties, new names for characters, new incidents for his plots, new scenery; but, Mr Pinfold maintained, most men harbour the germs of one or two books only; all else is professional trickery of which the most daemonic of the masters – Dickens and Balzac even – were flagrantly guilty.

At the beginning of this fifty-first year of his life Mr Pinfold presented to the world most of the attributes of well-being. Affectionate, high-spirited and busy in childhood; dissipated and often despairing in youth; sturdy and prosperous in early manhood; he had in middle-age degenerated less than many of his contemporaries. He attributed this superiority to his long, lonely, tranquil days at Lychpole, a secluded village some hundred miles from London.

He was devoted to a wife many years younger than himself, who actively farmed the small property. Their children were numerous, healthy, good-looking and good-mannered, and his income just sufficed for their education. Once he had travelled widely; now he spent most of the year in the shabby old house which, over the years, he had filled with pictures and books and furniture of the kind he relished. As a soldier he had sustained, in good heart, much discomfort and some danger. Since the end of the war his life had been strictly private. In his own village he took very lightly the duties which he might have thought incumbent on him. He contributed adequate sums to local causes but he had no interest in sport or in local government, no ambition to lead or to command. He had never voted in a parliamentary election, maintaining an idiosyncratic toryism which was quite unrepresented in the political parties of his time and was regarded by his neighbours as being almost as sinister as socialism.

These neighbours were typical of the English countryside of the period. A few rich men farmed commercially on a large scale; a few had business elsewhere and came home merely to hunt; the majority were elderly and in reduced circumstances; people who, when the Pinfolds settled at Lychpole, lived comfortably with servants and horses, and now lived in much smaller houses and met at the fishmonger's. Many of these were related to one another and formed a compact little clan. Colonel and Mrs Bagnold, Mr and Mrs Graves, Mrs and Miss Fawdle, Colonel and Miss Garbett, Lady Fawdle-Upton and Miss Clarissa Bagnold all lived in a radius of ten miles from Lychpole. All were in some way related. In the first years of their marriage Mr and Mrs Pinfold had dined in all these households and had entertained them in return. But after the war the decline of fortune, less sharp in the Pinfolds' case than their neighbours', made their meetings less frequent. The Pinfolds were addicted to nicknames and each of these surrounding families had its own private, unsuspected appellation at Lychpole, not malicious but mildly derisive, taking its origin in most cases from some half forgotten incident in the past. The nearest neighbour whom they saw most often was Reginald Graves-Upton, an uncle of the Graves-Uptons ten miles distant at Upper Mewling; a gentle, bee-keeping old bachelor who inhabited a thatched cottage up the lane less than a mile from the Manor. It was his habit on Sunday mornings to walk to church across the Pinfolds' fields and leave his Cairn terrier in the Pinfolds' stables while he attended Matins. He called for quarter of an hour when he came to fetch his dog, drank a small glass of sherry and described the wireless programmes he had heard during the preceding week. This refined, fastidious old gentleman went by the recondite name of 'the Bruiser', sometimes varied to 'Pug', 'Basher', and 'Old Fisticuffs', all of which sobriquets derived from 'Boxer'; for in recent years he had added to his interests an object which he reverently referred to as 'The Box'.

This Box was one of many operating in various parts of the country. It was installed, under the sceptical noses of Reginald Graves-Upton's nephew and niece, at Upper Mewling. Mrs Pinfold, who had been taken to see it, said it looked like a makeshift wireless-set. According to the Bruiser and other devotees The Box exercised diagnostic and therapeutic powers. Some part of a sick man or animal – a hair, a drop of blood preferably – was brought to The Box, whose guardian would then 'tune in' to the 'Life-Waves' of the patient, discern the origin of the malady and prescribe treatment.

Mr Pinfold was as sceptical as the younger Graves-Uptons. Mrs

Pinfold thought there must be something in it, because it had been tried, without her knowledge, on Lady Fawdle-Upton's nettle-rash and immediate relief had followed.

'It's all suggestion,' said young Mrs Graves-Upton.

'It can't be suggestion, if she didn't know it was being done,' said Mr Pinfold.

'No. It's simply a matter of measuring the Life-Waves,' said Mrs Pinfold.

'An extremely dangerous device in the wrong hands,' said Mr Pinfold.

'No, no. That is the beauty of it. It can't do any harm. You see it only transmits *Life* Forces. Fanny Graves tried it on her spaniel for worms, but they simply grew enormous with all the Life Force going into them. Like serpents, Fanny said.'

'I should have thought this Box counted as sorcery,' Mr Pinfold said to his wife when they were alone. 'You ought to confess it.'

'D'you really think so?'

'No, not really. It's just a lot of harmless nonsense.'

The Pinfolds' religion made a slight but perceptible barrier between them and these neighbours, a large part of whose activities centred round their parish churches. The Pinfolds were Roman Catholic, Mrs Pinfold by upbringing, Mr Pinfold by a later development. He had been received into the Church – 'conversion' suggests an event more sudden and emotional than his calm acceptance of the propositions of his faith – in early manhood, at the time when many Englishmen of humane education were falling into communism. Unlike them Mr Pinfold remained steadfast. But he was reputed bigoted rather than pious. His trade by its nature is liable to the condemnation of the clergy as, at the best, frivolous; at the worst, corrupting. Moreover by the narrow standards of the age his habits of life were self-indulgent and his utterances lacked prudence. And at the very time when the leaders of his Church were exhorting their people to emerge from the catacombs into the forum, to make their influence felt in democratic politics and to regard worship as a corporate rather than a private act, Mr Pinfold burrowed ever deeper into the rock. Away from his parish he sought the least frequented Mass; at home he held aloof from the multifarious organizations which have sprung into being at the summons of the hierarchy to redeem the times.

But Mr Pinfold was far from friendless and he set great store by his friends. They were the men and women who were growing old with him, whom in the 1920s and '30s he had seen constantly; who in the diaspora of the '40s and '50s kept more tenuous touch with one another, the men at Bellamy's Club, the women at the half-dozen poky, pretty houses of Westminster and Belgravia to which had descended the larger hospitality of a happier age.

He had made no new friends in late years. Sometimes he thought he detected a slight coldness among his old cronies. It was always he, it seemed to him, who proposed a meeting. It was always they who first rose to leave. In particular there was one, Roger Stillingfleet, who had once been an intimate but now seemed to avoid him. Roger Stillingfleet was a writer, one of the few Mr Pinfold really liked. He knew of no reason for their estrangement and, enquiring, was told that Roger had grown very odd lately. He never came to Bellamy's now, it was said, except to collect his letters or to entertain a visiting American.

It sometimes occurred to Mr Pinfold that he must be growing into a bore. His opinions certainly were easily predictable.

His strongest tastes were negative. He abhorred plastics, Picasso, sunbathing and jazz – everything in fact that had happened in his own lifetime. The tiny kindling of charity which came to him through his religion, sufficed only to temper his disgust and change it to boredom. There was a phrase in the '30s: 'It is later than you think', which was designed to cause uneasiness. It was never later than Mr Pinfold thought. At intervals during the day and night he would look at his watch and learn always with disappointment how little of his life was past, how much there was still ahead of him. He wished no one ill, but he looked at the world *sub specie aeternitatis* and he found it flat as a map; except when, rather often, personal annoyance intruded. Then he would come tumbling from his exalted point of observation. Shocked by a bad bottle of wine, an impertinent stranger, or a fault in syntax, his mind like a cinema camera trucked furiously forward to confront the offending object close-up with glaring lens; with the eyes of a drill sergeant inspecting an awkward squad, bulging with wrath that was half-facetious, and with half-simulated incredulity; like a drill sergeant he was absurd to many but to some rather formidable.

Once upon a time all this had been thought diverting. People quoted his pungent judgments and invented anecdotes of his aud-acity, which were recounted as 'typical Pinfolds'. Now, he realized, his singularity had lost some of its attraction for others, but he was too old a dog to learn new tricks.

As a boy, at the age of puberty when most of his school-fellows coarsened, he had been as fastidious as the Bruiser and in his early years of success diffidence had lent him charm. Prolonged prosperity had wrought the change. He had seen sensitive men make themselves a protective disguise against the rebuffs and injustices of manhood. Mr Pinfold had suffered little in these ways; he had been tenderly reared and, as a writer, welcomed and over-rewarded early. It was his modesty which needed protection and for this purpose, but without design, he gradually assumed this character of burlesque. He was neither a scholar nor a regular soldier; the part for which he cast himself was a combination of eccentric don and testy colonel and he acted it strenuously, before his children at Lychpole and his cronies in London, until it came to dominate his whole outward personality. When he ceased to be alone, when he swung into his club or stumped up the nursery stairs, he left half of himself behind and the other half swelled to fill its place. He offered the world a front of pomposity mitigated by indiscretion, that was as hard, bright and antiquated as a cuirass.

Mr Pinfold's nanny used to say: 'Don't care went to the gallows'; also: 'Sticks and stones can break my bones, but words can never hurt me'. Mr Pinfold did not care what the village or his neighbours said of him. As a little boy he had been acutely sensitive to ridicule. His adult shell seemed impervious. He had long held himself inaccessible to interviewers and the young men and women who were employed to write 'profiles' collected material where they could. Every week his press-cutting agents brought to his breakfast-table two or three rather offensive allusions. He accepted without much resentment the world's estimate of himself. It was part of the price he paid for privacy. There were also letters from strangers, some abusive, some adulatory. Mr Pinfold was unable to discover any particular superiority of taste or expression in the writers of either sort. To both he sent printed acknowledgments.

His days passed in writing, reading and managing his own small affairs. He had never employed a secretary and for the last two years he had been without a manservant. But Mr Pinfold did not repine. He was perfectly competent to answer his own letters, pay his bills, tie his parcels and fold his clothes. At night his most frequent recurring dream was of doing *The Times* crossword puzzle; his most disagreeable that he was reading a tedious book aloud to his family.

Physically, in his late forties, he had become lazy. Time was, he rode to hounds, went for long walks, dug his garden, felled small trees. Now he spent most of the day in an armchair. He ate less, drank more, and grew corpulent. He was very seldom so ill as to spend a day in bed. He suffered intermittently from various twinges and brief bouts of pain in his joints and muscles – arthritis, gout, rheumatism, fibrositis; they were not dignified by any scientific name. Mr Pinfold seldom consulted his doctor. When he did so it was as a 'private patient'. His children availed themselves of the National Health Act but Mr Pinfold was reluctant to disturb a relationship which had been formed in his first years at Lychpole. Dr Drake, Mr Pinfold's medical attendant, had inherited the practice from his father and had been there before the Pinfolds came to Lychpole. Lean, horsy and weather-beaten in appearance, he had deep roots and wide ramifications in the countryside, being brother of the local auctioneer, brother-in-law of the solicitor, and cousin of three neighbouring rectors. His recreations were sporting. He was not a man of high technical pretensions but he suited Mr Pinfold well. He too suffered, more sharply, from Mr Pinfold's troubles and when consulted remarked that Mr Pinfold must expect these things at his age; that the whole district was afflicted in this way and that Lychpole was notoriously the worst spot in it.

Mr Pinfold also slept badly. It was a trouble of long standing. For twenty-five years he had used various sedatives, for the last ten years a single specific, chloral and bromide which, unknown to Dr Drake, he bought on an old prescription in London. There were periods of literary composition when he would find the sentences he had written during the day running in his head, the words shifting and changing colour kaleidoscopically, so that he would again and again climb out of bed, pad down to the library, make a minute correction, return to his room, lie in the dark dazzled by the pattern of vocables until obliged once more to descend to the manuscript. But those days and nights of obsession, of what might without vainglory be called 'creative' work, were a small part of his year. On most nights he was neither fretful nor apprehensive. He was merely bored. After even the idlest day he demanded six or seven hours of insensibility. With them behind him, with them to look forward to, he could face another idle day with something approaching jauntiness; and these his doses unfailingly provided.

At about the time of his fiftieth birthday there occurred two events which seemed trivial at the time but grew to importance in his later adventures.

The first of these primarily concerned Mrs Pinfold. During the war Lychpole was let, the house to a convent, the fields to a grazier. This man, Hill, had collected parcels of grass-land in and around the parish and on them kept a nondescript herd of 'unattested' dairy-cattle. The pasture was rank, the fences dilapidated. When the Pinfolds came home in 1945 and wanted their fields back, the War Agricultural Committee, normally predisposed towards the sitting tenant, were in no doubt of their decision in Mrs Pinfold's favour. Had she acted at once, Hill would have been out, with his compensation, at Michaelmas, but Mrs Pinfold was tender-hearted and Hill was adroit. First he pleaded, then having established new rights, asserted them. Lady Day succeeded Michaelmas; Michaelmas, Lady Day for four full years. Hill retreated meadow by meadow. The committee, still popularly known as 'the War

Ag.', returned, walked the property anew, again found for Mrs Pinfold. Hill, who now had a lawyer, appealed. So it went on. Mr Pinfold held aloof from it all, merely noting with sorrow the anxiety of his wife. At length at Michaelmas 1949 Hill finally moved. He boasted in the village inn of his cleverness, and left for the other side of the county with a comfortable profit.

The second event occurred soon after. Mr Pinfold received an invitation from the BBC to record an 'interview'. In the previous twenty years there had been many such proposals and he had always refused them. This time the fee was more liberal and the conditions softer. He would not have to go to the offices in London. Electricians would come to him with their apparatus. No script had to be submitted; no preparation of any kind was required; the whole thing would take an hour. In an idle moment Mr Pinfold agreed and at once regretted it.

The day came towards the end of the summer holidays. Soon after breakfast there arrived a motor-car, and a van of the sort used in the army by the more important kinds of signaller, which immediately absorbed the attention of the younger children. Out of the car there came three youngish men, thin of hair, with horn-rimmed elliptical glasses, cord trousers and tweed coats; exactly what Mr Pinfold was expecting. Their leader was named Angel. He emphasized his primacy by means of a neat, thick beard. He and his colleagues, he explained, had slept in the district, where he had an aunt. They would have to leave before luncheon. They would get through their business in the morning. The signallers began rapidly uncoiling wires and setting up their microphone in the library, while Mr Pinfold drew the attention of Angel and his party to the more noticeable of his collection of works of art. They did not commit themselves to an opinion, merely remarking that the last house they visited had a gouache by Rouault.

'I didn't know he ever painted in gouache,' said Mr Pinfold. 'Anyway he's a dreadful painter.'

'Ah!' said Angel. 'That's very nice. Very nice indeed. We must try and work that into the broadcast.'

When the electricians had made their arrangements Mr Pinfold sat at his table with the three strangers, a microphone in their midst. They were attempting to emulate a series that had been cleverly done in Paris with various French celebrities, in which informal, spontaneous discussion had seduced the objects of inquiry into self-revelation.

They questioned Mr Pinfold in turn about his tastes and habits. Angel led and it was at him that Mr Pinfold looked. The commonplace face above the beard became slightly sinister, the accentless, but insidiously plebeian voice, menacing. The questions were civil enough in form but Mr Pinfold thought he could detect an underlying malice. Angel seemed to believe that anyone sufficiently eminent to be interviewed by him must have something to hide, must be an imposter whom it was his business to trap and expose, and to direct his questions from some basic, previous knowledge of something discreditable. There was the hint of the under-dog's snarl which Mr Pinfold recognized from his press-cuttings.

He was well equipped to deal with insolence, real or imagined, and answered succinctly and shrewdly, disconcerting his adversaries, if adversaries they were, point by point. When it was over Mr Pinfold offered his visitors sherry. Tension relaxed. He asked politely who was their next subject.

'We're going on to Stratford,' said Angel, 'to interview Cedric Thorne.'

'You evidently have not seen this morning's paper,' said Mr Pinfold.

'No, we left before it came.'

'Cedric Thorne has escaped you. He hanged himself yesterday afternoon in his dressing-room.'

'Good heavens, are you sure?'

'It's in *The Times*.'

'May I see?'

Angel was shaken from his professional calm. Mr Pinfold brought the paper and he read the paragraph with emotion.

'Yes, yes. That's him. I half expected this. He was a personal friend. I must get on to his wife. May I phone?'

Mr Pinfold apologized for the levity with which he had broken the news and led Angel to the business-room. He refilled the sherry glasses and attempted to appear genial. Angel returned shortly to say: 'I couldn't get through. I'll have to try again later.'

Mr Pinfold repeated his regrets.

'Yes, it is a terrible thing – not wholly unexpected though.'

A macabre note had been added to the discords of the morning.

Then hands were shaken; the vehicles turned on the gravel and drove away.

When they were out of sight down the turn of the drive, one of the children who had been listening to the conversation in the van said: 'You didn't like those people much, did you, papa?'

He had definitely not liked them and they left an unpleasant memory which grew sharper in the weeks before the record was broadcast. He brooded. It seemed to him that an attempt had been made against his privacy and he was not sure how effectively he had defended it. He strained to remember his precise words and his memory supplied various distorted versions. Finally the evening came when the performance was made public. Mr Pinfold had the cook's wireless carried into the drawing-room. He and Mrs Pinfold listened together. His voice came to him strangely old and fruity, but what he said gave him no regret. 'They tried to make an ass of me,' he said. 'I don't believe they succeeded.'

Mr Pinfold for the time forgot Angel.

Boredom alone and some stiffness in the joints disturbed that sunny autumn. Despite his age and dangerous trade Mr Pinfold seemed to himself and to others unusually free of the fashionable agonies of *angst*.

Chapter Two

COLLAPSE OF ELDERLY PARTY

Mr Pinfold's idleness has been remarked. He was halfway through a novel and had stopped work in early summer. The completed chapters had been typed, rewritten, retyped, and lay in a drawer of his desk. He was entirely satisfied with them. He knew in a general way what had to be done to finish the book and he believed he could at any moment set himself to do it. But he was not pressed for money. The sales of his earlier works had already earned him that year the modest sufficiency which the laws of his country allowed. Further effort could only bring him sharply diminishing rewards and he was disinclined to effort. It was as though the characters he had quickened had fallen into a light doze and he left them benevolently to themselves. Hard things were in store for them. Let them sleep while they could. All his life he had worked intermittently. In youth his long periods of leisure had been devoted to amusement. Now he had abandoned that quest. That was the main difference between Mr Pinfold at fifty and Mr Pinfold at thirty.

Winter set in sharp at the end of October. The central heating plant at Lychpole was ancient and voracious. It had not been used since the days of fuel shortage. With most of the children away at school Mr and Mrs Pinfold withdrew into two rooms, heaped the fires with such coal as they could procure and sheltered from draughts behind screens and sandbags. Mr Pinfold's spirits sank, he began to talk of the West Indies and felt the need of longer periods of sleep.

The composition of his sleeping-draught, as originally prescribed, was largely of water. He suggested to his chemist that it would save trouble to have the essential ingredients in full strength and to dilute them himself. Their taste was bitter and after various experiments he found they were most palatable in Crème de Menthe. He was not scrupulous in measuring the dose. He splashed into the glass as much as his mood suggested and if he took too little and woke in the small hours he would get out of bed and make unsteadily for the bottles and a second swig. Thus he passed many hours in welcome unconsciousness; but all was not well with him. Whether from too much strong medicine or from some other cause, he felt decidedly seedy by the middle of November. He found himself disagreeably flushed, particularly after drinking his normal, not illiberal, quantity of wine and brandy. Crimson blotches appeared on the backs of his hands.

He called in Dr Drake who said: 'That sounds like an allergy.'
'Allergic to what?'
'Ah, that's hard to say. Almost anything can cause an allergy nowadays. It might be something you're wearing or some plant growing near. The only cure really is a change.'
'I might go abroad after Christmas.'
'Yes, that's the best thing you could do. Anyway don't worry. No one ever died of an allergy. It's allied to hayfever,' he added learnedly, 'and asthma.'

Another thing which troubled him and which he soon began to attribute to his medicine, was the behaviour of his memory. It began to play him tricks. He did not grow forgetful. He remembered everything in clear detail but he remembered it wrong. He would state a fact, dogmatically, sometimes in print – a date, a name, a quotation – find himself challenged, turn to his books for verification and find most disconcertingly that he was at fault.

Two incidents of this kind slightly alarmed him. With the idea of cheering him up Mrs Pinfold invited a weekend party to Lychpole. On the Sunday afternoon he proposed a visit to a remarkable tomb in a neighbouring church. He had not been there since the war, but he had a clear image of it, which he described to them in technical detail; a recumbent figure of the mid-sixteenth century in gilded bronze; something almost unique in England. They found the place without difficulty; it was unquestionably what they sought; but the figure was of coloured alabaster. They laughed, he laughed, but he was shocked.

The second incident was more humiliating. A friend in London, James Lance, who shared his tastes in furniture, found, and offered him as a present, a most remarkable piece; a wash-hand stand of the greatest elaboration designed by an English architect of the 1860s, a man not universally honoured but of magisterial status to Mr Pinfold and his friends. This massive freak of fancy was decorated with metal work and mosaic, and with a series of panels painted in his hot youth by a rather preposterous artist who later became President of the Royal Academy. It was just such a trophy as Mr Pinfold most valued. He hurried to London, studied the object with exultation, arranged for its delivery and impatiently awaited its arrival at Lychpole. A fortnight later it came, was borne upstairs and set in the space cleared for it. Then to his horror Mr Pinfold observed that an essential part was missing. There should have been a prominent, highly ornamental, copper tap in the centre, forming the climax of the design. In its place there was merely a small socket. Mr Pinfold broke into lamentation. The carriers asserted that this was the condition of the piece when they fetched it. Mr Pinfold bade them search their van. Nothing was found. Mr Pinfold surcharged the receipt *'incomplete'* and immediately wrote to the firm ordering a diligent search of the warehouse where the wash-hand stand had reposed *en route* and enclosing a detailed drawing of the lost member. There was a brisk exchange of letters, the carriers denying all responsibility. Finally Mr Pinfold, decently reluctant to involve the donor in a dispute about a gift, wrote to James Lance asking for corroboration. James Lance replied: there never had been any tap such as Mr Pinfold described.

'You haven't always been altogether making sense lately,' said Mrs Pinfold when her husband showed her this letter, 'and you're a very odd colour. Either you're drinking too much or doping too much, or both.'

'I wonder if you're right,' said Mr Pinfold. 'Perhaps I ought to go slow after Christmas.'

The children's holidays were a time when Mr Pinfold felt a special need for unconsciousness at night and for stimulated geniality by day. Christmas was always the worst season. During that dread week he made copious use of wine and narcotics and his inflamed face shone like the florid squireens depicted in the cards that littered the house. Once catching sight of himself in the looking-glass, thus empurpled and wearing a paper crown, he took fright at what he saw.

'I *must* get away,' said Mr Pinfold later to his wife. 'I must go somewhere sunny and finish my book.'

'I wish I could come too. There's so much to be done getting Hill's horrible fields back into shape. I'm rather worried about you, you know. You ought to have someone to look after you.'

'I'll be all right. I work better alone.'

The cold grew intense. Mr Pinfold spent the day crouched over the library fire. To leave it for the icy passages made him shudder and stumble, half benumbed, while outside the hidden sun glared over a landscape that seemed all turned to metal; lead and iron and steel. Only in the evenings did Mr Pinfold manage a semblance of jollity, joining his family in charades or Up Jenkins, playing the fool to the loud delight of the youngest and the tolerant amusement of the eldest of his children, until in degrees of age they went happily to their rooms and he was released into his own darkness and silence.

At length the holidays came to an end. Nuns and monks received their returning charges and Lychpole was left in peace save for rare intrusions from the nursery. And now, just when Mr Pinfold was gathering himself as it were for a strenuous effort at reformation, he was struck down by the most severe attack of his 'aches' which he had yet suffered. Every joint, but especially feet, ankles and knees, agonized him. Dr Drake again advocated a warm climate and prescribed some pills which he said were 'something new and pretty powerful'. They were large and drab, reminding Mr Pinfold of the pellets of blotting-paper which used to be rolled at his private school. Mr Pinfold added them to his bromide and chloral and Crème de Menthe, his wine and gin and brandy, and to a new sleeping-draught which his doctor, ignorant of the existence of his other bottle, also supplied.

And now his mind became much overcast. One great thought

excluded all others, the need to escape. He, who even in this extremity eschewed the telephone, telegraphed to the travel agency with whom he dealt: *Kindly arrange immediate passage West Indies, East Indies, Africa, India, anywhere hot, luxury preferred, private bath, outside single cabin essential,* and anxiously awaited the reply. When it came it comprised a large envelope full of decorative folders and a note saying they awaited his further instructions.

Mr Pinfold became frantic. He knew one of the directors of the firm. He thought he had met others. It came to him in his daze quite erroneously that he had lately read somewhere that a lady of his acquaintance had joined the board. To all of them at their private addresses he despatched peremptory telegrams: *Kindly investigate wanton inefficiency your office. Pinfold.*

The director whom he really knew took action. There was little choice at that moment. Mr Pinfold was lucky to secure a passage in the *Caliban,* a one-class ship sailing in three days for Ceylon.

During the time of waiting Mr Pinfold's frenzy subsided. He became instead intermittently comatose. When lucid he was in pain.

Mrs Pinfold said, as she had often said before: 'You're doped, darling, up to the eyes.'

'Yes. It's those rheumatism pills. Drake said they were very strong.'

Mr Pinfold, who was normally rather deft, now became clumsy. He dropped things. He found his buttons and laces intractable, his handwriting in the few letters which his journey necessitated, uncertain, his spelling, never strong, wildly barbaric.

In one of his clearer hours he said to Mrs Pinfold: 'I believe you are right. I shall give up the sleeping-draughts as soon as I get to sea. I always sleep better at sea. I shall cut down on drink too. As soon as I get rid of these damned aches, I shall start work. I can always work at sea. I shall have the book finished before I get home.'

These resolutions persisted; there was a sober, industrious time ahead of him in a few days' time. He had to survive somehow until then. Everything would come right very soon.

Mrs Pinfold shared these hopes. She was busy with her plans

for the farm which the newly liberated territory made more elaborate. She could not get away. Nor did she think her presence was needed. Once her husband was safely on board, all would be well with him.

She helped him pack. Indeed he could do nothing except sit on a bedroom chair and give confused directions. He must take foolscap paper, he said, in large quantities; also ink, foreign ink was never satisfactory. And pens. He had once experienced great difficulty in New York in purchasing pen-nibs; he had in the end had recourse to a remote law-stationer's. All foreigners, he was now convinced, used some kind of stylographic instrument. He must take pens and nibs. His clothes were a matter of indifference. You could always get a Chinaman, anywhere out of Europe, to make you a suit of clothes in an afternoon, Mr Pinfold said.

That Sunday morning Mr Pinfold did not go to Mass. He lay in bed until midday and, when he came down, hobbled to the drawing-room window and gazed across the bare, icy park thinking of the welcoming tropics. Then he said: 'Oh God, here comes the Bruiser.'

'Hide.'

'No fire in the library.'

'I'll tell him you're ill.'

'No. I like the Bruiser. Besides, if you say I'm ill, he'll set his damned Box to work on me.'

Throughout the short visit Mr Pinfold exerted himself to be affable.

'You aren't looking at all well, Gilbert,' the Bruiser said.

'I'm all right really. A twinge of rheumatism. I'm sailing the day after tomorrow for Ceylon.'

'That's very sudden, isn't it?'

'The weather. Need a change.'

He sank into his chair and then, when the Bruiser left, got to his feet again with an enormous obvious effort.

'Please don't come out,' said the Bruiser.

Mrs Pinfold went with him to release his dog and when she returned found Mr Pinfold enraged.

'I know what you two have been talking about.'

'Do you? I was hearing about the Fawdles' row with the Parish Council about their right of way.'

'You've been giving him my hair for his Box.'

'Nonsense, Gilbert.'

'I could tell by the way he looked at me that he was measuring my Life-Waves.'

Mrs Pinfold looked at him sadly. 'You really are in rather a bad way, aren't you, darling?'

The *Caliban* was not a ship so large as to require a special train; carriages were reserved on the regular service from London. Mrs Pinfold accompanied him there the day before his departure. He had to collect his tickets from the travel agency, but when he arrived in London great lassitude came over him and he went straight to bed in his hotel, summoning a messenger from the agency to bring them to him. A young polite man came at once. He bore a small portfolio of documents, tickets for train and ship and for return by air, baggage forms, embarkation cards, carbon copies of letters of reservation and the like. Mr Pinfold had difficulty in understanding. He had trouble with his cheque book. The young man looked at him with more than normal curiosity. Perhaps he was a reader of Mr Pinfold's works. It was more probable that he found something bizarre in the spectacle of Mr Pinfold, lying there groaning and muttering, propped by pillows, purple in the face, with a bottle of champagne open beside him. Mr Pinfold offered him a glass. He refused. When he had gone Mr Pinfold said: 'I didn't at all like the look of that young man.'

'Oh, he was all right,' said Mrs Pinfold.

'There was something fishy about him,' said Mr Pinfold. 'He stared at me as though he was measuring my Life-Waves.'

Then he fell into a doze.

Mrs Pinfold lunched downstairs and rejoined her husband who said: 'I must go and say goodbye to my mother. Order a car.'

'Darling, you aren't well enough.'

'I *always* say goodbye to her before going abroad. I've told her we are coming.'

'I'll telephone and explain. Or shall I go out there alone?'

'I'm going. It's true I'm not well enough, but I'm going. Get the hall-porter to have a car here in half an hour.'

Mr Pinfold's widowed mother lived in a pretty little house at Kew. She was eighty-two years old, sharp of sight and hearing, but of recent years very slow of mind. In childhood Mr Pinfold had loved her extravagantly. There remained now only a firm *pietas*. He no longer enjoyed her company nor wished to communicate. She had been left rather badly off by his father. Mr Pinfold supplemented her income with payments under a deed of covenant so that she was now comfortably placed with a single, faithful old maid to look after her and all her favourite possessions, preserved from the larger house, set out round her. Young Mrs Pinfold, who would talk happily of her children, was very much more agreeable company to the old woman than was her son, but Mr Pinfold went to call dutifully several times a year and, as he said, always before an absence of any length.

A funereal limousine bore them to Kew. Mr Pinfold sat huddled in rugs. He hobbled on two sticks, one a blackthorn, the other a malacca cane, through the little gate up the garden path. An hour later he was out again, subsiding with groans into the back of the car. The visit had not been a success.

'It wasn't a success, was it?' said Mr Pinfold.

'We ought to have stayed to tea.'

'She knows I never have tea.'

'But I do, and Mrs Yercombe had it all prepared. I saw it on a trolley – cakes and sandwiches and a muffin-dish.'

'The truth is my mother doesn't like to see anyone younger than herself iller than herself – except children of course.'

'You were beastly snubbing about the children.'

'Yes. I know. Damn. Damn. Damn. I'll write to her from the ship. I'll send her a cable. Why does everyone except me find it so easy to be nice?'

When he reached the hotel he returned to bed and ordered

another bottle of champagne. He dozed again. Mrs Pinfold sat quietly reading a paper-covered detective story. He awoke and ordered a rather elaborate dinner, but by the time it came his appetite was gone. Mrs Pinfold ate well, but sadly. When the table was wheeled out, Mr Pinfold hobbled to the bathroom and took his blue-grey pills. Three a day was the number prescribed. He had a dozen left. He took a big dose of his sleeping-draught; the bottle was half full.

'I'm taking too much,' he said, not for the first time. 'I'll finish what I've got and never order any more.' He looked at himself in the glass. He looked at the backs of his hands which were again mottled with large crimson patches. 'I'm sure it's not really good for me,' he said and felt his way to bed, tumbled in and fell heavily asleep.

His train was at ten next day. The funereal limousine was ordered. Mr Pinfold dressed laboriously and, without shaving, went to the station. Mrs Pinfold came with him. He needed help to find a porter and to find his seat. He dropped his ticket and his sticks on the platform.

'I don't believe you ought to be going alone,' said Mrs Pinfold. 'Wait for another ship and I'll come too.'

'No, no. I shall be all right.'

But some hours later when he reached the docks Mr Pinfold did not feel so hopeful. He had slept most of the way, now and then waking to light a cigar and let it fall from his fingers after a few puffs. His aches seemed sharper than ever as he climbed out of the carriage. Snow was falling. The distance from the train to the ship seemed enormous. The other passengers stepped out briskly. Mr Pinfold moved slowly. On the quay a telegraph boy was taking messages. Mrs Pinfold would be back at Lychpole by now. Mr Pinfold with great difficulty wrote: *Safely embarked. All love.* Then he moved to the gangway and painfully climbed aboard.

A coloured steward led him to his cabin. He gazed round it unseeing, sitting on a bunk. There was something he ought to do; telegraph his mother. On the cabin table was some writing paper bearing the ship's name and the flag of the line at its head. Mr

Pinfold tried to compose and inscribe a message. The task proved to be one of insuperable difficulty. He threw the spoilt paper into the basket and sat on his bed, still in his hat and overcoat with his sticks beside him. Presently his two suitcases arrived. He gazed at them for some time, then began to unpack. That too proved difficult. He rang his bell and the coloured steward reappeared bowing and smiling.

'I'm not very well. I wonder if you could unpack for me?'

'Dinner seven-thirty o'clock, sir.'

'I said, could you unpack for me?'

'No, sir, bar not open in port, sir.'

The man smiled and bowed and left Mr Pinfold.

Mr Pinfold sat there, in his hat and coat, holding his cudgel and his cane. Presently an English steward appeared with the passenger list, some forms to fill, and the message: 'The Captain's compliments, sir, and he would like to have the honour of your company at his table in the dining-saloon.'

'Now?'

'No, sir. Dinner is at seven-thirty. I don't expect the Captain will be dining in the saloon tonight.'

'I don't think I shall either,' said Mr Pinfold. 'Thank the Captain. Very civil of him. Another night. Someone said something about the bar not being open. Can't you get me some brandy?'

'Oh yes, sir. I think so, sir. Any particular brand?'

'Brandy,' said Mr Pinfold. 'Large one.'

The chief steward brought it with his own hands.

'Good night,' said Mr Pinfold.

He found on the top of his case the things he needed for the night. Among them his pills and his bottle. The brandy impelled him to action. He must telegraph to his mother. He groped his way out and along the corridor to the purser's office. A clerk was on duty, very busy with his papers behind a grill.

'I want to send a telegram.'

'Yes, sir. There's a boy at the head of the gangway.'

'I'm not feeling very well. I wonder if you could be very kind and write it for me?'

The purser looked at him hard, observed his unshaven chin, smelled brandy, and drew on his long experience of travellers.

'Sorry about that, sir. Pleased to be any help.'

Mr Pinfold dictated, '*Everyone in ship most helpful. Love. Gilbert,*' fumbled with a handful of silver, then crept back to his cabin. There he took his large grey pills and a swig of his sleeping-draught. Then, prayerless, he got himself to bed.

Chapter Three

The SS. *Caliban*, Captain Steerforth master, was middle-aged and middle-class; clean, trustworthy and comfortable, without pretence to luxury. There were no private baths. Meals were not served in cabins, it was stated, except on the orders of the medical officer. Her public rooms were panelled in fumed oak in the fashion of an earlier generation. She plied between Liverpool and Rangoon, stopping at intermediate ports, carrying a mixed cargo and a more or less homogeneous company of passengers, Scotchmen and their wives mostly, travelling on business and on leave. Crew and stewards were Lascars.

When Mr Pinfold came to himself it was full day and he was rocking gently to and fro in his narrow bed with the slow roll of the high seas.

He had barely noticed his cabin on the preceding evening. Now he observed that it was a large one, with two berths. There was a little window made of slats of opaque glass, fitted with tight, ornamental muslin curtains, and a sliding shutter. This gave, not on the sea, but on a deck where people from time to time passed, casting a brief shadow but with no sound that was audible above the beat of the engine, the regular creak of plates and woodwork and the continuous insect-hum of the ventilator. The ceiling, at which Mr Pinfold gazed, was spanned as though by a cottage beam by a white, studded air-shaft and by a multiplicity of pipes and electric cable. Mr Pinfold lay for some time, gazing and rocking, not quite sure where he was but rather pleased than not to be there. His watch, unwound the night before, had run down. He had been called. On the shelf at his side a cup of tea, already quite cold, slopped in its saucer, and beside it, stained with spilt tea, was the ship's passenger list. He found himself entered as *Mr G. Penfold* and thought of Mr Pooter at the Mansion House. The misprint was welcome as an item of disguise, an uncovenanted addition to his privacy. He glanced idly through the other names – '*Dr Abercrombie, Mr Addison, Miss Amory, Mr and Mrs and Miss Margaret Angel, Mr and Mrs Benson, Mr Blackadder, Major and Mrs Cockson*', no one he knew, no one likely to annoy him. There were half a dozen Burmese on their way to Rangoon; the rest were solidly British. No one, he felt confident, would have read his books or would seek to draw him into literary conversation. He would be able to do a quiet three-weeks' work in this ship as soon as his health mended.

He sat up and put his feet to the floor. He was still crippled but a shade less painfully, he thought, than in the days before. He went to his basin. The looking-glass showed him a face which still looked alarmingly old and ill. He shaved, brushed his hair, took his grey pill, returned to bed with a book and at once fell into a doze.

The ship's hooter roused him. That must be twelve noon. A knock on his door, barely audible above the other sea noises, and the dark face of his steward appeared.

'No good today,' the man said. 'Plenty passengers sick.'

He took the cup of tea and slipped away.

Mr Pinfold was a good sailor. Only once in a war which had been largely spent bucketing about in various sorts of boat, had he ever been seasick and on that occasion most of the naval crew had been prostrate also. Mr Pinfold, who was neither beautiful nor athletic, cherished this one gift of parsimonious Nature. He decided to get up.

The main deck, when he reached it, was almost deserted. Two wind-blown girls in thick sweaters were tacking along arm-in-arm past the piles of folded chairs. Mr Pinfold hobbled to the after smoking-room bar. Four or five men sat together in one corner. He nodded to them, found a chair on the further side and ordered brandy and ginger-ale. He was not himself. He knew in a distant way, as he knew, or thought he knew, certain facts of history, that he was in a ship, travelling for the good of his health, but, as with much of his historical knowledge, he was vague about the date. He did not know that twenty-four hours ago he had been in the train from London to Liverpool. His phases of sleeping and waking in the last few days were not related to night and day. He sat still in the smoking-room gazing blankly ahead.

After a time two cheerful women entered. The men greeted them:

'Morning, Mrs Cockson. Glad to see you're on your feet this merry morning.'

'Good morning, good morning, good morning all. You know Mrs Benson?'

'I don't think I've had that pleasure. Will you join us, Mrs Benson? I'm in the chair,' and he turned and called to the steward: 'Boy.'

Mr Pinfold studied this group with benevolence. No one among them would be a Pinfold fan. Presently, at one o'clock, a steward appeared with a gong and Mr Pinfold followed him submissively down to the dining-saloon.

The Captain's table was laid for seven. The 'fiddles' were up and the cloth damped; barely quarter of the places in the saloon were taken.

Only one other of the Captain's party came to luncheon, a tall young Englishman who fell into easy conversation with Mr Pinfold, informing him that he was named Glover and was manager of a tea plantation in Ceylon; an idyllic life, as he described it, lived on horseback with frequent long leave at a golf club. Glover was keen on golf. In order to keep himself in condition for the game on board ship he had a weighted club, its head on a spring, which he swung, he said, a hundred times morning and evening. His cabin, it transpired, was next to Mr Pinfold's.

'We have to share a bathroom. When do you like your bath?'

Glover's conversation did not demand sharp attention. Mr Pinfold found himself recalled into a world beyond which he had momentarily wandered, to answer: 'Well, really, I hardly ever have a bath at sea. One keeps so clean and I don't like hot salt water. I tried to book a private bathroom. I can't think why.'

'There aren't any private baths in this ship.'

'So I learned. It seems a very decent sort of ship,' said Mr Pinfold, gazing sadly at his curry, at his swaying glass of wine, at the surrounding deserted table, wishing to be pleasant to Glover.

'Yes. Everyone knows everyone else. The same people travel in her every year. People sometimes complain they feel rather out of things if they aren't regulars.'

'I shan't complain,' said Mr Pinfold. 'I've been rather ill. I want a quiet time.'

'Sorry to hear that. You'll find it quiet enough. Some find it too quiet.'

'It can't be too quiet for me,' said Mr Pinfold.

He took rather formal leave of Glover and at once forgot him until, reaching his cabin, he found added to its other noises the strains of a jazz band. Mr Pinfold stood puzzled. He was not musical. All he knew was that somewhere quite near him a band was playing. Then he remembered.

'It's the golfer,' he thought. 'That young man next door. He's got a gramophone. What's more,' he suddenly observed, 'he's got a *dog*.' Quite distinctly on the linoleum outside his door, between his door and Glover's, he heard the pattering of a dog's feet. 'I bet he's not allowed it. I've never been in a ship where they allowed dogs in the cabins. I daresay he bribed the steward. Anyway, one can't reasonably object. I don't mind. He seemed a very pleasant fellow.'

He noticed his grey pills, took one, lay down, opened his book and then to the sound of dance tunes and the snuffling of the dog, he fell asleep once more.

Perhaps he dreamed. He forgot on the instant whatever had happened in the hours between. It was dark. He was awake and there was a very curious scene being played near him; under his feet, it seemed. He heard distinctly a clergyman conducting a religious meeting. Mr Pinfold had no first-hand acquaintance with evangelical practice. His home and his schools had professed a broad-to-high anglicanism. His ideas of non-conformity derived from literature, from Mr Chadband and Philip Henry Gosse, from charades and from back numbers of *Punch*. The sermon, which was just rising to its peroration, was plainly an expression of that kind of faith, scriptural in diction, emotional in appeal. It was addressed presumably to members of the crew. Male voices sang a hymn which Mr Pinfold remembered from his nursery where his nanny, like almost all nannies, had been Calvinist: '*Pull for the shore, sailor. Pull for the shore.*'

'I want to see Billy alone after you dismiss,' said the clergyman. There followed an extempore, rather perfunctory prayer, then a great shuffling of feet and pushing about of chairs; then a hush; then the clergyman, very earnestly: 'Well, Billy, what have you got to say to me?' and the unmistakable sound of sobbing.

Mr Pinfold began to feel uneasy. This was something that was not meant to be overheard.

'Billy, you must tell me yourself. I am not accusing you of anything. I am not putting words into your mouth.'

Silence except for sobbing.

'Billy, you know what we talked about last time. Have you done it again? Have you been impure, Billy?'

'Yes, sir. I can't help it, sir.'

'God never tempts us beyond our strength, Billy. I've told you that, haven't I? Do you suppose I do not feel these temptations, too, Billy? Very strongly at times. But I resist, don't I? You know I resist, don't I, Billy?'

Mr Pinfold was horror-struck. He was being drawn into participation in a scene of gruesome indecency. His sticks lay by the bunk. He took the blackthorn and beat strongly on the floor.

'Did you hear anything then, Billy? A knocking. That is God knocking at the door of your soul. He can't come and help you unless you are pure, like me.'

This was more than Mr Pinfold could bear. He took painfully to his feet, put on his coat, brushed his hair. The voices below him continued:

'I can't help it, sir. I want to be good. I try. I can't.'

'You've got pictures of girls stuck up by your bunk, haven't you?'

'Yes, sir.'

'Filthy pictures.'

'Yes, sir.'

'How can you say you want to be good when you keep temptation deliberately before your eyes. I shall come and destroy those pictures.'

'No, please sir. I want them.'

Mr Pinfold hobbled out of his cabin and up to the main deck. The sea was calmer now. More passengers were about in the lounge and the bar. It was half-past six. A group were throwing dice for drinks. Mr Pinfold sat alone and ordered a cocktail. When the steward brought it, he asked: 'Does this ship carry a regular chaplain?'

'Oh no, sir. The Captain reads the prayers on Sundays.'

'There's a clergyman, then, among the passengers?'

'I haven't seen one, sir. Here's the list.'

Mr Pinfold studied the passenger list. No name bore any prefix indicating Holy Orders. A strange ship, thought Mr Pinfold, in which laymen were allowed to evangelize a presumably heathen crew; religious mania perhaps on the part of one of the officers.

Waking and sleeping he had lost count of time. It seemed he had been many days at sea in this strange ship. When Glover came into the bar, Mr Pinfold said affably: 'Nice to see you again.'

Glover looked slightly startled by this greeting.

'I've been down in my cabin,' he said.

'I had to come up. I was embarrassed by that prayer-meeting. Weren't you?'

'Prayer-meeting?' said Glover. 'No.'

'Right under our feet. Couldn't you hear it?'

'I heard nothing,' said Glover.

He began to move away.

'Have a drink,' said Mr Pinfold.

'I won't, thanks. I don't. Have to be careful in a place like Ceylon.'

'How's your dog?'

'My dog?'

'Your crypto-dog. The stowaway. Please don't think I'm complaining. I don't mind your dog. Nor your gramophone for that matter.'

'But I haven't a dog. I haven't a gramophone.'

'Oh well,' said Mr Pinfold huffily. 'Perhaps I am mistaken.'

If Glover did not wish to confide in him, he would not try to force himself on the young man.

'See you at dinner,' said Glover, making off.

He was wearing a dinner jacket, Mr Pinfold noticed, as were several other passengers. Time to change. Mr Pinfold went back to his cabin. No sound came now from below; the pseudo-priest and the unchaste seaman had left. But the jazz band was going full blast. So it was not Glover's gramophone. As he changed, Mr Pinfold considered the matter. During the war he had travelled in troop-ships which were fitted with amplifiers on every deck. Unintelligible alarms and orders had issued from these devices and at certain hours popular music. The *Caliban*, plainly, was equipped in this way. It would be a great nuisance when he began to write. He would have to enquire whether there was some way of cutting it off.

It took him a long time to dress. His fingers were unusually clumsy with studs and tie, and his face in the glass was still blotched and staring. By the time he was ready the gong was sounding for dinner. He did not attempt to wear his evening shoes. Instead he slipped into the soft, fur-lined boots in which he had come aboard. With one hand firmly on the rail, the other on his cane, he made his way laboriously down to the saloon. On the stairs he noticed a bronze plaque recording that this ship had been manned by the Royal Navy during the war and had served in the landings in North Africa and Normandy.

He was first at his table, one of the earliest diners in the ship. He noticed a small dark man in day clothes sitting at a table alone. Then the place began to fill. He watched his fellow passengers in a slightly dazed way. The purser's table, as is common in ships of the kind, had the gayest party, the few girls and young women, the more jovial men from the bar. A plate of soup was set before Mr Pinfold. Two or three coloured stewards stood together by a service table talking in undertones. Suddenly Mr Pinfold was surprised to hear from them three obscene epithets spoken in clear

English tones. He looked and glared. One of the men immediately slid to his side.

'Yes, sir; something to drink, sir.'

There was no hint of mockery in the gentle face, no echo in that soft South Indian accent of the gross tones he had overheard. Baffled, Mr Pinfold said: 'Wine.'

'Wine, sir?'

'You have some champagne on board, I suppose?'

'Oh yes, sir. Three names. I show list.'

'Don't bother about the name. Just bring half a bottle.'

Glover came and sat opposite.

'I owe you an apology,' said Mr Pinfold. 'It wasn't your gramophone. Part of the naval equipment left over from the war.'

'Oh,' said Glover. 'That was it, was it?'

'It seems the most likely explanation.'

'Perhaps it does.'

'Very odd language the servants use.'

'They're from Travancore.'

'No. I mean the way they swear. In front of us, I mean. I daresay they don't mean to be insolent but it shows bad discipline.'

'I've never noticed it,' said Glover.

He was not at his ease with Mr Pinfold.

Then the table filled up. Captain Steerforth greeted them and took his place at the head. He was an unremarkable man at first sight. A pretty, youngish woman introduced as Mrs Scarfield sat next to Mr Pinfold. He explained that he was temporarily a cripple and could not stand up. 'My doctor has given me some awfully strong pills to take. They make me feel rather odd. You must forgive me if I'm a dull companion.'

'We're all very dull, I'm afraid,' she said. 'You're the writer, aren't you? I'm afraid I never seem to get any time for reading.'

Mr Pinfold was inured to this sort of conversation but tonight he could not cope. He said: 'I wish I didn't' and turned stupidly to his wine. 'She probably thinks I'm drunk,' he thought and made an attempt to explain: 'They are big grey pills. I don't know

34

what's in them. I don't believe my doctor does either. Something new.'

'That's always exciting, isn't it?' said Mrs Scarfield.

Mr Pinfold despaired and spent the rest of dinner, at which he ate very little, in silence.

The Captain rose, his party with him. Mr Pinfold, slow to move, was still in his chair, fumbling for his stick, when they passed behind him. He got to his feet. He would have dearly liked to go to his cabin but he was held back, partly by the odd fear that he would be suspected of sea-sickness but more by an odder sentiment, a bond of duty which he conceived held him to Captain Steerforth. It seemed to him that he was in some way under this man's command and that it would be a grave default to leave him until he was dismissed. So, laboriously, he followed them to the lounge and lowered himself into an armchair between the Scarfields. They were drinking coffee. He offered them all brandy. They refused and for himself he ordered brandy and Crème de Menthe mixed. As he did so Mr and Mrs Scarfield exchanged a glance, which he intercepted, as though to confirm some previous confidence – 'My dear, that man next to me, the author, was completely tight.' 'Are you sure?' 'Simply plastered.'

Mrs Scarfield was really extremely pretty, Mr Pinfold thought. She would not keep that skin long in Burma.

Mr Scarfield was in the timber trade, teak. His prospects depended less on his own industry and acumen than on the action of politicians. He addressed the little circle on this subject.

'In a democracy,' said Mr Pinfold with more weight than originality, 'men do not seek authority so that they may impose a policy. They seek a policy so that they may achieve authority.'

He proceeded to illustrate this theme with examples.

At one time or another he had met most of the Government Front Bench. Some were members of Bellamy's whom he knew well. Oblivious of his audience he began to speak of them with familiarity, as he would have done among his friends. The Scarfields again exchanged glances and it occurred to him, too late, that he was not among people who thought it on the whole rather discreditable to know politicians. These people thought he was showing off. He stopped in the middle of a sentence, silent with shame.

'It must be very exciting to move behind the scenes,' said Mrs Scarfield. 'We only know what we see in the papers.'

Was there malice behind her smile? At first meeting she had seemed frank and friendly. Mr Pinfold thought he discovered sly hostility now.

'Oh, I hardly ever read the political columns,' he said.

'You don't have to, do you? Getting it all first hand.'

There was no doubt in Mr Pinfold's mind. He had made an ass of himself. Reckless now of his reputation as a good sailor, he attempted a little bow to include the Captain and the Scarfields.

'If you'll excuse me, I think I'll go to my cabin.'

He had difficulty getting out of his deep chair, he had difficulty with his stick, he had difficulty keeping his balance. They had barely said 'Goodnight', he was still struggling away from them, when something the Captain said made them laugh. Three distinct laughs, all, in Mr Pinfold's ears, cruelly derisive. On his way out he passed Glover. Moved to explain himself he said: 'I don't know anything about politics.'

'No?' said Glover.

'Tell them I don't know anything.'

'Tell who?'

'The Captain.'

'He's just behind you over there.'

'Oh well, it doesn't matter.'

He hobbled away and looking back from the doors saw Glover talking to the Scarfields. They were ostensibly arranging a four for bridge but Mr Pinfold knew they had another darker interest – *him*.

It was not yet nine o'clock. Mr Pinfold undressed. He hung up his clothes, washed and took his pill. There were three tablespoon-fuls left in his bottle of sleeping-draught. He decided to try and spend the night without it, to delay anyway until after midnight. The sea was much calmer now; he could lie in bed without rolling.

He lay at his ease and began to read one of the novels he had brought on board.

Then, before he had turned a page, the band struck up. This was no wireless performance. It was a living group just under his feet, rehearsing. They were in the same place, as inexplicably audible, as the afternoon bible-class; young, happy people, the party doubtless from the purser's table. Their instruments were drums and rattles and some sort of pipe. The drums and rattles did most of the work. Mr Pinfold knew nothing of music. It seemed to him that the rhythms they played derived from some very primitive tribe and were of anthropological rather than artistic interest. This guess was confirmed.

'Let's try the Pocoputa Indian one,' said the young man who acted, without any great air of authority, as leader.

'Oh not *that*. It's so *beastly*,' said a girl.

'I know,' said the leader. 'It's the three-eight rhythm. The Gestapo discovered it independently, you know. They used to play it in the cells. It drove the prisoners mad.'

'Yes,' said another girl. 'Thirty-six hours did for anyone. Twelve was enough for most. They could stand any torture but that.'

'It drove them absolutely mad.' 'Raving mad.' 'Stark, staring mad.' 'It was the worst torture of all.' 'The Russians use it now.' The voices, some male, some female, all young and eager, came tumbling like puppies. 'The Hungarians do it best.' 'Good old three-eight.' 'Good old Pocoputa Indians.' 'They were mad.'

'I suppose no one can hear us?' said a sweet girlish voice.

'Don't be so wet, Mimi. Everyone's up on the main deck.'

'All right then,' said the band leader. 'The three-eight rhythm.' And off they went.

The sound throbbed and thrilled in the cabin which had suddenly become a prison cell. Mr Pinfold was not one who thought and talked easily to a musical accompaniment. Even in early youth he had sought the night-clubs where there was a bar out of hearing of the band. Friends he had, Roger Stillingfleet among them, to whom jazz was a necessary drug – whether stimulant or narcotic Mr Pinfold did not know. He preferred silence. The three-eight rhythm was indeed torture to him. He could not read. It was not a quarter of an hour since he had entered the cabin. Unendurable hours lay ahead. He emptied the bottle of sleeping-draught and, to the strains of the jolly young people from the purser's table, fell into unconsciousness.

He awoke before dawn. The bright young people below him had dispersed. The three-eight rhythm was hushed. No shadow passed between the deck-light and the cabin window. But overhead there was turmoil. The crew, or a considerable part of it, was engaged on an operation of dragging the deck with what from the sound of it might have been an enormous chain-harrow, and they were not happy in their work. They were protesting mutinously in their own tongue and the officer in command was roaring back at them in the tones of an old sea-dog: 'Get on with it, you black bastards. Get on with it.'

The Lascars were not so easily quelled. They shouted back unintelligibly.

'I'll call out the Master-at-Arms,' shouted the officer. An empty threat, surely? thought Mr Pinfold. It was scarcely conceivable that the *Caliban* carried a Master-at-Arms. 'By God, I'll shoot the first man of you that moves,' said the officer.

The hubbub increased. Mr Pinfold could almost see the drama overhead, the half-lighted deck, the dark frenzied faces, the solitary bully with the heavy old-fashioned ship's pistol. Then there was a crash, not a shot but a huge percussion of metal as though a hundred pokers and pairs of tongs had fallen into an enormous fender, followed by a wail of agony and a moment of complete silence.

'There,' said the officer more in the tones of a nanny than a sea-dog, 'just see what you've gone and done now.'

Whatever its nature this violent occurrence entirely subdued the passions of the crew. They were docile, ready to do anything to retrieve the disaster. The only sounds now were the officer's calmer orders and the whimpering of the injured man.

'Steady there. Easy does it. You, cut along to the sickbay and get the surgeon. You, go up and report to the bridge . . .'

For a long time, two hours perhaps, Mr Pinfold lay in his bunk listening. He was able to hear quite distinctly not only what was said in his immediate vicinity, but elsewhere. He had the light on, now, in his cabin, and as he gazed at the complex of tubes and wires which ran across his ceiling, he realized that they must form some kind of general junction in the system of communication. Through some trick or fault or war-time survival everything spoken in the executive quarters of the ship was transmitted to him. A survival seemed the most likely explanation. Once during the blitz in London he had been given an hotel bedroom which had been hastily vacated by a visiting allied statesman. When he lifted the telephone to order his breakfast, he had found himself talking on a private line direct to the Cabinet Office. Something of that kind must have happened in the *Caliban*. When she was a naval vessel this cabin had no doubt been the office of some operational head-quarters and when she was handed back to her owners and re-adapted for passenger service, the engineers had neglected to disconnect it. That alone could explain the voices which now kept him informed of every stage of the incident.

The wounded man seemed to have got himself entangled in some kind of web of metal. Various unsuccessful and agonizing attempts were made to extricate him. Finally the decision was taken to cut him out. The order once given was carried out with surprising speed but the contraption, whatever it was, was ruined in the process and was finally dragged across the deck and thrown overboard. The victim continuously sobbed and whimpered. He was taken to the sickbay and put in charge of a kind but not, it appeared, very highly qualified nurse. 'You must be brave,' she said. 'I will say the rosary for you. You must be brave,' while the wireless telegraphist got into touch with a hospital ashore and was given instructions in first aid. The ship's surgeon never appeared. Details of treatment were dictated from the shore and passed to the sick-bay. The last words Mr Pinfold heard from the bridge were Captain Steerforth's 'I'm not going to be bothered with a sick man on board. We'll have to signal a passing homebound ship and have him transferred.'

Part of the treatment prescribed by the hospital was a sedative injection, and as this spread its relief over the unhappy Lascar, Mr Pinfold too grew drowsy until finally he fell asleep to the sound of the nurse murmuring the Angelic Salutation.

He was awakened by the coloured cabin steward bringing him tea.

'Very disagreeable business that last night,' said Mr Pinfold.

'Yes, sir.'

'How is the poor fellow?'

'Eight o'clock, sir.'

'Have they managed to get into touch with a ship to take him off?'

'Yes, sir. Breakfast eight-thirty, sir.'

Mr Pinfold drank his tea. He felt disinclined to get up. The intercommunication system was silent. He picked up his book and began to read. Then with a click the voices began again.

Captain Steerforth seemed to be addressing a deputation of the crew. 'I want you to understand,' he was saying, 'that a great quantity of valuable metal was sacrificed last night for the welfare of a single seaman. That metal was pure *copper*. One of the most valuable metals in the world. Mind you I don't regret the sacrifice and I am sure the Company will approve my action. But I want you all to appreciate that only in a British ship would such a thing be done. In the ship of any other nationality it would have been the seaman not the metal that was cut up. You know that as well as I do. Don't forget it. And another thing, instead of taking the man with us to Port Said and the filth of a Wog hospital, I had him carefully transhipped and he is now on his way to England. He couldn't have been treated more handsomely if he'd been a director of the Company. I know the hospital he's going to; it's a sweet, pretty place. It's the place all seamen long to go to. He'll have the best attention there and live, if he does live, in the greatest comfort. That's the kind of ship this is. Nothing is too good for the men who serve in her.'

The meeting seemed to disperse. There was a shuffling and muttering and presently a woman spoke. It was a voice which was soon to become familiar to Mr Pinfold. To all men and women there is some sound – grating, perhaps, or rustling, or strident, deep or shrill, a note of inflection of speech – which causes peculiar pain; which literally 'makes the hair stand on end' or metaphorically 'sets the teeth on edge'; something which Dr Drake would have called an 'allergy'. Such was this woman's voice. It clearly did not affect the Captain in this way but to Mr Pinfold it was excruciating.

'Well,' said this voice. 'That should teach them not to grumble.'

'Yes,' said Captain Steerforth. 'We've settled that little mutiny, I think. We shouldn't have any trouble now.'

'Not till the next time,' said the cynical woman. 'What a contemptible exhibition that man made of himself – crying like a child. Thank God we've seen the last of him. I liked your touch about the sweet, pretty hospital.'

'Yes. They little know the Hell-spot I've sent him to. Spoiling my copper indeed. He'll soon wish he were in Port Said.'

And the woman laughed odiously. 'Soon wish he was dead,' she said.

There was a click (someone seemed to be in control of the apparatus, Mr Pinfold thought), and two passengers were speaking. They seemed to be elderly, military gentlemen.

'I think the passengers should be told,' one said.

'Yes, we ought to call a meeting. It's the sort of thing that so often passes without proper recognition. We ought to pass a vote of thanks.'

'A ton of copper, you say?'

'Pure copper, cut up and chucked overboard. All for the sake of a nigger. It makes one proud of the British service.'

The voices ceased and Mr Pinfold lay wondering about this meeting; was it his duty to attend and report what he knew of the true characters of the Captain and his female associate? The difficulty, of course, would be to prove his charges; to explain satisfactorily how he came to overhear the Captain's secret.

Soft music filled the cabin, an oratorio sung by a great but distant choir. 'That *must* be a gramophone record,' thought Mr Pinfold. 'Or the wireless. They can't be performing this on board.' Then he slept for some time, until he was woken by a change of music. The bright young people were at it again with their Pocoputa Indian three-eight rhythm. Mr Pinfold looked at his watch. Eleven-thirty. Time to get up.

As he laboriously shaved and dressed, he reasoned closely about his situation. Now that he knew of the intercommunication system, it was plain to him that the room used by the band might be anywhere in the ship. The prayer-meeting too. It had seemed odd at the time that the quiet voices had come so clearly through the floor; that they had been audible to him and not to Glover. That was now explained. But he was puzzled by the irregularity, by the changes of place, the clicking on and off. It was improbable that anyone at a switchboard was directing the annoyances into his cabin. It was certain that the Captain would not deliberately broadcast his private and compromising conversations. Mr Pinfold wished he knew more of the mechanics of the thing. He remembered that in London just after the war when everything was worn out, telephones used sometimes to behave in this erratic way; the line would go dead; then crackle; then, when the tangled wire was given a twist and a jerk, normal conversation was rejoined. He supposed that somewhere over his head, in the ventilation shaft probably, there were a number of frayed and partly disconnected wires which every now and then with the movement of the ship came into contact and so established communication now with one, now with another part of the ship.

Before leaving his cabin he considered his box of pills. He was not well. Much was wrong with him, he felt, beside lameness. Dr Drake did not know about the sleeping-draught. It might be that the pills, admittedly new and pretty strong, warred with the bromide and chloral; perhaps with gin and brandy too. Well, the sleeping-draught was finished. He would try the pills once or twice more. He swallowed one and crept up to the main deck.

Here there was light and liveliness, a glitter of cool sunshine and a brisk breeze. The young people had abandoned the concert in the short time it had taken Mr Pinfold to climb the stairs. They were on the after deck playing quoits and shuffle-board and watching one another play; laughing boisterously as the ship rolled and jostled them against one another. Mr Pinfold leant on the rail and looked down, thinking it odd that such healthy-seeming, good-natured creatures should rejoice in the music of the Pocoputa Indians. Glover stood by himself in the stern swinging his golf-club. On the sunny side of the main deck the older passengers sat wrapped in rugs, some with popular biographies, some with knitting. The young Burmese paced together in pairs, uniformly and neatly dressed in blazers and pale fawn trousers, like officers waiting to fall in at a battalion parade.

Mr Pinfold sought the military gentlemen whose ill-informed eulogies of the Captain he believed it to be his duty to correct. From the voices, elderly, precise, conventional, he had formed a clear idea of their appearance. They were major-generals, retired now. They had been gallant young regimental officers – line-cavalry probably – in 1914 and had commanded brigades at the end of that war. They had passed at the Staff College and waited patiently for another battle only to find in 1939 that they were passed over for active command. But they had served loyally in offices, done their turn at fire-watching, gone short of whisky and razor-blades. Now they could just afford an inexpensive winter cruise every other year; admirable old men in their way. He did not find them on deck or in any of the public rooms.

As noon was sounded there was a movement towards the bar for the announcement of the ship's run and the result of the sweepstake. Scarfield was the winner of a modest prize. He ordered drinks for all in sight including Mr Pinfold. Mrs Scarfield stood near him and Mr Pinfold said: 'I say, I'm afraid I was an awful bore last night.'

'Were you?' she said. 'Not while you were with us.'

'All that nonsense I talked about politics. It's those pills I have to take. They make me feel rather odd.'

'I'm sorry about that,' said Mrs Scarfield, 'but I assure you, you didn't bore *us* in the least. I was fascinated.'

Mr Pinfold looked hard at her but could detect no hint of irony. 'Anyway I shan't hold forth like that again.'

'Please do.'

The ladies who had been identified as Mrs Benson and Mrs Cockson were in the same chairs as on the day before. They liked their glass, that pair, thought Mr Pinfold with approval; good sorts. He greeted them. He greeted anyone who caught his eye. He was feeling very much better.

One figure alone remained aloof from the general conviviality, the dark little man whom Mr Pinfold had noticed dining alone.

Presently the steward passed by, tapping his little musical gong, and Mr Pinfold followed the company down to luncheon. Knowing what he did of Captain Steerforth's character, Mr Pinfold found it rather repugnant to sit at the table with him. He gave him a perfunctory nod and addressed himself to Glover.

'Noisy night, wasn't it?'

'Oh,' said Glover, 'I didn't hear anything.'

'You must sleep very sound.'

'As a matter of fact, I didn't. I usually do, but I am not getting the exercise I'm used to. I was awake half the night.'

'And you didn't hear the accident?'

'No.'

'Accident?' said Mrs Scarfield overhearing. 'Was there an accident last night, Captain?'

'No one told me of one,' said Captain Steerforth blandly.

'The villain,' thought Mr Pinfold. 'Remorseless, treacherous, lecherous, kindless villain,' for though Captain Steerforth had shown no other symptoms of lechery, Mr Pinfold knew instinctively that his relations with the harsh-voiced woman – stewardess, secretary, passenger, whatever she might be – were grossly erotic.

'What accident, Mr Pinfold?' asked Mrs Scarfield.

'Perhaps I was mistaken,' said Mr Pinfold stiffly. 'I often am.'

There was another couple at the Captain's table. They had been there the night before, had been part of the group in which Mr Pinfold had talked so injudiciously, but he had barely noticed them; a pleasant, middle-aged nondescript, rather rich-looking couple, not English, Dutch perhaps or Scandinavian. The woman now leant across and said in thick, rather arch tones:

'There are two books of yours in the ship's library, I find.'

'Ah.'

'I have taken one. It is named *The Last Card*.'

'*The Lost Chord*,' said Mr Pinfold.

'Yes. It is a humorous book, yes?'

'Some people have suggested as much.'

'I find it so. It is not your suggestion also? I think you have a peculiar sense of humour, Mr Pinfold.'

'Ah.'

'That is what you are known for, yes, your peculiar sense of humour?'

'Perhaps.'

'May I have it after you?' asked Mrs Scarfield. 'Everyone says I have a peculiar sense of humour too.'

'But not so peculiar as Mr Pinfold?'

'That remains to be seen,' said Mrs Scarfield.

'I think you're embarrassing the author,' said Mr Scarfield.

'I expect he's used to it,' she said.

'He takes it all with his peculiar sense of humour,' said the foreign lady.

'If you'll excuse me,' said Mr Pinfold, struggling to rise.

'You see he is embarrassed.'

'No,' said the foreign lady. 'It is his humour. He is going to make notes of us. You see, we shall all be in a humorous book.'

As Mr Pinfold rose, he gazed towards the little dark man at his solitary table. That is where he should have been, he thought. The last sound he heard as he left the dining-saloon was merry young laughter from the purser's table.

Since he left it not much more than an hour before, the cabin had been tidied and the bed-clothes stretched taut, hospital-like, across the bunk. He took off his coat and his soft boots, lit a cigar and lay down. He had barely eaten at all that day but he was not hungry. He blew smoke up towards the wires and pipes on the ceiling and wondered how without offence he could escape from the Captain's table to sit and eat alone, silent and untroubled, like that clever, dark, enviable little fellow, and as though in response

45

to these thoughts the device overhead clicked into life and he heard this very subject being debated by the two old soldiers.

'My dear fellow, *I* don't care a damn.'

'No, of course you don't. Nor do I. All the same I think it very decent of him to mention it.'

'*Very* decent. What did he say exactly?'

'Said he was very sorry he hadn't room for you and me and my missus. The table only takes six passengers. Well, he had to have the Scarfields.'

'Yes, of course. He *had* to have the Scarfields.'

'Yes, he had to have them. Then there's the Norwegian couple – foreigners you know.'

'Distinguished foreigners.'

'Got to be civil to them. Well that makes four. Then if you please, he got an order from the Company to take this fellow Pinfold. So he only had one place. Knew he couldn't separate you and me and the missus, so he asked that decent young fellow – the one with the uncle in Liverpool.'

'Has he got an uncle in Liverpool?'

'Yes, yes. That's why he asked him.'

'But why did he ask Pinfold?'

'Company's orders. *He* didn't want him.'

'No, no, of course not.'

'If you ask me Pinfold drinks.'

'Yes, so I have always heard.'

'I saw him come on board. He was tight then. In a beastly state.'

'He's been in a beastly state ever since.'

'He says it's pills.'

'No, no, drink. I've seen better men than Pinfold go that way.'

'Wretched business. He shouldn't have come.'

'If you ask me he's been *sent* on this ship as a *cure*.'

'Ought to have someone to look after him.'

'Have you noticed that little dark chap who sits alone? I shouldn't be surprised if *he* wasn't keeping an eye on him.'

'A male nurse?'

'A warder more likely.'

'Put on him by his missus without his knowing?'

'That's my appreciation of the situation.'

The voices of the two old gossips faded and fell silent. Mr Pinfold lay smoking, without resentment. It was the sort of thing one expected to have said behind one's back – the sort of thing one said about other people. It was slightly unnerving to overhear it. The idea of his wife setting a spy on him was amusing. He would write and tell her. The question of his drunkenness interested him more. Perhaps he did give that impression. Perhaps on that first evening at sea – how long ago was that now? – when he had talked politics after dinner, perhaps he *had* drunk too much. He had had too much of something certainly, pills or sleeping-draught or liquor. Well, the sleeping-draught was finished. He resolved to take no more pills. He would stick to wine and a cocktail or two and a glass of brandy after dinner and soon he would be well and active once more.

He had reached the last inch of his cigar, a large one, an hour's smoking, when his reverie was interrupted from the Captain's cabin.

The doxy was there. In her harsh voice she said: 'You've got to teach him a lesson.'

'I will.'

'A *good* lesson.'

'Yes.'

'One he won't forget.'

'Bring him in.'

There was a sound of scuffling and whimpering, a sound rather like that of the wounded seaman whom Mr Pinfold had heard that morning; which morning? One morning of this disturbing voyage. It seemed that a prisoner was being dragged into the Captain's presence.

'Tie him to the chair,' said the leman, and Mr Pinfold at once thought of *King Lear.* 'Bind fast his corky arms.' Who said that? Goneril? Regan? Perhaps neither of them. Cornwall? It was a man's voice, surely? in the play. But it was the voice of the woman, or what passed as a woman, here. Addict of nicknames as he was, Mr Pinfold there and then dubbed her 'Goneril'.

'All right,' said Captain Steerforth, 'you can leave him to me.'
'And to me,' said Goneril.

Mr Pinfold was not abnormally squeamish nor had his life been particularly sheltered, but he had no experience of personal, physical cruelty and no liking for its portrayal in books or films. Now, lying in his spruce cabin in this British ship, in the early afternoon, a few yards distance from Glover and the Scarfields, Mrs Benson and Mrs Cockson, he was the horrified witness of a scene which might have come straight from the kind of pseudo-American thriller he most abhorred.

There were three people in the Captain's cabin, Steerforth, Goneril and their prisoner, who was one of the coloured stewards. Proceedings began with a form of trial. Goneril gave her evidence, vindictively but precisely accusing the man of an attempted sexual offence against her. It sounded to Mr Pinfold rather a strong case. Knowing the ambiguous position which the accuser held in the ship, remembering the gross language he had overheard in the dining-saloon and the heavy, unhealthy discourse of the preacher, Mr Pinfold considered the incident he heard described, exactly the sort of thing he would expect to happen in this beastly ship. Guilty, he thought.

'Guilty,' said the Captain and at the word Goneril vented a hiss of satisfaction and anticipation. Slowly and deliberately, as the ship steamed South with its commonplace load of passengers, the Captain and his leman with undisguised erotic enjoyment settled down to torture their prisoner.

Mr Pinfold could not surmise what form the torture took. He could only listen to the moans and sobs of the victim and the more horrific, ecstatic, orgiastic cries of Goneril:

'More. More. Again. Again. Again. You haven't had anything yet, you beast. Give him some more, more, more, more.'

Mr Pinfold could not endure it. He must stop this outrage at once. He lurched from his bunk, but even as he felt for his boots, silence fell in the Captain's cabin and a suddenly sobered Goneril said: 'That's enough.'

Not a sound came from the victim. After a long pause Captain Steerforth said: 'If you ask me, it's too much.'

'He's shamming,' said Goneril without conviction.

'He's dead,' said the Captain.

'Well,' said Goneril. 'What are you going to do about it?'

'Untie him.'

'I'm not going to touch him. I never touched him. It was all *you*.'

Mr Pinfold stood in his cabin, just as, no doubt, the Captain was standing in his, uncertain what to do, and as he hesitated, he realized through his horror that the pains in his legs had suddenly entirely ceased. He rose on his toes; he bent his knees. He was cured. It was the way in which these attacks of his always came and went, quite unpredictably. In spite of his agitation he had room in his mind to consider whether perhaps they were nervous in origin, whether the shock he had just endured might not have succeeded where the grey pills had failed; whether he had not been healed by the steward's agony. It was a hypothesis which momentarily distracted him from the murderer above.

Presently he turned to listen to them.

'As master of the ship I shall make out a death-certificate and have him put overboard after dark.'

'How about the surgeon?'

'He must sign too. The first thing is to get the body into the sickbay. We don't want any more trouble with the men. Get Margaret.'

The situation, as Mr Pinfold saw it, was appalling but it did not call for action.

Whatever had to be done, need not be done now. He could not burst alone into the Captain's cabin and denounce him. What was the proper procedure, if any existed, for putting a Captain in irons in his own ship? He would have to take advice. The military men, that sage, authoritative couple, were the obvious people. He would find them and explain the situation. They would know what to do. A report must be made, he assumed, depositions taken. Where? At the first consulate they came to, at Port Said; or should they wait until they reached a British port? Those old campaigners would know.

Meanwhile Margaret, the kind nurse, a sort of Cordelia, seemed to have charge of the body. 'Poor boy, poor boy,' she was saying. 'Look at these ghastly marks. You can't say these are "natural causes".'

'That's what the Captain says,' said a new voice, the ship's surgeon's presumably. 'I take my orders from him. There's a lot goes on aboard this ship that I don't like. The best you can do, young lady, is to see nothing, hear nothing and say nothing.'

'But the poor boy. He must have suffered so.'

'Natural causes,' said the doctor. And then there was silence.

Mr Pinfold removed his soft boots and put on shoes. He propped his two sticks in a corner of the wardrobe. 'I shan't need those again,' he reflected, little knowing what the coming days had in store, and walked almost blithely to the main deck.

No one was about except two Lascars, slung overhead, painting the davits. It was half-past three, a time when all the passengers were in their cabins. Like a lark on a battlefield Mr Pinfold's spirits rose, free and singing. He rejoiced in his power to walk. He walked round the ship, again and again, up and down. Was it possible, in this bright and peaceful scene, to believe in the abomination that lurked up there, just overhead, behind the sparkling paint? Could he possibly be mistaken? He had never seen Goneril. He barely knew the Captain's voice. Could he really identify it? Was it not possible that what he had heard was a piece of acting – a charade of the bright young peoples? A broadcast from London?

Wishful thinking, perhaps, born on the exhilaration of sun and sea and wind and his own new-found health?

Time alone would show.

Chapter Four

THE HOOLIGANS

That evening Mr Pinfold felt the renewal of health and cheerfulness and clarity of mind greater, it seemed to him, than he had known for weeks. He looked at his hands, which for days now had been blotched with crimson; now they were clear and his face in the glass had lost its congested, mottled hue. He dressed more deftly and as he dressed the wireless in his cabin came into action.

'This is the BBC Third Programme. Here is Mr Clutton-Cornforth to speak on Aspects of Orthodoxy in Contemporary Letters.'

Mr Pinfold had known Clutton-Cornforth for thirty years. He was now the editor of a literary weekly, an ambitious, obsequious fellow. Mr Pinfold had no curiosity about his opinions on any subject. He wished there were a way of switching off the fluting, fruity voice. He tried instead to disregard it until, just as he was leaving, he was recalled by the sound of his own name.

'Gilbert Pinfold,' he heard, 'poses a precisely antithetical problem, or should we say? the same problem in antithetical form. The basic qualities of a Pinfold novel seldom vary and may be enumerated thus: conventionality of plot, falseness of characterization, morbid sentimentality, gross and hackneyed farce alternating with grosser and more hackneyed melodrama; cloying religiosity, which will be found tedious or blasphemous according as the reader shares or repudiates his doctrinal preconceptions; an adventitious and offensive sensuality that is clearly introduced for commercial motives. All this is presented in a style which, when it varies from the trite, lapses into positive illiteracy.'

Really, thought Mr Pinfold, this was not like the Third Programme; it was not at all like Algernon Clutton-Cornforth. 'My word,' he thought, 'I'll give that booby such a kick on the sit-upon

51

next time I see him waddling up the steps of the London Library.'

'Indeed,' continued Clutton-Cornforth, 'if one is asked – and one *is* often asked – to give one name which typifies all that is decadent in contemporary literature, one can answer without hesitation – Gilbert Pinfold. I now turn from him to the equally deplorable but more interesting case of a writer often associated with him – Roger Stillingfleet.'

Here, by a quirk of the apparatus, Clutton-Cornforth was cut off and succeeded by a female singer:

> *'I'm Gilbert, the filbert,*
> *The knut with the K,*
> *The pride of Piccadilly,*
> *The blasé roué.'*

Mr Pinfold left his cabin. He met the steward on his rounds with the dinner-gong and ascended to the maindeck. He stepped out into the wind, leaned briefly on the rail, looked down into the surge of lighted water. The music rejoined him there emanating from somewhere quite near where he stood.

> *'For Gilbert, the filbert,*
> *The Colonel of the Knuts.'*

Other people in the ship were listening to the wireless. Other people, probably, had heard Clutton-Cornforth's diatribe. Well, he was accustomed to criticism (though not from Clutton-Cornforth). He could take it. He only hoped no one bored him by talking about it; particularly not that Norwegian woman at the Captain's table.

Mr Pinfold's feelings towards the Captain had moderated in the course of the afternoon. As to whether the man were guilty of murder or no, his judgment was suspended, but the fact of his having fallen under a cloud, of Mr Pinfold's possession of secret knowledge which might or might not bring him to ruin, severed the bond of loyalty which had previously bound them. Mr Pinfold felt disposed to tease the Captain a little.

Accordingly at dinner, when they were all seated, and he had ordered himself a pint of champagne, he turned the conversation rather abruptly to the subject of murder.

'Have you ever actually met a murderer?' he asked Glover.

Glover had. In his tea garden a trusted foreman had hacked his wife to pieces.

'I expect he smiled a good deal, didn't he?' asked Mr Pinfold.

'Yes, as a matter of fact he did. Always a most cheerful chap. He went off to be hanged laughing away with his brothers as though it was no end of a joke.'

'*Exactly.*'

Mr Pinfold stared full in the eyes of the smiling Captain. Was there any sign of alarm in that broad, plain face?

'Have *you* ever known a murderer, Captain Steerforth?'

Yes, when he first went to sea, Captain Steerforth had been in a ship with a stoker who killed another with a shovel. But they brought it in that the man was insane, affected by the heat of the stoke-hold.

'In my country in the forests in the long winter often the men become drunken and fight and sometimes they kill one another. Is not hanging in my country for such things. Is a case for the doctor we think.'

'If you ask me all murderers are mad,' said Scarfield.

'And always smiling,' said Mr Pinfold. 'That's the only way you can tell them – by their inevitable good-humour.'

'This stoker wasn't very cheerful. Surly fellow as I remember him.'

'Ah, but he was mad.'

'Goodness,' said Mrs Scarfield, 'what a morbid subject. However did we get on to it?'

'Not so morbid by half as Clutton-Cornforth,' said Mr Pinfold rather truculently.

'Who?' asked Mrs Scarfield.

'As what?' asked the Norwegian woman.

Mr Pinfold looked from face to face round the table. Clearly no one had heard the broadcast.

'Oh,' he said, 'if you don't know about him, the less said the better.'

'Do tell,' said Mrs Scarfield.

'No, really, it's nothing.'

She gave a little shrug of disappointment and turned her pretty face towards the Captain.

Later Mr Pinfold tried to raise the topic of burial at sea, but this was not taken up with any enthusiasm. Mr Pinfold had devoted some thought to the matter during the late afternoon. Glover had said that the stewards came from Travancore, in which case there was a good chance of their being Christians of one or other of the ancient rites that prevailed in that complex culture. They would insist on some religious observance for one of their number. If he wished to avert suspicion, the Captain could not bundle the body overboard secretly. Once in a troopship Mr Pinfold had assisted at the committal to the sea of one of his troop who shot himself. The business he remembered took some time. Last Post had been sounded. Mr Pinfold rather thought the ship had hove-to. In the *Caliban* the sports-deck seemed the most likely place for the ceremony. Mr Pinfold would keep watch. If the night passed without incident, Captain Steerforth would stand acquitted.

That evening, as on the evening before, Captain Steerforth played bridge. He smiled continuously rubber after rubber. Early hours were kept in the *Caliban*. The bar shut at half-past ten, lights began to be turned off and ash trays emptied; the passengers went to their cabins. Mr Pinfold saw the last of them go below, then went aft to a seat overlooking the sports-deck. It was very cold. He went down to his cabin for an overcoat. It was warm there and welcoming. It occurred to him, he could keep his vigil perfectly well below deck. When the engines stopped, he would know that the game was on. The last faint cobwebs of his sleeping-draught had now been swept up. He was wide awake. Without undressing he lay on his bunk with a novel.

Time passed. No sound came through the intercommunication; the engines beat regularly, the plates and panelling creaked; the low hum of the ventilator filled the cabin.

There were no funeral obsequies, no panegyric; no dirge on board the *Caliban* that night. Instead there was enacted on the deck immediately outside Mr Pinfold's window a dramatic cycle lasting five hours – six? Mr Pinfold did not notice the time at which the disturbance began – of which he was the solitary audience. Had it appeared behind footlights on a real stage, Mr Pinfold would have condemned it as grossly overplayed.

There were two chief actors, juvenile leads, one of whom was called Fosker; the other, the leader, was nameless. They were drunk when they first arrived and presumably carried a bottle from which they often swigged for the long hours of darkness were of no avail in sobering them. They raged more and more furiously until their final lapse into incoherence. By their voices they seemed to be gentlemen of a sort. Fosker, Mr Pinfold was pretty sure, had been in the jazz band; he thought he had noticed him in the lounge after dinner, amusing the girls, tall, very young, shabby, shady, vivacious, bohemian, with long hair, a moustache and the beginning of side-whiskers. There was something in him of the dissolute law students and government clerks of mid-Victorian fiction. Something too of the young men who had now and then crossed his path during the war – the sort of subaltern who was disliked in his regiment and got himself posted to SOE. When Mr Pinfold came to consider the matter at leisure he could not explain to himself how he had formed so full an impression during a brief, incurious glance, or why Fosker, if he were what he seemed, should be travelling to the East in such incongruous company. The image of him, however, remained sharp cut as a cameo. The second, dominant young man was a voice only; rather a pleasant well-bred voice for all its vile utterances.

'He's gone to bed,' said Fosker.

'We'll soon get him out,' said the pleasant well-bred voice.

'Music.'

'Music.'

> *'I'm Gilbert, the filbert,*
> *The knut with the K,*
> *The pride of Piccadilly,*
> *The blasé roué.*

> *Oh Hades, the ladies*
> *Who leave their wooden huts*
> *For Gilbert, the filbert,*
> *The Colonel of the Knuts.'*

'Come on, Gilbert. Time to leave your wooden hut.'

Damned impudence, thought Mr Pinfold. Oafs, bores.

'D'you think he's enjoying this?'

'He's got a most peculiar sense of humour? He's a most peculiar man. Queer, aren't you, Gilbert? Come out of your wooden hut, you old queer.'

Mr Pinfold drew the wooden shutter across his window but the noise outside was undiminished.

'He thinks that'll keep us out. It won't, Gilbert. We aren't going to climb through the window, you know. We shall come in at the door and then, by God, you're going to cop it. Now he's locked the door.' Mr Pinfold had done no such thing. 'Not very brave, is he? Locking himself in. Gilbert doesn't want to be whipped.'

'But he's going to be whipped.'

'Oh yes, he's going to be whipped all right.'

Mr Pinfold decided on action. He put on his dressing-gown, took his blackthorn and left his cabin. The door which led out to the deck was some way down the corridor. The voices of the two hooligans followed him as he went to it. He thought he knew the Fosker type, the aggressive under-dog, vainglorious in drink, very easily put in his place. He pushed open the heavy door and stepped resolutely into the wind. The deck was quite empty. For the length of the ship the damp planks shone in the lamp-light. From above came shrieks of laughter.

'No, no, Gilbert, you can't catch us that way. Go back to your little hut, Gilbert. We'll come for you when we want you. Better lock the door.'

Mr Pinfold returned to his cabin. He did not lock the door. He sat, stick in hand, listening.

The two young men conferred.

'We'd better wait till he goes to sleep.'

'Then we'll pounce.'

'He doesn't seem very sleepy.'

'Let's get the girls to sing him to sleep. Come on, Margaret, give Gilbert a song.'

'Aren't you being rather beastly?' The girl's voice was clear and sober.

'No, of course not. It's all a joke. Gilbert's a sport. Gilbert's enjoying it as much as we are. He often did this sort of thing when he was our age – singing ridiculous songs outside men's rooms at Oxford. He made a row outside the Dean's rooms. That's why he got sent down. He accused the Dean of the most disgusting practices. It was all a great joke.'

'Well, if you're sure he doesn't mind . . .'

Two girls began singing very prettily.

> '*When first I saw Mabel,*' they sang,
> '*In her fair Russian sable*
> *I knew she was able*
> *To satisfy me.*
> *Her manners were careless . . .*'

The later lines of the song – one well known to Mr Pinfold – are verbally bawdy, but as they rose now on the passionless, true voices of the girls, they were purged and sweetened; they floated over the sea in perfect innocence. The girls sang this and other airs. They sang for a long time. They sang intermittently throughout the night's disturbances, but they were powerless to sooth Mr Pinfold. He sat wide awake with his stick to deal with intruders.

Presently the father of the nameless young man came to join them. He was, it appeared, one of the generals.

'Go to bed, you two,' he said. 'You're making an infernal nuisance of yourselves.'

'We're only mocking Pinfold. He's a beastly man.'

'That's no reason to wake up the whole ship.'

'He's a Jew.'

'Is he? Are you sure? I never heard that.'

'Of course he is. He came to Lychpole in 1937 with the German refugees. He was called Peinfeld then.'

'We're out for Peinfeld's blood,' said the pleasant voice. 'We want to beat Hell out of him.'

'You don't really mind, do you, sir,' said Fosker, 'if we beat Hell out of him.'

'What's wrong with the fellow particularly?'

'He's got a dozen pairs of shoes in his little hut, all beautifully polished on wooden trees.'

'He sits at the Captain's table.'

'He's taken the only bathroom near our cabin. I tried to use it tonight and the steward said it was private, for Mr Pinfold.'

'Mr Peinfeld.'

'I hate him. I hate him. I hate him. I hate him. I hate him,' said Fosker. 'I've got my own score to settle with him for what he did to Hill.'

'That farmer who shot himself?'

'Hill was a decent, old-fashioned yeoman. The salt of the country. Then this filthy Jew came and bought up the property. The Hills had farmed it for generations. They were thrown out. That's why Hill hanged himself.'

'Well,' said the general. 'You won't do any good by shouting outside his window.'

'We're going to do more than that. We're going to give him the hiding of his life.'

'Yes, you could do that, of course.'

'You leave him to us.'

'I'm certainly not going to stay up here and be a witness. He's just the sort of fellow to take legal action.'

'He'd be far too ashamed. Can't you see the headlines "Novelist whipped in liner".'

'I don't suppose he'd care a damn. Fellows like that live on publicity.' Then the general changed his tone. 'All the same,' he added wistfully, 'I wish I was young enough to help, good luck to you. Give it to him good and strong. Only remember; if there's trouble, *I* know nothing about it.'

The girls sang. The youths drank. Presently the mother came to plead. She spoke in yearning tones that reminded Mr Pinfold of his deceased Anglican aunts.

'I can't sleep,' she said. 'You know I can never sleep when you're in this state. My son, I beg you to go to bed. Mr Fosker, how can you lead him into this escapade? Margaret, darling, what are you doing here at this time of night? *Please* go to your cabin, child.'

'It's only a joke, mama.'

'I very much doubt whether Mr Pinfold thinks it a joke.'

'I hate him,' said her son.

'Hate?' said the mother. 'Hate? Why do all you young people *hate* so much? What has come over the world? You were not brought up to *hate*. Why do you hate Mr Pinfold?'

'I have to share a cabin with Fosker. That swine has a cabin to himself.'

'I expect he paid for it.'

'Yes, with the money he cheated Hill out of.'

'He behaved badly to Hill certainly. But he isn't used to country ways. I've not met him, though we have lived so near all these years. I think perhaps he rather looks down on all of us. We aren't so clever as he, nor as rich. But that's no reason to *hate* him.'

At this the son broke into a diatribe in the course of which he and Fosker were left alone. There had been an element of jollity in the pair at the beginning of their demonstration. Now they were possessed by hatred, repeating and elaborating a ferocious, rambling denunciation full of obscenities. The eviction of Hill and responsibility for his suicide were the chief recurring charges but interspersed with them were other accusations. Mr Pinfold, they said, had let his mother die in destitution. He was ashamed of her because she was an illiterate immigrant, had refused to help her or go near her, had let her die alone, uncared for, had not attended her pauper's funeral. Mr Pinfold had shirked in the war. He had used it as an opportunity to change his name and pass himself off as an Englishman, to make friends with people who did not know his origin, to get into Bellamy's Club. Mr Pinfold had in some way been implicated in the theft of a moonstone. He had paid a large sum of money to sit at the Captain's table. Mr Pinfold typified the decline of England, of rural England in particular. He was a reincarnation (Mr Pinfold, not they, drew the analogy) of the 'new men' of the Tudor period who had despoiled the Church and the peasantry. His religious profession was humbug, assumed in order to ingratiate himself with the aristocracy. Mr Pinfold was a sodomite. Mr Pinfold must be chastened and chastised.

The night wore on, the charges became wilder and wider, the threats more bloody. The two young men were like prancing savages working themselves into a frenzy of blood-lust. Mr Pinfold awaited their attack and prepared for it. He made an operational plan. They would come through the door singly. The cabin was not spacious but there was room to swing a stick. He turned out the light and stood by the door. The young men coming suddenly into the dark from the lighted corridor would not know where to lay hands on him. He would fell the first with his blackthorn, then change this weapon for the malacca cane. The second young man no doubt would stumble over his fallen friend. Mr Pinfold would then turn on the light and carefully thrash him. They were far too drunk to be really dangerous. Mr Pinfold was quite confident of the outcome. He awaited them calmly.

The incantations were rising to a climax.

'Now's the time. Ready, Fosker?'

'Ready.'

'In we go then.'

'You first, Fosker.'

Mr Pinfold stood ready. He was glad that Fosker should be the man to be painlessly stunned; the instigator, the man to receive full punishment. There was justice in that order.

Then came anticlimax. 'I can't get in,' said Fosker. 'The bastard has locked the door.'

Mr Pinfold had not locked the door. Moreover Fosker had not tried it. There had been no movement of the handle. Fosker was afraid.

'Go on. What are you waiting for?'

'I tell you he's locked us out.'

'That's torn it.'

Crestfallen, the two returned to the deck.

'We've got to get him. We must get him tonight,' said the one who was not Fosker, but the fire had gone out of him and he added: 'I feel awfully sick suddenly.'

'Better put it off for tonight.'

'I feel frightful. Oh!'

There followed the ghastly sounds of vomiting and then a whimper; the same abject sound that seemed to re-echo through the *Caliban*, the sob of the injured seaman, of the murdered steward.

His mother was there now to comfort him.

'I haven't been to bed, dear. I couldn't leave you like that. I've been waiting and praying for you. You're ready to come now, aren't you?'

'Yes, mother, I'm ready.'

'I love you so. All loving is suffering.'

Silence fell. Mr Pinfold put his weapons away and drew back the shutter. It was dawn. He lay on his bed wide awake, his rage quite abated, calmly considering the events of the night.

There had been no funeral. So much seemed certain. Indeed the whole incident of Captain Steerforth and Goneril and the murdered steward had become insubstantial under the impact of the new assault. Mr Pinfold's orderly, questing mind began to sift the huge volume of charges which had been made against him. Some – that he was Jewish and homosexual, that he had stolen a moonstone and left his mother to die a pauper – were totally preposterous. Others were inconsistent. If, for example, he were a newly arrived immigrant, he could not have been a rowdy undergraduate at Oxford; if he were so anxious to establish himself as a countryman, he would not have slighted his neighbours. The young men in their drunken rage had clearly roared out any abuse that came to mind, but there emerged from the chaotic uproar the basic facts that he was generally disliked on board the *Caliban*, that two at least of his fellow-passengers were possessed by fanatical hate, and that they had some sort of indirect personal acquaintance with him. How else could they have heard, even in its wildly garbled form, of his wife's transactions with Hill (who was well and prosperous when Mr Pinfold last heard of him)? They came from his part of the country. It was not unlikely that Hill, while boasting of his astuteness among his cronies, had told a story of oppression elsewhere. If that was the sort of thing that was being said in the district, Mr Pinfold should correct it. Mr Pinfold had to consider also his comfort during the coming voyage. He required peace of mind in which to work. These dreadful young men were likely, whenever they got drunk, to come caterwauling outside his cabin. On a later occasion, moreover, they might attempt physical assault, might even succeed in it. The result could only be humiliating; it might be painful. The world teemed with journalists. He imagined his wife reading in her morning paper a cable from Aden or Port Soudan describing the *fracas*. Something must be done. He could lay the matter before the Captain, the natural guardian of law in his ship, but with his thought there emerged again from oblivion the matter of the Captain's own culpability. Mr Pinfold was going to have the Captain arrested for murder at the earliest opportunity. Nothing would suit that black heart better than to have the only witness against him involved in a brawl – or silenced in one. A new suspicion took shape. Mr Pinfold had been indiscreet at dinner in revealing his private knowledge. Was it not probable that Captain Steerforth had instigated the whole attack? Where had the young men been drinking after the bar was shut, if not in the Captain's cabin?

Mr Pinfold began to shave. This prosaic operation recalled him to strict reason. The Captain's guilt was not proven. First things first. He must deal with the young men. He studied the passenger-list. There was no Fosker on it. Mr Pinfold himself, when crossing the Atlantic, avoided interviewers by remaining incognito. It seemed unlikely that Fosker would have the same motive. Perhaps the police were after him. The other man was ostensibly respectable; four of a name should be easy to find. But there seemed to be no family of father, mother, son and daughter in that list. Mr Pinfold lathered his face for the second shave. He was puzzled. It was unlikely that so large a party would join the ship at the last moment, after the list had been printed. They did not sound the kind of people given to impetuous dashes abroad – and anyway, such people travelled by air nowadays. And there was that other general travelling with them. Mr Pinfold gazed at his puzzled, soapy face. Then he saw light. Step-father, that was it. He and the mother would bear one name, the children another. Mr Pinfold would keep his eyes and ears open. It should not be difficult to identify them.

Mr Pinfold dressed carefully. He chose a Brigade tie to wear that morning and a cap that matched his tweed suit. He went on deck, where seamen were at work swabbing. They had already cleaned up all traces of the night's disgusting climax. He ascended to the main, promenade deck. It was a morning such as at any other time would have elated him. Even now, with so much to harass him, he was conscious of exhilaration. He stood alone breathing deeply, making light of his annoyances.

Margaret, somewhere quite near, said: 'Look, he's left his cabin. Doesn't he look smart today? Now's our chance to give him our presents. It's much better than giving them to his steward as we meant to. Now we can arrange them ourselves.'

'D'you think he'll like them?' said the other girl.

'He ought to. We've taken enough trouble. They're the best we could possibly get.'

'But, Meg, he's so *grand*.'

'It's because he's grand he'll like them. Grand people are always pleased with *little* things. He *must* have his presents this morning. After the silly way the boys behaved last night it will show him *we* weren't in it. At least not in it in the way they were. He'll see that as far as we're concerned it was all fun and love.'

'Suppose he comes in and finds us?'

'You keep *cave*. If he starts going down sing.'

' "When first I saw Mabel"?'

'Of course. *Our* song.'

Mr Pinfold was tempted to trap Margaret. He relished the simple male pleasure, rather rare to him in recent years, of being found attractive, and was curious to see this honey-tongued girl. But she

63

inevitably would lead him to the brother and to Fosker, and he was constrained by honour. These presents, whatever they were, constituted a flag of truce. He could not snatch advantage from the girls' generosity.

Presently Margaret rejoined her friend.

'He hasn't moved.'

'No, he's just stood there all the time. What do you suppose he's thinking about?'

'Those beastly boys, I expect.'

'Do you think he's very upset?'

'He's so brave.'

'Often brave people are the most sensitive.'

'Well it will be all right when he gets back to his cabin and finds our presents.'

Mr Pinfold walked the decks for an hour. No passengers were about.

As the gong sounded for breakfast, Mr Pinfold went below. He stopped first at his cabin to see what Margaret had left for him. All he found was the cup of tea, cold now, which the steward had put there. The bed was made. The place was squared up and ship-shape. There were no presents.

As he left, he met the cabin-steward.

'I say, did a young lady leave anything for me in my cabin?'

'Yes, sir, breakfast now, sir.'

'No. Listen. I think something was left for me here about an hour ago.'

'Yes, sir, gong for breakfast just now.'

'Oh,' said Margaret, 'he hasn't found it.'

'He must *look*.'

'*Look* for it, Gilbert, *look*.'

He searched the little wardrobe. He peered under the bunk. He opened the cupboard over the washhand-basin. There was nothing there.

'There's nothing there,' said Margaret. 'He can't find it. He can't find anything,' she said on a soft note of despair. 'The sweet brave idiot, he can't find anything.'

So he went down alone to breakfast.

He was the first of the passengers to appear. Mr Pinfold was hungry. He ordered coffee and fish and eggs and fruit. He was about to eat when, Ping; the little, rose-shaded electric lamp which stood on the table before him came into action as a transmitter. The delinquent youths were awake and up and on the air again, their vitality unimpaired by the excesses of the night.

'Halloo-loo-loo-loo-loo. Hark-ark-ark-ark-ark,' they holloaed. 'Loo in there. Fetch him out. Yoicks.'

'I fear Fosker is not entirely conversant with sporting parlance,' said the general.

'Hark-ark-ark-ark. Come out, Peinfeld. We know where you are. We've got you.' A whip-crack. 'Ow,' from Fosker, 'look out what you're doing with that hunting crop.'

'Run, Peinfeld, run. We can see you. We're coming for you.'

The steward at that moment was at Mr Pinfold's side serving him with haddock. He seemed unconscious of the cries emanating from the lamp; to him presumably they were all one with the unreasonable variety of knives and forks and the superfluity of inedible foods; all part of the complexity of this remote and rather disgusting western way of life.

Mr Pinfold ate stolidly. The young men resumed the diatribe repeating again in clear, morning voices the garbled accusations of the night before. Interspersed with them was the challenge: 'Come and meet us, Gilbert. You're afraid, Peinfeld. We want to talk to you, Peinfeld. You're hiding, aren't you? You're afraid to come and talk.'

Margaret spoke: 'Oh, Gilbert, what are they doing to you? Where are you? You mustn't let them find you. Come to me. I'll hide you. You never found your presents and now they are after you again. Let *me* look after you, Gilbert. It's me, Mimi. Don't you trust me?'

Mr Pinfold turned to his scrambled eggs. He had forgotten,

when he ordered them, that they would not be fresh. Now he beckoned to the steward to remove them.

'Off your feed, Gilbert? You're in a funk, aren't you? Can't eat when you're in a funk, can you? Poor Gilbert, too scared to eat.' They began to give instructions for a place of meeting. '. . . D. Deck, turn right. Got that? You'll see some lockers. The next bulk-head. We're waiting for you. Better come now and get it over. You've got to meet us some time, you know. We've got you, Gilbert. We've got you. There's no escape. Better get it over . . .'

Mr Pinfold's patience was exhausted. He must put a stop to this nonsense. Recalling some vague memories of signal procedure in the army, he drew the lamp towards him and spoke into it curtly: 'Pinfold to Hooligans. Rendezvous Main Lounge 0930 hours. Out.'

The lamp was not designed to be moved. His pull disconnected it in some way. The bulb went out and the voices abruptly ceased. At the same moment Glover came in to breakfast. 'Hullo, something gone wrong with the light?'

'I tried to move it. I hope you slept better last night?'

'Like a log. No more disturbances, I hope?'

Mr Pinfold considered whether or not to confide in Glover and decided immediately, no.

'No,' he said, and ordered some cold ham.

The dining-saloon filled. Mr Pinfold exchanged greetings. He went on deck, keeping alert, hoping to spot his persecutors, thinking it possible that Margaret would make herself known to him. But he saw no hooligans; half a dozen healthy girls passed him, some in trousers and duffle coats, some in tweed skirts and sweaters; one might be Margaret but none gave him a sign. At half-past nine he took an armchair in a corner of the lounge and waited. He had his blackthorn with him; it was just conceivable that the youths were so frenzied that they might attempt violence even here, in the daylight.

He began to rehearse the coming interview. He was the judge. He had summoned these men to appear before him. Something like a regimental orderly room, he thought, would be the proper atmosphere. He was the commanding officer hearing a charge of brawling. His powers of punishment were meagre. He would admonish them severely, and threaten them with civil penalties.

He would remind them that they were subject to British law in the *Caliban* just as much as on land; that defamation of character and physical assault were grave crimes which would prejudice their whole future careers. He would 'throw the whole book' at them. He would explain icily that he was entirely indifferent to their good or bad opinion; that he regarded their friendship and their enmity as equally impertinent. But he would also hear what they had to say for themselves. A good officer knows the enormous ills that can arise from men brooding on imaginary grudges. These defaulters were clearly suffering from a number of delusions about himself. It was better that they should get it off their chests, hear the truth and then shut up for the rest of the voyage. Moreover if, as seemed certain, these delusions derived from rumours which were in circulation among Mr Pinfold's neighbours, he must plainly investigate and scotch them.

He had the lounge to himself. The rest of the passengers were ranged along the deck in their chairs and rugs. The unvarying hum of marine mechanical-life was the only sound. The clock over the little bandstand read a quarter to ten. Mr Pinfold decided to give them till ten; then he would go to the wireless office and inform his wife of his recovery. It was beneath his dignity to attend on these dreadful young men.

Some similar point of pride seemed to influence them. Above the hum he presently heard them discussing him. The voices came from the panelling near his head. First in his cabin, then in the dining-saloon, now here, the surviving strands of war-time inter-communication were fitfully active. The whole wiring of the ship was in need of a thorough overhaul, Mr Pinfold thought; for all he knew there might be a danger of fire.

'We'll talk to Peinfeld when it suits us and not a moment before.'

'Who'll do the talking?'

'I will, of course.'

'Do you know what you're going to say?'

'Of course.'

'Not really much point in my coming at all, is there?'

'I may need you as a witness.'

'All right, come on then. Let's see him now.'

'When it suits *me*, Fosker, not before.'

'What are we waiting for?'

'To let him get into a thorough funk. Remember at school one was always kept waiting for a beating? Just to make it taste sweeter? Well, Peinfeld can wait for *his* beating.'

'He's scared stiff.'

'He's practically blubbing now.'

At ten o'clock Mr Pinfold took out his watch, verified the time shown on the clock, and rose from the corner. 'He's going away.' 'He's running away.' 'Funk' came faintly from the fumed oak panelling. Mr Pinfold climbed to the wireless office on the boat-deck, composed a message and handed it in: *Pinfold. Lychpole. Entirely cured. All love. Gilbert.*

'Is that address enough?' asked the clerk.

'Yes. There's only one telegraph office called Lychpole in the country.'

He walked the decks, thought his blackthorn superfluous and returned to his cabin where the BBC was loudly in possession. '. . . in the studio Jimmy Lance, who is well known to all listeners, and Miss June Cumberleigh, who is new to listeners. Jimmy is going to let us see what is probably a unique collection. He has kept every letter he ever received. That's so, isn't it, Jimmy?'

'Well, not letters from the Income Tax Collector.'

'Ha. Ha.'

'Ha. Ha.'

A great burst of unrestrained laughter from the unseen audience.

'No, none of us like to be reminded of that kind of letter, Jimmy, do we? Ha ha. But I think in your time you have had letters from a great many celebrities?'

'And from some pretty dim people, too.'

'Ha. Ha.'

'Ha. Ha. Ha.'

'Well, June is going to take letters at random out of your file and read them. Ready, June? Right. The first letter is from – '

Mr Pinfold knew June Cumberleigh and liked her. She was a wholly respectable, clever, funny-faced girl who had got drawn into Bohemia through her friendship with James Lance. It was not her natural voice that she now used. Through some mechanical distortion she spoke in almost identical tones to Goneril's.

'Gilbert Pinfold,' she said.

'And do you count him among the celebrities or the dim people, Jimmy?'

'A celebrity.'

'Do you?' said June. 'I think he's a dreadfully dim little man.'

'Well, what's the dim little man got to say?'

'It is so badly written I can't read it.'

Enormous amusement in the audience.

'Try another.'

'Who is it this time?'

'Why. This is *too* much. Gilbert Pinfold again.'

'Ha, ha, ha, ha, ha.'

Mr Pinfold left his cabin, slamming the door on this deplorable entertainment. James, he knew, did a lot of broadcasting. He was a poet and artist by nature who had let himself become popularized; but this exhibition was a bit thick, even for him. And what was June doing? She must have lost all sense of decency.

Mr Pinfold walked the decks. He was still troubled by the unsolved problem of the hooligans. Something would have to be done about them. But he felt reassured about Captain Steerforth. Now that it was apparent that many of the sounds in his cabin emanated from Broadcasting House, he became certain that what he had overheard was part of a play. The similarity of June's voice and Goneril's seemed to confirm it. He had been an ass to suppose Captain Steerforth a murderer; it was part of the confusion of mind caused by Dr Drake's pills. And if Captain Steerforth were innocent, then he was a potential, a natural ally against his enemies.

Thus comforted, Mr Pinfold returned to his listening post in the corner of the lounge. Father and son were in conference.

'Fosker's wet.'

'Yes. I've never thought anything of him.'

'I'm leaving him out of this business from now on.'

'Very wise. But you've got to go through with it yourself, you know. You didn't come very creditably out of last night's affair. I've no great objection to your knocking the fellow about a bit if he deserves it. Anyway you've threatened him and you've got to do something about it. You can't just drop the matter at this stage. But you want to go about it in the right way. You're up against something rather more dangerous than you realize.'

'Dangerous? That cowardly, common little communist pansy –'

'Yes, yes. I know how you feel. But I've seen a bit more of the world than you have, my boy. I think I'd better put you up to a few wrinkles. In the first place Pinfold is utterly unscrupulous. He has no gentlemanly instincts. He's quite capable of taking you to the courts. Have you any proof of your charges?'

'Everyone knows they're true.'

'That may be but it won't mean a thing in a court of law unless you can prove it. You need evidence so strong that Pinfold daren't sue you. And, so far, you haven't got it. Another thing, Pinfold is extremely rich. I daresay for example he owns a controlling share in this shipping line. The long-nosed, curly-headed gentlemen don't pay taxes like us poor Christians, you know. Pinfold has money salted away in half a dozen countries. He has friends everywhere.'

'*Friends*?'

'Well, no, not friends as *we* understand them. But he has influence – with politicians, with the police. You've lived in a small world, my boy. You have no conception of the ramifications of power of a man like Pinfold in the modern age. He's attractive to women – homosexuals always are. Margaret is distinctly taken with him. Even your mother doesn't really dislike him. We've got to work cautiously and build up a party against him. I'll send off a few radiograms. There are one or two people I know who, I think, may be able to give us some *facts* about Pinfold. It's facts we need. We've got to make out an absolutely water-tight case. Till then, lie low.'

'You don't think I ought to beat him up?'

'Well, I wouldn't go so far as to say that. If you find him alone, you might have a smack at him. I know what I should have done myself at your age. But I'm old now and wise and my advice is lie low, work under cover. Then in a day or two we may have something to surprise our celebrated fellow passenger . . .'

When noon was sounded Mr Pinfold went aft and ordered himself a cocktail. There was the usual jollity over the sweepstake. He looked at the flag on the chart. The *Caliban* had rounded Cape St Vincent and was well on the way to Gibraltar. She should pass the straits that night into the Mediterranean. When he went down to luncheon he was in a hopeful mood. The hooligans had fallen out and their rage had been tempered. The Mediterranean had always welcomed Mr Pinfold in the past. His annoyance would be over, he believed, once he was in those hallowed waters.

In the dining-saloon he noticed that the dark man who had sat alone, was now at a table with Mrs Cockson and Mrs Benson. In a curious way that too seemed a good omen.

Chapter Five

THE INTERNATIONAL INCIDENT

It was the conversation of the two generals, overheard as he lay in his cabin after luncheon, which first made Mr Pinfold aware of the international crisis which had been developing while he lay ill. There had been no hint of it in the newspapers he had listlessly scanned before embarkation; or, if there had been, he had not, in his confused state, appreciated its importance. Now, it appeared, there was a first class row about the possession of Gibraltar. Some days ago the Spaniards had laid formal, peremptory claim to the fortress and were now exercising the very dubious right of stopping and searching ships passing through the straits in what they defined as their territorial waters. During luncheon the *Caliban* had hove-to and Spanish officials had come on board. They were demanding that the ship put into Algeciras for an examination of cargo and passengers.

The two generals were incensed against General Franco and made free use of 'tin-pot dictator', 'twopenny-half-penny Hitler', 'dago', 'priest-ridden puppet', and similar opprobrious epithets. They also spoke contemptuously of the British government who were prepared to 'truckle' to him.

'It's nothing short of a blockade. If I were in command I'd call their bluff, go full steam ahead and tell them to shoot and be damned.'

'That would be an act of war, of course.'

'Serve 'em right. We haven't sunk so low that we can't lick the Spaniards, I hope.'

'It's all this UNO.'

'And the Americans.'

'Anyway, this is one thing that can't be blamed on Russia.'

'It means the end of NATO.'

'Good riddance.'

'The Captain has to take his orders from home, I suppose.'

'That's the trouble. He can't get any orders.'

Captain Steerforth was now fully restored to Mr Pinfold's confidence. He saw him as a simple sailor obliged to make a momentous decision, not only for the safety of his own vessel but for the peace of the world. Throughout that long afternoon Mr Pinfold followed the frantic attempts of the signalmen to get into touch with the shipping company, the Foreign Office, the Governor of Gibraltar, the Mediterranean fleet. All were without avail. Captain Steerforth stood quite alone as the representative of international justice and British prestige. Mr Pinfold thought of Jenkins's ear and the Private of the Buffs. Captain Steerforth was a good man forced into an importance quite beyond his capabilities. Mr Pinfold wished he could stand beside him on the bridge, exhort him to defiance, run the ship under the Spanish guns into the wide, free inland sea where all the antique heroes of history and legend had sailed to glory.

As factions resolve in common danger, Mr Pinfold forgot the enmity of the young hooligans. All on board the *Caliban* were comrades-in-arms against foreign aggression.

The Spanish officials were polite enough. Mr Pinfold could hear them talking in the Captain's cabin. In excellent English they explained how deeply repugnant they, personally, found the orders they had to carry out. It was a question of politics, they said. No doubt the matter would be adjusted satisfactorily at a congress. Meanwhile they could only obey. They spoke of some enormous indemnity which, if it were forthcoming from London, would immediately ensure the *Caliban*'s free passage. A time was mentioned, midnight, after which if no satisfactory arrangements were made, the *Caliban* would be taken under escort to Algeciras.

'Piracy,' said Captain Steerforth, 'blackmail.'

'We cannot allow such language about the Head of the State.'

'Then you can bloody well get off my bridge,' said the Captain. They withdrew but nothing was settled by the tiff. They remained on board and the ship lay motionless.

Towards evening Mr Pinfold went on deck. There was no sign of land, nor of the Spanish ship which had brought the officials and, presumably, was lying off somewhere below the horizon. Mr Pinfold leaned over the rail and looked down at the flowing sea. The sun was dead astern of them sinking low over the water. Had he not known better, he would have supposed they were still steaming forward, so swiftly and steadily ran the current. He recalled that he had once been taught that through the Suez Canal the Indian Ocean emptied itself into the Atlantic. He thought of the multitudinous waters that supplied the Mediterranean, the ice-flows of the Black Sea that raced past Constantinople and Troy; the great rivers of history, the Nile, the Euphrates, the Danube, the Rhône. They it was that broke across the bows and left a foaming wake.

The passengers seemed quite unaware of the doom which threatened the ship. Fresh from their siestas they sat about that afternoon just as they had sat before, reading and talking and knitting. There was the same little group on the sports-deck. Mr Pinfold met Glover.

'Did you see the Spaniards come on board?' he asked.

'Spaniards? Come on board? How could they? When?'

'They're causing a lot of trouble.'

'I'm awfully sorry,' said Glover. 'I simply don't know what you're talking about.'

'You will,' said Mr Pinfold. 'Soon enough, I fear.'

Glover looked at him with the keen, perplexed air which he often assumed now when Mr Pinfold spoke to him.

'There aren't any Spaniards on board that I know of.'

It was not Mr Pinfold's duty to spread alarm and despondency or explain his unique sources of information. The Captain plainly wanted the secret kept as long as possible.

'I daresay I'm mistaken,' said Mr Pinfold loyally.

'There are the Burmese and the Norwegian couple at our table. They're the only foreigners I've seen.'

'Yes. A misunderstanding no doubt.'

Glover went to the space in the bows where he swung his club.

He swung it methodically, with concentration, without a thought of Spaniards.

Mr Pinfold withdrew to his listening post in the corner of the lounge but nothing was to be heard there except the tapping of morse as the signalmen sent out their calls for help. One of them said: 'Nothing coming in at all. I don't believe our signals are going out.'

'It's that new device,' said his mate. 'I heard something had been invented to create wireless silence. It's not been tried before, as far as I know. It was developed too late to use in the war. Both sides were at work on it but it was still in the experimental stage in 1945.'

'More effective than jamming.'

'Different principle altogether. They can only do it at short range so far. In a year or two it'll develop so that they can isolate whole countries.'

'Where will our jobs be then?'

'Oh, someone'll find a counter-system. They always do.'

'Anyway all we can do now is keep on trying.'

The tapping recommenced. Mr Pinfold went to the bar and ordered himself a glass of gin and bitters. The English steward came in from the deck, tray in hand, and went to the serving hatch.

'Those Spanish bastards are asking for whisky,' he said.

'I'll not serve them,' said the man who handled the bottles.

'Captain's order,' said the steward.

'What's come over the old man? It isn't like him to take a thing like this lying down.'

'He's got a plan. Trust him. Now give me those four whiskies and I hope it poisons them.'

Mr Pinfold finished his drink and returned to his listening post. He was curious to know more of the Captain's plan. He had no sooner settled in his chair and attuned his ear to the panelling than he heard the Captain; he was in his cabin addressing the officers.

'. . . all question of international law and convention apart,' he was saying, 'there is a particular reason why we cannot allow this ship to be searched. You all know we have an extra man on board. He's not a passenger. He's not one of the crew. He doesn't appear on any list. He's got no ticket or papers. I don't even know his name myself. I daresay you've noticed him sitting alone in the dining saloon. All I've been told is that he's very important indeed to HMG. He's on a special mission. That's why he's travelling with us instead of on one of the routes that are watched. It's him, of course, that the Spaniards are after. All this talk about territorial waters and right of search is pure bluff. We've got to see that that man gets through.'

'How are you going to manage that, skipper?'

'I don't know yet. But I've got an idea. I think I shall have to take the passengers into my confidence – not all of them, of course, and not fully into my confidence. But I'm going to collect half a dozen of the more responsible men and put them in the picture – into a bit of the picture anyway. I'll ask them up here, casually, after dinner. With their help the plan *may* work.'

The generals received their invitation early and were not deceived by its casual form. They were discussing it while Mr Pinfold dressed for dinner.

'It looks as though he's decided to put up a fight.'

'We'll all stand by him.'

'Can we trust those Burmese?'

'That's a question to raise at the meeting tonight.'

'Wouldn't trust 'em myself. Yellow-bellies.'

'The Norwegians?'

'They seem sound enough but this is a British affair.'

'Always happier on our own, eh?'

It did not occur to Mr Pinfold that he might be omitted from the Captain's *cadre*. But no invitation reached him although in various other parts of the ship he heard confidential messages . . . 'the Captain's compliments and he would be grateful if you could find it convenient to come to his cabin for a few minutes after dinner . . .'

At table Captain Steerforth carried his anxieties with splendid composure. Mrs Scarfield actually asked him: 'When do we go through the straits?' and he replied without any perceptible nuance: 'Early tomorrow morning.'

'It ought to get warmer then?'

'Not at this time of year,' he answered nonchalantly. 'You must wait for the Red Sea before you go into whites.'

During their brief acquaintance Mr Pinfold had regarded this man with sharply varying emotions. Unquestionable admiration filled him when, at the end of dinner, Mrs Scarfield asked: 'Are you joining us for a rubber?' and he replied: 'Not this evening, I'm afraid. I've one or two things to see to,' but though Mr Pinfold hung back so that he left the dining-saloon at the Captain's side, giving him the chance to invite him to the conference, they parted at the head of the stair without the word being said. Rather nonplussed Mr Pinfold hesitated, then decided to go to his cabin. It was essential that he should be easily found when he was wanted.

Soon it was apparent that he was not wanted at all. Captain Steerforth had his party promptly assembled and he began by giving them a résumé of the situation as Mr Pinfold already understood it. He said nothing of the secret agent. He merely explained that he had been unable to obtain authorization from his company to pay the preposterous sum demanded. The alternative offered by the Spaniards was that he should put into Algeciras until the matter had been settled between Madrid and London. That, he said, would be a betrayal of every standard of British seamanship. The *Caliban* would not strike her flag. There was a burst of restrained, husky, emotional, male applause. He explained his plan: at midnight the Spanish ship would come alongside. The officials now on board would tranship to her to report the results of their demand. They intended to take with them under arrest himself and a party of hostages and to put an officer of their own on his bridge to sail her into the Spanish port. It was in the dark, on the gangway, that the resistance would disclose itself. The English would overpower the Spaniards, throw them back into their ship – 'and if one or two go into the drink in the process, so much the better' – and the *Caliban* would then make full steam ahead. 'I don't think when it comes to the point, they'll open fire. Anyway their gunnery is pretty moderate and I consider it's a risk we have to take. You are all agreed?'

'Agreed. Agreed. Agreed.'

'I knew I could trust you,' said the Captain. 'You're all men who've seen service. I am proud to have you under my command. The yellow-bellies will be locked in their cabins.'

'How about Pinfold?' asked one of the generals. 'Shouldn't he be here?'

'There is a rôle assigned to Captain Pinfold. I don't think I need go into that at the moment.'

'Has he received his orders?'

'Not yet,' said Captain Steerforth. 'We have some hours before us. I suggest, gentlemen, that you go about the ship in the normal way, turn in early, and rendezvous here at 11.45. Midnight is zero hour. Perhaps, general, you will remain behind for a few minutes. For the present, good night, gentlemen.'

The meeting broke up. Presently only the general remained with the first and second officers in the Captain's cabin.

'Well,' said Captain Steerforth, 'how did that sound?'

'Pretty thin, skipper, if you ask me,' said the first officer.

'I take it,' said the general, 'that what we have just heard was merely the cover-plan?'

'Precisely. I could hardly hope to deceive an old campaigner like you. I am sorry not to be able to take your companions into my confidence, but in the interest of security I have had to limit those in the know to an absolute minimum. The rôle of the committee who have just left us is to create sufficient diversion to enable us to carry out the real purpose of the operation. That, of course, is to prevent a certain person falling into the hands of the enemy.'

'Pinfold?'

'No, no, quite the contrary. Captain Pinfold, I fear, has to be written off. The Spaniards will not let us pass until they think they have their man. It has not been an easy decision, I assure you. I am responsible for the safety of all my passengers, but at a time like this sacrifices have to be accepted. The plan briefly is this.

Captain Pinfold is to impersonate the agent. He will be provided with papers identifying him. The Spaniards will take him ashore and the ship will sail on unmolested.'

There was a pause while this proposition was considered. The first officer at length spoke: 'It might work, skipper.'

'It *must* work.'

'What do you suppose will happen to him?'

'Can't say. I suppose they'll hold him under arrest while they investigate. They won't let him communicate with our embassy, of course. When they find out their mistake, if they ever do, they'll be in rather a jam. They may let him out or they may find it more convenient just to let him disappear.'

'I see.'

It was the general who voiced the thought uppermost in Mr Pinfold's mind. 'Why Pinfold?' he asked.

'It was a painful choice,' said Captain Steerforth, 'but not a difficult one. He is the obvious man, really. No one else on board would take them in for a moment. He looks like a secret agent. I think he was one during the war. He's a sick man and therefore expendable. And, of course, he's a Roman Catholic. That ought to make things a little easier for him in Spain.'

'Yes,' said the general, 'yes. I see all that. But all the same I think it's pretty sporting of him to agree. In his place I must own I'd think twice before taking it on.'

'Oh, *he* doesn't know anything about it.'

'The devil he doesn't?'

'No, that would be quite fatal to security. Besides he might *not* agree. He has a wife, you know, and a large family. You can't really blame a man who thinks of domestic responsibilities before volunteering for hazardous service. No, Captain Pinfold must be kept quite in the dark. That's the reason for the counter-plan, the diversion. There's got to be a schemozzle on the gangway so that Captain Pinfold can be pushed into the corvette. You, number one, will be responsible for hauling him out of his cabin and planting the papers on him.'

'Aye, aye, sir.'

'That boy of mine will laugh,' said the general. 'He took against Pinfold from the start. Now he hears he's deserted to the enemy . . .'

The voices ceased. For a long time Mr Pinfold sat paralysed with horror and rage. When at length he looked at his watch he found that it was nearly half-past nine. Then he took off his evening clothes and put on his tweeds. Whatever outrage the night brought forth should find him suitably dressed. He pocketed his passport and his traveller's cheques. Then, blackthorn in hand, he sat down again and began patiently and painfully as he had learned in the army, to 'appreciate the situation'. He was alone, without hope of reinforcement. His sole advantage was that he knew, and they did not know he knew, their plan of action. He examined the Captain's plan in the light of the quite considerable experience he had acquired in small-scale night operations and he found it derisory. The result of a scuffle in the dark on a gangway was quite unpredict-able but he was confident that, forewarned, he could easily evade or repulse any attempt to put him into the corvette against his will. Even if they succeeded and the *Caliban* attempted to sail away, the corvette, of course, would open fire and, of course, would sink or disable her long before the Spaniards began examining the forged papers that were to be planted on him.

And here Mr Pinfold experienced scruples. He was not what is generally meant by the appellation a 'philanthropic' man; he totally lacked what was now called a 'social conscience'. But apart from his love of family and friends he had a certain basic kindliness to those who refrained from active annoyance. And in an old-fashioned way he was patriotic. These sentiments sometimes did service for what are generally regarded as the higher loyalties and affections. This was such an occasion. He rather liked Mrs Scarfield, Mrs Cockson, Mrs Benson, Glover and all those simple, chatting, knitting, dozing passengers. For the unseen, enigmatic Margaret he felt tender curiosity. It would be a pity for all these to be precipitated into a watery bier by the ineptitude of Captain Steer-forth. For himself he had little concern, but he knew that his disappearance, and possible disgrace, would grieve his wife and family. It was intolerable that this booby Captain should handle so many lives so clumsily. But there was also the question of the secret agent. If this man, as seemed likely, was really of vital importance to his country, he must be protected. Mr Pinfold felt responsible for his protection. He had been chosen as victim. That doom was inescapable. But he would go to the sacrifice a garlanded hero. He would not be tricked into it.

No precise tactical plan could be made. Whatever his action, it would be improvised. But the intention was plain. He would, if necessary, consent to impersonate the agent, but Captain Steerforth and his cronies must understand that he went voluntarily as a man of honour and Mrs Pinfold must be fully informed of the circumstances. That established, he would consent to his arrest.

As he pondered all this, he was barely conscious of the voices that came to him. He waited.

At a quarter to twelve there was a hail from the bridge answered from the sea in Spanish. The corvette was coming alongside and at once the ship came to life with a multitude of voices. This, Mr Pinfold decided, was his moment to act. He must deliver his terms to the Captain before the Spaniards came on board. Gripping his blackthorn he left the cabin.

Immediately his communications were cut. The lighted corridor was empty and completely silent. He strode down it to the stairway, mounted to the main deck. No one was about. There was no ship near or anywhere in sight; not a light anywhere on the dark horizon; not a sound from the bridge; only the rush and slap of the waves along the ship's side, and the keen sea wind. Mr Pinfold stood confounded, the only troubled thing in a world at peace.

He had been dauntless a minute before in the face of his enemies. Now he was struck with real fear, something totally different from the superficial alarms he had once or twice known in moments of danger, something he had quite often read about and dismissed as over-writing. He was possessed from outside himself with atavistic panic. 'O let me not be mad, not mad, sweet heaven,' he cried.

And in that moment of agony there broke not far from him in the darkness peal upon rising peal of mocking laughter – Goneril's. It was not an emollient sound. It was devoid of mirth, an obscene cacophony of pure hatred. But it fell on Mr Pinfold's ears at that moment like a nursery lullaby.

'A hoax,' he said to himself.

It was all a hoax on the part of the hooligans. He understood all. They had learned the secret of the defective wiring in his cabin. Somehow they had devised a means of controlling it, somehow they had staged this whole charade to tease him. It was spiteful and offensive, no doubt; it must not happen again. But Mr Pinfold felt nothing but gratitude in his discovery. He might be unpopular; he might be ridiculous; but he was not mad.

He returned to his cabin. He had been awake now for thirty or forty hours. He lay down at once in his clothes and fell into deep, natural sleep. He lay motionless and unconscious for six hours.

When he next went on deck the sun was up, directly over the bows. Square on the port beam rose the unmistakable peak of the Rock. The *Caliban* was steaming into the calm Mediterranean.

Chapter Six

THE HUMAN TOUCH

While Mr Pinfold was shaving, he heard Margaret say: 'It was an absolutely beastly joke and I'm glad it fell flat.'

'It came off very nicely,' said her brother. 'Old Peinfeld was jibbering with funk.'

'He wasn't – and he isn't called Peinfeld. He was a hero. When I saw him standing there alone on deck I thought of Nelson.'

'He was drunk.'

'He says it's not drink, dear,' said their mother, gently uncommitted to either side. 'He *says* it's some medicine he has to take.'

'Medicine from a brandy bottle.'

'I know you're wrong,' said Margaret. 'You see it just happens *I know* what he's thinking, and you don't.'

Then Goneril's steely voice cut in: '*I* can tell you what he was doing on deck. He was screwing up his courage to jump overboard. He longs to kill himself, don't you, Gilbert. All right, I know you're listening down there. You can hear me, can't you Gilbert? You wish you were dead, don't you, Gilbert. And a very good idea, too. Why don't you do it, Gilbert? Why not? Perfectly easy. It would save us all – you too, Gilbert – great deal of trouble.'

'Beast,' said Margaret and broke into weeping.

'Oh God,' said her brother, 'now you've turned on the waterworks again.'

Mr Pinfold was fortified by his six hours' sleep. He went above, leaving the nagging voices of the cabin for the silent and empty decks for an hour. The Rock had dropped below the horizon and there was no land in sight. The sea might have been any sea by the look of it, but he knew it was the Mediterranean, that splendid enclosure which held all the world's history and half the happiest memories of his own life; of work and rest and battle, of aesthetic adventure and of young love.

After breakfast he took a book to the lounge, not to his listening post in the panelled corner, but to an isolated chair in the centre, and read undisturbed. He must get out of that haunted cabin, he thought; but not yet; later, in his own time.

Presently he rose and began once more to walk the decks. They were thronged now. All the passengers seemed to be there, occupied as before in reading, knitting, dozing or strolling like himself, but that morning he found a kind of paschal novelty in the scene and rejoiced in it until he was rudely disturbed in his benevolence.

The passengers, too, seemed aware of change. They must all at one time or another in the last few days have caught sight of Mr Pinfold. Now, however, it was as though he were a noteworthy, unaccompanied female, newly appearing in the evening promenade of some stagnant South American town. He had been witness of such an event on many a dusty plaza; he had seen the sickly faces of the men brighten, their lassitude take sudden life; he had observed the little flourishes of seedy dandyism; he had heard the jungle whistles and, without fully understanding them, the frank, anatomical appraisals; had seen the sly following and pinching of the unwary tourist. In just that way Mr Pinfold, wherever he went that day, found himself to be such a cynosure; everyone was talking about him, loudly and unashamedly, but not in his praise.

'That's Gilbert Pinfold, the writer.'

'That common little man? It can't be.'

'Have you read his books? He has a very *peculiar* sense of humour, you know.'

'He is very peculiar altogether. His hair is very long.'

'He's wearing lipstick.'

'He's painted up to the eyes.'

'But he's so shabby. I thought people like that were always smart.'

'There are different types of homosexual, you know. What are called "poufs" and "nancies" – that is the dressy kind. Then there are the others they call "butch". I read a book about it. Pinfold is a "butch".'

That was the first conversation Mr Pinfold overheard. He stopped, turned and tried to stare out of countenance the little group of middle-aged women who were speaking. One of them smiled at him and then, turning, said: 'I believe he's trying to get to know us.'

'How disgusting.'

Mr Pinfold walked on but wherever he went he was the topic.

'. . . Lord of the Manor of Lychpole.'

'Anyone can be that. It's often a title that goes with some tumbledown farmhouse these days.'

'Oh, Pinfold lives in great style I can tell you. Footmen in livery.'

'I can guess what he does with the footmen.'

'Not any more. He's been impotent for years, you know. That's why he's always thinking of death.'

'Is he always thinking of death?'

'Yes. He'll commit suicide one of these days, you'll see.'

'I thought he was a Catholic. They aren't allowed to commit suicide, are they?'

'That wouldn't stop Pinfold. He doesn't really *believe* in his religion, you know. He just pretends to because he thinks it aristocratic. It goes with being Lord of the Manor.'

'There's only one Lychpole in the world, he told the wireless man.'

'Only one Lychpole and Pinfold is its Lord . . .'

'. . . There he is, drunk again.'

'He looks ghastly.'

'A dying man, if ever I saw one.'

'Why doesn't he kill himself?'

'Give him time. He's doing his best. Drink and drugs. He daren't go to a doctor, of course, for fear he'd be put in a home.'

'Best place for him, I should have thought.'

'Best place for him would be over the side.'

'Rather a nuisance for poor Captain Steerforth.'

'It's a great nuisance for Captain Steerforth having him on board.'

'And at his own table.'

'That's being taken care of. Haven't you heard? There's going to be a petition.'

'. . . Yes, I've signed. Everyone has, I believe.'

'Except those actually at the table. The Scarfields wouldn't, or Glover.'

'I see it might be a little awkward for them.'

'It's a very well-worded petition.'

'Yes. The general did that. It makes no specific accusation, you see, that might be libellous. Simply: "*We the undersigned, for reasons which we are prepared to state in confidence, consider it to be an insult to us, as passengers in the* Caliban, *that Mr Gilbert Pinfold should sit at the Captain's table, a position of honour for which he is notoriously unsuitable.*" That's very neatly put.'

'. . . the Captain ought to lock him up. He has full authority.'

'But he hasn't actually *done* anything yet, on board.'

This was a pair of genial businessmen with whom and the Scarfields Mr Pinfold had spent half an hour one evening.

'For his own protection. It was a very near thing the other night that those boys didn't beat him up.'

'They were drunk.'

'They may get drunk again. It would be most unpleasant for everyone if there was a police court case.'

'Couldn't something be put in our petition about that?'

'It was discussed. The generals thought it could best be left to the interview. The Captain is bound to ask them to give their reasons.'

'Not in writing.'

'Exactly. They don't suggest putting him in the cell. Simply confining him to his cabin.'

'He probably has certain legal rights, having paid his fare, to his cabin and his meals.'

'But *not* to his meals at the Captain's table.'

'There you have the crux.'

'. . . No,' the Norwegian was saying, 'I did not sign anything. It is a British matter. All I know is that he is a fascist. I have heard him speak ill of democracy. We had a few such men in the time of Quisling. We knew what to do with them. But I will not mix in these British affairs.'

'I've got a photograph of him in a black shirt taken at one of those Albert Hall meetings before the war.'

'That might be useful.'

'He was up to his eyes in it. He'd have been locked up under 18B but he escaped by joining the army.'

'He did pretty badly there, I suppose?'

'*Very* badly. There was a scandal in Cairo that had to be hushed up when his brigade-major shot himself.'

'Blackmail?'

'The next best thing.'

'I see he's wearing the Guards tie.'

'He wears any kind of tie – old Etonian usually.'

'*Was* he ever at Eton?'

'He says he was,' said Glover.

'Don't you believe it. Board-school through and through.'

'Or at Oxford?'

'No, no. His whole account of his early life is a lie. No one had ever heard of him until a year or two ago. He's one of a lot of nasty people who crept into prominence during the war . . .'

'. . . I don't say he's an actual card-carrying member of the communist party, but he's certainly mixed up with them.'

'Most Jews are.'

'Exactly. And those "missing diplomats". They were friends of his.'

'He doesn't know enough to make it worth the Russians' while to take him to Moscow.'

'Even the Russians wouldn't want Pinfold.'

*

The most curious encounter of that morning was with Mrs Cockson and Mrs Benson. They were sitting as usual on the verandah of the deck-bar, each with her glass, and they were talking French with what seemed to Mr Pinfold, who spoke the language clumsily, pure accent and idiom. Mrs Cockson said: 'Ce Monsieur Pinfold essaye toujours de pénétrer chez moi, et il a essayé de se faire présenter à moi par plusieurs de mes amis. Naturellement j'ai refusé.'

'Connaissez-vous un seul de ses amis? Il me semble qu'il a des relations très ordinaires.'

'On peut toujours se tromper dans le premier temps sur une relation étrangère. On a fini par s'apercevoir à Paris qu'il n'est pas de notre société . . .'

It was a put-up job, Mr Pinfold decided. People did not normally behave in this way.

When Mr Pinfold first joined Bellamy's there was an old earl who sat alone all day and every day in the corner of the stairs wearing an odd, hard hat and talking loudly to himself. He had one theme, the passing procession of his fellow members. Sometimes he dozed, but in his long waking hours he maintained a running commentary – 'That fellow's chin is too big; dreadful-looking fellow. Never saw him before. Who let him in? . . . Pick your feet up, you. Wearing the carpets out . . . Dreadfully fat young Crambo's getting. Don't eat, don't drink, it's just he's hard up. Nothing fattens a man like getting hard up . . . Poor old Nailsworth, his mother was a whore, so's his wife. They say his daughter's going the same way' . . . and so on.

In the broad tolerance of Bellamy's this eccentric had been accepted quite fondly. He was dead many years now. It was not conceivable, Mr Pinfold thought, that all the passengers in the *Caliban* should suddenly have become similarly afflicted. This chatter was designed to be overheard. It was a put-up job. It was in fact the generals' subtle plan, substituted for the adolescent violence of their young.

Twenty-five years ago or more Mr Pinfold, who was in love with one of them, used to frequent a house full of bright, cruel girls who spoke their own thieves' slang and played their own games. One of these games was a trick from the schoolroom polished for drawing-room use. When a stranger came among them, they would all – if the mood took them – put out their tongues at him or her; all, that is to say, except those in his immediate line of sight. As he turned his head, one group of tongues popped in, another popped out. Those girls were adept in dialogue. They had rigid self-control. They never giggled. Those who spoke to the stranger assumed an unnatural sweetness. The aim was to make him catch another with her tongue out. It was a comic performance – the turning head, the flickering, crimson stabs, the tender smiles turning to sudden grimaces, the artificiality of the conversation which soon engendered an unidentifiable discomfort in the most insensitive visitor, made him feel that somehow he was making a fool of himself, made him look at his trouser buttons, at his face in the glass to see whether there was something ridiculous in his appearance.

Some sort of game as this, enormously coarsened, must, Mr Pinfold supposed, have been devised by the passengers in the *Caliban* for their amusement and his discomfort. Well, he was not going to give them the satisfaction of taking notice of it. He no longer glanced to see who was speaking.

'. . . His mother sold her few little pieces of jewellery, you know, to pay his debts . . .'

'. . . Were his books ever any good?'

'Never *good*. His earlier ones weren't quite as bad as his latest. He's written out.'

'He's tried every literary trick. He's finished now and he knows it.'

'I suppose he's made a lot of money?'

'Not as much as he pretends. And he's spent every penny. His debts are enormous.'

'And of course they'll catch him for income-tax soon.'

'Oh, yes. He's been putting in false returns for years. They're investigating him now. They don't hurry. They always get their man in the end.'

'They'll get Pinfold.'

'He'll have to sell Lychpole.'

'His children will go to the board-school.'

'Just as he did himself.'

'No more champagne for Pinfold.'

'No more cigars.'

'I suppose his wife will leave him?'

'Naturally. No home for her. Her family will take her in.'

'But not Pinfold.'

'No. Not Pinfold . . .'

Mr Pinfold would not give ground. There must be no appearance of defeat. But in his own time, when he had sauntered long enough, he retired to his cabin.

'Gilbert,' said Margaret. 'Gilbert. Why don't you speak to me? You passed quite close to me on deck and you never looked at me. *I* haven't offended you, have I? You know it isn't me who's saying all these beastly things, don't you? Answer me, Gilbert. I can hear you.'

So Mr Pinfold, not uttering the words but pronouncing them in his mind, said: 'Where are you? I don't even know you by sight. Why don't we meet, now? Come and have a cocktail with me.'

'Oh, Gilbert, darling, you know that's not possible. The *Rules*.'

'What rules? Whose? Do you mean your father won't let you?'

'No, Gilbert, not *his* rules, *the* Rules. Don't you understand? It's against *the Rules* for us to meet. I can talk to you now and then but we must never meet.'

'What do you look like?'

'I mustn't tell you that. You must find out for yourself. That's one of the Rules.'

'You talk as though we were playing some kind of game.'

'That's all we are doing – playing a kind of game. I must go now. But there's one thing I'd like to say.'

'Well?'

'You won't be offended?'

'I don't expect so.'

'Are you sure, darling?'

'What is it?'

'Shall I tell you? Dare I? You won't be offended? Well . . .' Margaret paused and then in a thrilling whisper said: '*Get your hair cut.*'

'Well, I'll be damned,' said Mr Pinfold; but Margaret was gone and did not hear him.

He looked in the glass. Yes, his hair was rather long. He would get it cut. Then he pondered the new problem: how had Margaret heard his soundless words? That could not be explained on any theory of frayed and crossed wires. As he considered the matter Margaret briefly returned to say: 'Not *wires*, darling. *Wireless*,' and then was gone again.

That perhaps should have given him the clue he sought; should have dispelled the mystery that enveloped him. He would learn in good time; at that moment Mr Pinfold was baffled, almost stupefied, by the occurrences of the morning and he went down to luncheon at the summons of the gong thinking vaguely in terms of telepathy, a subject on which he was ill-informed.

At the table he tackled Glover at once on a question that vexed him. 'I was not at Eton,' he said suddenly, with a challenge in his tone.

'Nor was I,' said Glover. 'Marlborough.'

'I never said I was at Eton,' Mr Pinfold insisted.

'No. Why should you, I mean, if you weren't?'

'It is a school for which I have every respect, but I was not there myself.' Then he turned across to the table to the Norwegian. 'I never wore a black shirt in the Albert Hall.'

'No?' said the Norwegian, interested but uncomprehending.

'I had every sympathy with Franco during the Civil War.'

'Yes? It is so long ago I have rather forgotten what it was all about. In my country we did not pay so much attention as the French and some other nations.'

'I never had the smallest sympathy with Hitler.'

'No, I suppose not.'

'Once I had hopes of Mussolini. But I was never connected with Mosley.'

'Mosley? What is that?'

'Please, please,' cried pretty Mrs Scarfield, 'don't let's get on to politics.'

For the rest of the meal Mr Pinfold sat silent.

Later he went to the barber's shop and from there to his listening post in the empty lounge. He saw the ship's surgeon pass the windows. He was on his way, evidently, to the Captain's cabin for almost immediately Mr Pinfold heard him say: '. . . I thought I ought to report it to you, skipper.'

'Where was he last seen?'

'In the barber's shop. After that he completely disappeared. He's not in his cabin.'

'Why should he have gone overboard?'

'I've had my eye on him ever since we sailed. Haven't you noticed anything odd about him?'

'I've noticed he drinks.'

'Yes, he's a typical alcoholic. Several of the passengers asked me to look him over, but I can't you know, unless he calls me in or unless he does something violent. Now they're all saying he's jumped overboard.'

'I'm not going to stop the ship and put out a boat simply because a passenger isn't in his cabin. He's probably in someone else's cabin with one of my female passengers doing you know what.'

'Yes, that's the most likely explanation.'

'Is there anything the matter with him apart from the bottle?'

'Nothing a day's hard work wouldn't cure. The best thing for him would be to be put swabbing decks for a week . . .'

And after that the ship, like an aviary, was noisy with calls and chatter.

'. . . He can't be found.'

'. . . Overboard.'

'. . . No one's seen him since he left the barber . . .'

'. . . The Captain thinks he's got a woman somewhere . . .'

Very wearily Mr Pinfold tried to shut his mind to these distractions and to read his book. Presently the note changed. 'It's all right, he's found.'

'. . . False alarm.'

'. . . Pinfold's found.'

'I'm glad of that,' said the general gravely. 'I was afraid we might have gone too far.'

And the rest was silence.

The cutting of Mr Pinfold's hair fomented relations with Margaret. She prattled off and on all that afternoon and evening, gloating fondly over the change in Mr Pinfold's appearance; he looked younger, she said, smarter, altogether more lovable. Gazing long and earnestly into his looking-glass, turning his head this way and that, Mr Pinfold saw nothing very different from what he was used to, nothing to justify this enthusiasm. Margaret's gratification, he surmised, sprang less from his enhanced beauty than from the evidence he had given of his trust in her.

Interspersed with her praises there was an occasional hint of some deeper significance: '. . . Think Gilbert. *Barber's shop*. Doesn't that tell you anything?'

'No. Should it?'

'It's the *clue*, Gilbert. It's what you most want to know, what you *must* know.'

'Well, tell me.'

'I can't do that, darling. It's against the *Rules*. But I can hint. *Barber's shop*, Gilbert. What do barbers do beside cutting hair?'

'They try and sell one hairwash.'

'No. No.'

'They make conversation. They massage the scalp. They iron moustaches. They sometimes, I believe, cut people's corns.'

'Oh, Gilbert, something much simpler. Think, darling. Sh . . . Sh . . .'

'Shave?'

'Got it.'

'But I shaved this morning. You're not asking me to shave again?'

'Oh, Gilbert, I think you're sweet. Is your chin a little bit rough, darling? How long after you shave does it get rough again? I *think* I should like it rough . . .' And she was off again on her galloping declaration of love.

More than once Mr Pinfold – or rather a fanciful image of him derived from his books – had been the object of adolescent infatuation. Margaret's fervent, naive tones reminded him of the letters which used to come, two a day usually for periods of a week or ten days, written in bed probably. They were confidences and avowals of love, bearing no address; asking no reciprocation or sign of recognition; the series ending as abruptly as it had begun. As a rule, he read none after the first, but here on the hostile *Caliban*, these guileless words uttered in Margaret's sweet, breathless tones fell softly on Mr Pinfold's ear and he listened complacently. Indeed he began to relish these moments of unction which compensated for much of the ignorant abuse. That morning he had determined to change his cabin. That evening he was loth to cut himself off from this warm spring.

But night wrought a change.

Mr Pinfold did not dress or dine. He was very weary and he sat alone on deck until the passengers began to come up from dinner. Then he went to his cabin and for the first time for three days put on pyjamas, said his prayers, got into bed, turned off the light, composed himself for sleep, and slept.

He was awakened by Margaret's mother.

'Mr Pinfold. Mr Pinfold. Surely you haven't gone to sleep? Everyone is in bed now. Surely you haven't forgotten your promise to Margaret?'

'Mother, he didn't make any promise.' Margaret's voice was tearful and strained, almost hysterical. 'Not really. Not really what you could call a *promise*. Don't you see how awful it is for *me*, if you upset him now? He never *promised*.'

'When I was young, dear, any man would be proud of a pretty girl taking notice of him. He wouldn't try and get out of it by pretending to be asleep.'

'I asked for it. I expect I bore him. He's a man of the world. He's had hundreds of other girls, all sorts of horrible, fashionable, vicious old hags in London and Paris and Rome and New York. Why should he look at *me*? But I *do* love him so,' and in her anguish she uttered the whimper which Mr Pinfold had heard before in this ship on other lips.

'Don't cry, my dear. Mother will talk to him.'

'Please, *please* not, Mother. I forbid you to interfere.'

' "Forbid" isn't a very nice word, is it, dear? You leave it to me. I'll talk to him. Mr Pinfold. *Gilbert*. Wake up. Margaret's got something to say to you. He's awake now, dear, I know. Just tell her you're awake and listening, Gilbert.'

'I'm awake and listening,' said Mr Pinfold.

'All right then, hold on' – she was like a telephone operator, Mr Pinfold thought – 'Margaret's going to speak to you. Come along, Margaret, speak up.'

'I can't, Mother, I can't.'

'You see, Gilbert, you've upset her. Tell her you love her. You do love her, don't you?'

'But I've never met her,' said Mr Pinfold desperately. 'I'm sure she's a delightful girl, but I've never set eyes on her.'

'Oh, Gilbert, Gilbert, that's not a very gallant thing to say, is it? Not really like you, not like the *real* you. You just pretend to be hard and worldly, don't you? and you can't blame people if they take you at your own estimate. Everyone in the ship, you know, has been saying the most odious things about you. But I know better. Margaret wants to come and say good night to you, Gilbert, but she's not sure you really love her. Just tell Mimi you love her, Gilbert.'

'I can't, I don't,' said Mr Pinfold. 'I'm sure your daughter is a most charming girl. It so happens I have never met her. It also happens that I have a wife. I love *her*.'

'Oh, Gilbert, what a very middle-class thing to say!'

'He doesn't love me,' wailed Margaret. 'He doesn't love me any more.'

'Gilbert, Gilbert, you're breaking my little girl's heart.'

Mr Pinfold was exasperated.

'I'm going to sleep now,' he said. 'Good night.'

'Margaret's coming to see you.'

'Oh, shut up, you old bitch,' said Mr Pinfold.

He should not have said it. The moment the words crossed his lips – or, rather, his mind – he knew it was not the right thing to say. The whole sturdy ship seemed to tremble with shock. There was a single piteous wail from Margaret, from her mother an inarticulate but plainly audible hiss of outrage, an attempt at bluster from the son: 'My God, Peinfeld, you'll pay for that. If you think you can talk to my mother like . . .' And then, most unexpectedly came a hearty chuckle from the general.

'Upon my soul, my dear, he called you an old bitch. Good for Peinfeld. That's something I've been longing to say to you for thirty years. You *are* an old bitch, you know, a thorough old bitch. Now perhaps you'll allow *me* to handle the situation. Clear out, the lot of you, I want to talk to my daughter. Come here, Meg, Peg o' my heart, my little Mimi.' The voices became thick, the diction strangely Celtic as sentiment overpowered the military man. 'You'll not be my little Mimi ever again, any more after tonight and I'll not forget it. You're a woman now and you've set your heart on a man as a woman should. The choice is yours, not mine. He's old for you, but there's good in that. Many a young couple spend a wretched fortnight together through not knowing how to set about what has to be done. And an old man can show you better than a young one. He'll be gentler and kinder and cleaner; and then, when the right time comes, you in your turn can teach a younger man – and that's how the art of love is learned and the breed survives. I'd like dearly to be the one myself to teach you, but you've made your own choice and who's to grudge it you?'

'But, Father, he doesn't love me. He said not.'

'Fiddlesticks. You're as pretty a girl as he'll meet in a twelvemonth. There's certainly no one in this ship to touch you and if he's the man I think, he'll be feeling the need of an armful by now. Go in and get him, lass. How do you think your mother got me? Not by waiting to be asked, I can tell you. She was a soldier's daughter. She always rode straight at her fences. She rode straight at me, I can tell you. Don't forget you're a soldier's daughter too. If you want this fellow Pinfold, go in and take him. But for God's sake come on parade looking like a soldier. Get yourself cleaned up. Wash your face, brush your hair, take your clothes off.'

Margaret went obediently to her cabin. There she was joined by her friend, several friends, it seemed, a whole choir of bridesmaids who chanted an epithalamium as they disrobed her and tied her hair.

Mr Pinfold listened with conflicting resentment and fascination. He was a man accustomed to his own preferences and decisions. It seemed to him that Margaret's parents were being officious and presumptuous, were making altogether too free with his passions. He had never, even in his bachelor days, been a strenuous philanderer. Abroad, especially in remote places, he used to patronize brothels with the curiosity of a traveller who sought to taste all flavours of the exotic. In England he was rather constant and rather romantic in his affections. Since marriage he had been faithful to his wife. He had, since his acceptance of the laws of the Church, developed what approximated to a virtuous disposition; a reluctance to commit deliberate grave sins, which was independent of the fear of Hell; he had assumed a personality to which such specifically forbidden actions were inappropriate. And yet amorous expectations began to stir in Mr Pinfold. That acquired restraint and dignity of his had suffered some hard knocking-about during the last few days. Margaret's visit was exciting. He started to plan her reception.

The cabin with its two narrow bunks was ill-designed for such purposes. He began by tidying it, putting away his clothes and straightening the bed. He succeeded only in making it look unoccupied. She would enter by that door. She must not find him reclining like a pasha. He must be on his feet. There was one chair only. Should he offer it to her? Somehow he must dispose her, supine, on the bunk. But how to get her there silently and gracefully. How to shift her? Was she portable? He wished that he knew her dimensions.

He took off his pyjamas and hung them in his cupboard, put on his dressing-gown, and sat in the chair facing the door, waiting, while the folk-ritual of Margaret's preparations filled the cabin with music. As he waited his mood changed. Doubt and dismay intruded on his loving fancies. What on earth was he up to? What was he letting himself in for? He thought with disgust of Clutton-Cornforth and his tedious succession of joyless, purposeful seductions. He thought of his own enfeebled condition. 'Feeling the need of an armful' indeed! Would he be able to sustain his interest during all the patient exploration required of him? Then as he gazed at the tidy bunk, he filled it with delicate, shrinking, yielding, yearning nudity, with a nymph by Boucher or Fragonard, and his mood changed again. Let her come. Let her come speedily. He was strongly armed for the encounter.

But Margaret did not hurry. The attendant virgins completed their services. She was inspected by both parents.

'Oh my darling, my own. You're so young. Are you sure? Are you quite sure you love him. You can always turn back. It's not too late. I shall never see you again as I am seeing you now, my innocent daughter.'

'Yes, mother, I love him.'

'Be kind to her, Gilbert. You have not been kind to me. You used an expression to me that I never expected to hear on a man's lips. I meant never to speak to you again. But this is no moment for pride. My daughter's happiness is in your hands. Treat her *husbandly*. I'm entrusting something very precious to you . . .'

And the general: 'That's my beauty. Go and take what's coming to you. Listen, my Peg, you know what you're in for, don't you?'

'Yes, father, I think so.'

'It's always a surprise. You may think you know it all on paper, but like everything else in life it's never quite what you expect when it comes to action. There's no going back now. Come and see me when it's all over. I'll be waiting up to hear the report. In you go, bless you.'

But still the girl delayed.

'Gilbert, Gilbert. Do you want me?' she asked. 'Really and truly?'

'Yes, of course, come along.'

'Say something sweet to me.'

'I'll be sweet enough when you get here.'

'Come and fetch me.'

'Where are you?'

'Here. Just outside your cabin.'

'Well, come along in. I've left the door open.'

'I can't. I can't. You've got to come and fetch me.'

'Oh, don't be such a little ass. I've been sitting here for goodness knows how long. Come in if you're coming. If you're not, I want to go back to bed.'

At this Margaret broke into weeping and her mother said: 'Gilbert, that wasn't kind. It wasn't like you. You love her. She loves you. Can't you understand? A young girl; the first time; woo her, Gilbert, coax her. She's a little wild, woodland thing.'

'What the hell's going on?' asked the general. 'You ought to be in position by now. Haven't had a Sitrep. Isn't the girl over the Start Line?'

'Oh, Father, I can't. I *can't*. I thought I could, but I *can't*.'

'Something's gone wrong, Pinfold. Find out. Send out patrols.'

'Go and find her, Gilbert. Lure her in, tenderly, *husbandly*. She's just there waiting for you.'

Rather crossly Mr Pinfold strode into the empty corridor. He could hear Glover snoring. He could hear Margaret weeping quite close to him. He looked in the bathroom; not there. He looked round each corner, up and down the stairs; not there. He even looked in the lavatories, men's and women's; not there. Still the sobbing continued piteously. He returned to his cabin, fixed the door open on its hook and drew the curtain. He was overcome by weariness and boredom.

'I'm sorry, Margaret,' he said, 'I'm too old to start playing hide and seek with schoolgirls. If you want to come to bed with me, you'll have to come and join me there.'

He put on his pyjamas and lay down, pulling the blankets up to his chin. Presently he stretched out his arm and turned off the light. Then the passage light was disturbing. He shut the door. He rolled over on his side and lay between sleep and waking. Just as he was falling into unconsciousness he heard his door open and quickly shut. He opened his eyes too late to see the momentary gleam of light from the corridor. He heard slippered feet scurrying away and Margaret's despairing wail.

'I did go to him. I did. I did. I did. And when I got there he was lying in the dark snoring.'

'Oh, my Margaret, my daughter. You should never have gone. It was all your father's fault.'

'Sorry about that, Peg,' said the general. 'False appreciation.'

The last voice Mr Pinfold heard before he fell asleep was Goneril's: 'Snoring? Shamming. Gilbert knew he wasn't up to it. He's impotent, aren't you, Gilbert? Aren't you?'

'It was Glover snoring,' said Mr Pinfold, but nobody seemed to hear him.

Chapter Seven

THE VILLAINS UNMASKED — BUT NOT FOILED

Mr Pinfold did not sleep for very long. He awoke as usual when the men began washing the deck overhead and he woke with the firm resolution of changing his cabin that day. His bond with Margaret was severed. He wished to be rid of the whole set of them and to sleep in peace in a cabin free of electrical freaks. He resolved, too, to move from the Captain's table. He had never wished to sit there. Anyone who coveted the place was welcome to it. Mr Pinfold was going to be strictly private for the rest of the voyage.

This resolution was confirmed by the last of the many communications that had come to him in that cabin.

Shortly before the breakfast hour, the device brought him into contact with what he might have supposed would be its most natural source, the wireless office; he found himself listening not as before to the normal traffic of the ship, but to the conversation of the wireless operator, and this man was entertaining a party of early-risers, the bright young people, by reading to them the text of Mr Pinfold's own messages.

'"*Everyone in ship most helpful. Love. Gilbert.*"'

'That's a good one.'

'Everyone?'

'I wonder if poor Gilbert thinks that now?'

'*Love.* Love from Gilbert. That's funny.'

'Show us some more.'

'Strictly speaking, you know, I oughtn't to. They're supposed to be confidential.'

'Oh, come off it, Sparks.'

'Well, this is rather rich. "*Entirely cured. All love.*"'

'Cured? Ha. Ha.'

'*Entirely* cured.'

'Our Gilbert *entirely cured*! Yes, that's delicious. Oh, Sparks, read us some more.'

'I've never known a chap spend so much on radiograms. They're mostly just about money and often he was so drunk I couldn't read what he'd written. There are an awful lot just refusing invitations. Oh, here's a good series. "*Kindly arrange immediate luxury private bath. Kindly investigate wanton inefficiency your office.*" He sent out dozens of those.'

'Thank God for our Gilbert. What should we do without him?'

'Was his luxury private bath inefficient?'

'"Wanton" is good coming from Gilbert. Does he wanton in his bath?'

To Mr Pinfold this little scene was different in kind from the earlier annoyances. The bright young people had gone too far. It was one thing to play practical jokes on him; it was something quite else to read confidential messages. They had put themselves outside the law. Mr Pinfold left his cabin for the dining-saloon with set purpose. He would put them on a charge.

He met the Captain making his morning round.

'Captain Steerforth, may I speak to you for a moment?'

'Surely.' The Captain paused.

'In your cabin?'

'Yes, if you want to. I shall be through in ten minutes. Come up then. Or is it very urgent?'

'It can wait ten minutes.'

Mr Pinfold climbed to the cabin behind the bridge. Few personal additions embellished the solid ship's furniture. There were family photographs in leather frames; an etching of an English cathedral on the panelled wall which might have been the Captain's property or the company's; some pipes in a rack. Mr Pinfold could not imagine this place the scene of orgy, outrage or plot.

Presently the Captain returned.

'Well, sir, and what can I do for you?'

'First, I want to know whether radiograms sent from your ship are confidential documents?'

'I'm sorry. I'm afraid I don't understand you.'

'Captain Steerforth, since I came on board I have sent out a large number of messages of an entirely private character. This morning, early, there were a group of passengers reading them aloud in the wireless-room.'

'Well, we can easily get the facts about that. How many of these radiograms were there?'

'I don't know exactly. About a dozen.'

'And when did you send them?'

'At various times during the early days of the voyage.'

Captain Steerforth looked perplexed. 'This is only our fifth day out, you know,' he said.

'Oh,' said Mr Pinfold, disconcerted, 'are you quite sure?'

'Yes, of course I'm sure.'

'It seems longer.'

'Well, come along to the office and we'll look into the matter.'

The wireless-room was only two doors from the Captain's cabin.

'This is Mr Pinfold, a passenger.'

'Yes, sir. We've seen him before.'

'He wants to enquire about some radiograms he sent.'

'We can easily check on that, sir. We've had practically no private traffic!' He opened a file at his side and said: 'Yes. Here we are. The day before yesterday. It went out within an hour of being handed in.'

He showed Mr Pinfold's holograph: *Entirely cured. All love.*

'But the others?' said Mr Pinfold, bewildered.

'There were no others, sir.'

'A dozen or more.'

'Only this one. I should know, I can assure you.'

'There was one I sent at Liverpool, the evening I came on board.'

'That would have gone by Post Office Telegraph, sir.'

'And you wouldn't have a copy here?'

'No, sir.'

'Then how,' said Mr Pinfold, 'was it possible for a group of passengers to read it aloud in this office at eight o'clock this morning?'

'Quite impossible,' said the wireless operator. 'I was on duty myself at that time. There were no passengers here.'

He and the Captain exchanged glances.

'Does that satisfy all your questions, Mr Pinfold?' asked the Captain.

'Not quite. May I come back to your cabin?'

'If you wish it.'

When they were seated Mr Pinfold said: 'Captain Steerforth, I am the victim of a practical joke.'

'Something of the sort, it seems,' said the Captain.

'Not for the first time. Ever since I came on board this ship – you say it has only been five days?'

'Four actually.'

'Ever since I came on board, I have been the victim of hoaxes and threats. Mind you I am not making any accusation. I don't know the names of these people. I don't even know what they look like. I am *not* asking for an official investigation – yet. What I do know is that the leaders comprise a family of four.'

'I don't believe we have any families on board,' said the Captain, taking the passenger list off his desk, 'except the Angels. I hardly think they're the sort of people to play practical jokes on anyone. A very quiet family.'

'There are several people travelling who aren't on that list.'

'No one, I assure you.'

'Fosker for one.'

Captain Steerforth turned the pages. 'No,' he said. 'No Fosker.'

'And that dark little man who used to sit alone in the dining-saloon.'

'Him? I know him well. He often travels with us. Mr Murdoch – here he is on the list.'

Baffled, Mr Pinfold turned to another course suggested by Mr Murdoch's solitary meals.

'Another thing, Captain. I greatly appreciate the honour of being invited to sit at your table in the dining-saloon. But the truth is I'm not fit for human society, just at the moment. I've been taking some grey pills – pretty strong stuff, for rheumatism, you know. I'm really better alone. So if you won't think it rude . . .'

'Sit where you like, Mr Pinfold. Just tell the chief steward.'

'Please understand I am not going because of any pressure from outside. It is simply that I am not well.'

'I quite understand, Mr Pinfold.'

'I reserve the right to return if I feel better.'

'Please sit exactly where you like, Mr Pinfold. Is that all you wanted to say?'

'No. There's another thing. The cabin I'm in. You ought to get the wiring seen to. I don't know whether you know it, but I can often hear anything that's being said up here, on the bridge and in other parts of the ship.'

'I didn't know,' said Captain Steerforth. 'That is most unusual.'

'They've used this defect in their practical jokes. It's most disturbing. I should like to change cabins.'

'That should be easy. We have two or three vacant. If you'll tell the purser . . . Is *that* everything, Mr Pinfold?'

'Yes,' said Mr Pinfold. 'Thank you very much. I am most grateful to you. And you *do* understand about my changing tables? You don't think it rude?'

'No offence whatever, Mr Pinfold. Good morning.'

Mr Pinfold left the cabin far from content with his interview. It seemed to him that he had said too much or too little. But he had achieved certain limited objectives and he set about his business with the purser and chief steward with alacrity. He was given the very table where Mr Murdoch had sat. Of several cabins he chose a small one near the verandah-bar which gave immediate access to the promenade-deck. Here, he was sure, he would be safe from physical attack.

He returned to his old cabin to direct the removal of his possessions. The voices began at once but he was very busy with the English-speaking steward and did not listen until he had seen his clothes and belongings packed and carried away. Then briefly he surveyed the scene of his suffering and lent them his ears. He was gratified to find that, however incomplete it looked to him, his morning's work had dismayed his enemies.

'Dirty little sneak,' – there was a note of fear in Goneril's hatred that morning – 'what have you been saying to the Captain? We'll get even with you. Have you forgotten the three-eight rhythm? Did you tell him our names? Did you? Did you?'

Margaret's brother was positively conciliatory: 'Look here, Gilbert, old boy, we don't want to bring other people into our business, do we? We can settle it between ourselves can't we, Gilbert?'

Margaret was reproachful; not because of the drama of the night; all that storm of emotion seemed to have passed leaving no more trace than thunder clouds in the blue of summer. Indeed in all their subsequent acquaintance she never mentioned that fiasco; she chid him instead gently for his visit to the Captain. 'It's *against the Rules*, darling, don't you see? We *must* all play by the Rules.'

'I'm not playing at all.'

'Oh yes, darling, you are. We all are. We can't help ourselves. And it's a Rule that no one else must be told. If there's anything you don't understand, ask me.'

Poor waif, Mr Pinfold thought, she has kept bad company and been corrupted. After the embarrassments of the night Margaret had forfeited his trust, but he loved her a little and felt it unmannerly to be leaving her flat, as he planned to do. It had proved easy to move out of their reach. They had confided too much, these aggressive young people, in their mechanical toy. And now he was breaking it.

'Margaret,' he said, 'I don't know anything about your rules and I am not playing any game with any of you. But I should like to see you. Come and join me on deck any time you like.'

'Darling, you know I long to. But I can't, can I? You do see, don't you?'

'No,' said Mr Pinfold, 'frankly I don't see. I leave it to you. I'm off now,' and he left the haunted cabin for the last time.

It was the social hour of noon when the sweepstake was paid and the cocktails ordered. From his new cabin, where his new steward was unpacking, he could hear the chatter from the bar.

He stood alone thinking how smoothly he had made the transition.

He repeated to himself all that had been said in the Captain's cabin: '. . . *no families on board except the Angels?*' Angel. And suddenly Mr Pinfold understood, not everything, but the heart of the mystery. Angel, the quizzical man from the BBC. ' – *not wires, darling. Wireless*' – Angel, the man with the technical skill to use the defects of the *Caliban*'s communications, perhaps to cause them. Angel, the man with the beard – '*What do barbers do besides cut hair?*' – Angel, who had an aunt near Lychpole and could have heard from her the garbled gossip of the countryside. Angel who had 'half expected' Cedric Thorne to kill himself; Angel who bore a grudge for the poor figure he had cut at Lychpole and had found Mr Pinfold by chance alone and ill and defenceless, ripe for revenge. Angel was the villain, he and his sinister associate – mistress? colleague? – whom Mr Pinfold had dubbed 'Goneril'. And Angel had gone too far. He was afraid now that his superiors in London might get wind of his escapade. And they would, too; Mr Pinfold would see to that, when he returned to England. He might even write from the ship. If, as seemed probable, he was travelling on duty, the BBC would have something to say to young Angel, bearded or shaven.

There were many passages in the story of the last few days that remained obscure under this new, bright light. Mr Pinfold felt as though he had come to the end of an ingenious, old-fashioned detective novel which he had read rather inattentively. He knew the villain now and began turning back the pages to observe the clues he had missed.

It was not the first time in the *Caliban* that noon had brought an illusion of shadowless commonplace.

The change of cabin was not the tactical triumph Mr Pinfold briefly supposed. He was like a commander whose attack 'hit air'. The post he had captured, which had seemed the key of the enemy's position, proved to be empty, a mere piece of deception masking an elaborate and strongly held system; the force he supposed routed was reinforced and ready for the counter-attack.

Mr Pinfold discovered, before he went down to his first lonely luncheon, that Angel's range of action was not limited to the original cabin and the corner of the lounge. From some mobile point of control he could speak and listen in every part of the ship and in the following days Mr Pinfold, wherever he stood, could hear, could not keep himself from hearing, everything that was said in Angel's headquarters. Living and moving and eating now quite alone, barely nodding to Glover or Mrs Scarfield, Mr Pinfold listened and spoke only to his enemies and hour by hour, day by day, night by night, carefully assembled the intricate pieces of a plot altogether more modern and horrific than anything in the classic fictions of murder.

Mr Pinfold's change of cabin had momentarily disconcerted Angel and his staff (there were about half a dozen of them, male and female, all young, basically identical with the three-eight orchestra); moreover it seemed likely that the scare of the day before, when it was put about the ship that he had gone overboard, was genuine enough. At any rate Angel's first concern was that Mr Pinfold should be kept under continual observation. Immediate reports were made to headquarters of his every move. These reports were concise and factual.

'Gilbert has sat down at his table . . . He's reading the menu . . . He's ordering wine . . . He's ordered a plate of cold ham.'

When he moved he was passed on to relays of observers.

'Gilbert coming up to main deck. Take over, B.'

'OK A. Gilbert now approaching door on port side, going out on to deck. Take over, C.'

'OK B. Gilbert walking the deck anti-clockwise. He's approaching the main door, starboard side. Over to you B.'

'He's sitting down with a book.'

'OK B. Stay on duty in the lounge. Report any move. I'll have you relieved at three.'

Mr Pinfold, looking from one to another of the occupants of the lounge, wondered which was B. Later it transpired that about half the passengers had been recruited by Angel for observation duties. They considered it an innocuous parlour game. Of the rest some knew nothing of what was afoot – this group included Glover and the Scarfields – others thought the whole thing silly. The inner circle manned the staff office where reports were collated and inquiries instigated. Every few hours a conference was held at which Angel collected and discussed the notes of his observers, drafted them into a coherent report and gave them to a girl to be typed. He maintained a rollicking good humour and zest.

'Great stuff. Splendid . . . My word, Gilbert's given himself away here . . . Most valuable . . . We could do with a little more detail on these points . . .'

Anything Mr Pinfold had said or done or thought, that day or in his past life seemed significant. Angel was mocking, but appreciative. At intervals two older men – not the generals, but men more akin to them than to the boisterous youngsters – subjected Mr Pinfold to direct questioning. This inquisition, it appeared, was the essence of the enterprise. It was prosecuted whenever Mr Pinfold sat in the lounge or lay in his cabin, and so curious was he about the motives and mechanics of the thing that for the first twenty-four hours he, to some extent, collaborated. The inquisitors, it seemed, possessed a huge but incomplete and wildly inaccurate dossier covering the whole of Mr Pinfold's private life. It was their task to fill the gaps. In manner they were part barristers, part bureaucrats.

'Where were you in January 1929, Pinfold?'

'I really don't know.'

'Perhaps I can refresh your memory. I have here a letter from you written at Mena House Hotel, Cairo. Were you in Egypt in 1929?'

'Yes, I believe I was.'

'And what were you doing there?'

'Nothing.'

'Nothing? That won't do, Pinfold. I want a better answer than that.'

'I was just travelling.'

'Of course you were travelling. You could hardly get to Egypt without travelling, could you? I want the truth, Pinfold. *What were you doing* in Egypt in 1929?'

On another occasion: 'How many pairs of shoes do you possess?'

'I really don't know.'

'You *must* know. Would you say a dozen?'

'Yes, I daresay.'

'We have you down here as possessing ten.'

'Perhaps.'

'Then why did you tell me a dozen, Pinfold? He did say a dozen, didn't he?'

'Quite distinctly.'

'I don't like this, Pinfold. You have to be truthful. Only the truth can help you.'

Sometimes they turned to more immediate topics.

'On more than one occasion you have complained of suffering from the effects of some grey pills. Where did they come from?'

'My doctor.'

'Do you suppose he manufactured them himself?'

'No, I suppose not.'

'Well then answer my question properly. Where did those pills come from?'

'I really don't know. Some chemist, I suppose.'

'Exactly. Would it surprise you to hear they came from Wilcox and Bredworth?'

'Not particularly.'

'*Not particularly*, Pinfold? I must warn you to be careful. Don't you know that Wilcox and Bredworth are one of the most respected firms in the country?'

'Yes.'

'And you accuse them of purveying dangerous drugs?'

'I expect they manufacture great quantities of poison.'

'You mean you accuse Wilcox and Bredworth of conspiring with your doctor to poison you?'

'Of course I don't.'

'Then what *do* you mean?'

Sometimes they made in their stern, precise voices accusations as fantastic as those of the hooligans and the gossips. They pressed him for information about the suicide of a staff-officer in the Middle East – a man who to the best of Mr Pinfold's knowledge had ended the war healthily and prosperously – which they attributed to Mr Pinfold's malice. They brought up the old charges of the eviction of Hill and of Mrs Pinfold senior's pauper's funeral. They examined him about a claim he had never made, to be the nephew of an Anglican bishop.

Once or twice during these days Angel organized a rag, but since Mr Pinfold could hear the preparations, he was not dismayed as he had been by the previous exercises.

Early one morning he heard Angel announce: 'We will mount Operation Storm today,' and as soon as the ship came to life and the passengers began their day, all conversation, when they passed Mr Pinfold, or he them, was about a gale warning. '. . . The Captain says we're coming right into it.'

'One of the worst storms he's ever known in the Mediterranean . . .'

The day was bright and calm. Mr Pinfold had no fear – if anything he had rather a relish – for rough weather. After an hour of this charade Angel called it off. 'No good,' he said, 'operation cancelled. Gilbert isn't scared.'

'He's a good sailor,' said Margaret.

'He doesn't mind missing his lunch,' said Goneril. 'The food isn't good enough for him.'

'Operation Stock Exchange,' said Angel.

This performance was even more fatuous than its predecessor. The method was the same, a series of conversations designed for him to hear. The subject was a financial slump which had suddenly thrown the stock-markets of the world into chaos. As they sauntered past or sat over their knitting the passengers dutifully recounted huge falls in the prices of stocks and shares in the world capital cities, the suicide of financiers, the closing of banks and corporations. They quoted figures. They named the companies which had failed. All this, even had he believed it, would have been of very remote interest to Mr Pinfold.

'They say Mr Pinfold's fortune is entirely wiped out,' said Mrs

Benson to Mrs Cockson (these ladies had now resumed their mother tongue).

Mr Pinfold had no fortune. He owned a few fields, a few pictures, a few valuable books, his own copyrights. At the bank he had a small overdraft. He had never in his life put out a penny at interest. The rudimentary technicalities of finance were Greek to him. It was very odd, he thought, that these people could go to so much trouble to investigate his affairs and know so little about them.

'Operation cancelled,' announced Angel at length.

'What went wrong?'

'I wish I knew. Gilbert is no longer responding to treatment. We had him on the run in the early days. Now he seems punch-drunk.'

'He's in a sort of daze.'

'He's not sleeping enough.'

This was indeed true. Since he finished his sleeping-draught Mr Pinfold had seldom had more than an hour at a time of uneasy dozing. The nights were a bad time for him. He would sit in the lounge, alone in his dinner jacket, observing his fellow passengers, distracted a little by their activities from the voices of his enemies, trying to decide which were his friends, which were neutral, until the last of them had gone below and the lights were turned down. Then, knowing what to expect, he would go to his cabin and undress. He had given up any attempt at saying his prayers; the familiar, hallowed words provoked a storm of blasphemous parody from Goneril.

He lay down expecting little rest. Angel had in his headquarters an electric instrument which showed Mr Pinfold's precise state of consciousness. It consisted, Mr Pinfold surmised, of a glass tube containing two parallel lines of red light which continually drew together or moved apart like telegraph wires seen from a train. They approached one another as he grew drowsy and, when he fell asleep, crossed. A duty officer followed their fluctuations.

'. . . Wide awake . . . now he's getting sleepy . . . they're almost touching . . . a single line . . . they're going to cross . . . no, wide awake again . . .' And when he awoke after his brief spells of insensibility, his first sensation was always the voice of the observer: 'Gilbert's awake again. Fifty-one minutes.'

'That's better than the time before.'

'But it isn't enough.'

One night they tried to soothe him by playing a record specially made by Swiss scientists for the purpose. These savants had decided from experiments made in a sanatorium for neurotic industrial workers that the most soporific noises were those of a factory. Mr Pinfold's cabin resounded to the roar and clang of machinery.

'You bloody fools,' he cried in exasperation, '*I'm* not a factory worker. You're driving me mad.'

'No, no, Gilbert, you *are* mad already,' said the duty officer. 'We're driving you sane.'

The hubbub continued until Angel came on his round of inspection.

'Gilbert not asleep yet? Let me see the log. "*0312 hours. You bloody fools, I'm not a factory worker.*" Well nor he is. "*You're driving me mad.*" I believe we are. Turn off that record. Give him something rural.'

From then for a long time nightingales sang to Mr Pinfold but still he did not sleep. He stepped out on deck and leaned on the rail.

'Go on, Gilbert. Jump. In you go,' said Goneril. Mr Pinfold did not feel the smallest temptation to obey. 'Water-funk.'

'I know all about that actor, you know,' said Mr Pinfold. 'The one who was a friend of Angel's and hanged himself in his dressing-room.'

This was the first time that he disclosed his knowledge of Angel's identity. The effect was immediate. All Angel's assumed good humour was dispelled. 'Why do you call me Angel?' he asked fiercely. 'What the devil do you mean by it?'

'It's your name. I know exactly what you are doing for the BBC' – this was bluff – 'I know exactly what you did to Cedric Thorne. I know exactly what you are trying to do to me.'

'Liar. You don't know anything.'

'Liar,' said Goneril.

'I told you,' said Margaret, 'Gilbert's no fool.'

Silence fell on the headquarters. Mr Pinfold returned to his bunk, lay down and slept until the steward came in with his tea. Angel spoke to him at once. He was in a chastened mood. 'Look here, Gilbert, you've got us all wrong. What we're doing is nothing to do with the BBC. It's a private enterprise entirely. And as for Cedric – that wasn't our fault. He came to us too late. We did everything we could for him. He was a hopeless case. Why don't you answer? Can't you hear me, Gilbert? Why don't you answer?'

Mr Pinfold held his peace. He was getting near to a full explanation.

Mr Pinfold was never able to give a completely coherent account either to himself or to anyone else of how he finally unravelled the mystery. He heard so much, directly and indirectly; he reasoned so closely; he followed so many false clues and reached so many absurd conclusions; but at length he was satisfied that he knew the truth. He then sat down and wrote about it at length to his wife.

Darling, he wrote,

As I said in my telegram I am quite cured of my aches and pains. In that way the trip has been a success but this has not proved a happy ship and I have decided to get off at Port Said and go on by aeroplane.

Do you remember the tick with a beard who came to Lychpole from the BBC. He is on board with a team bound for Aden. They are going to make recordings of Arab dance music. The tick is called Angel. He has shaved his beard. That is why I didn't spot him at first. He has some of his family with him – rather a nice sister – travelling I suppose for pleasure. They seem to be cousins of a lot of our neighbours. You might enquire. These BBC people have made themselves a great nuisance to me on board. They have got a lot of apparatus with them, most of it new and experimental. They have something which is really a glorified form of Reggie Upton's Box. I shall never laugh at the poor Bruiser again. There is a great deal in it. More in fact than he imagines. Angel's Box is able to speak and to hear. In fact I spend most of my days and nights carrying on conversations with people I never see. They are trying to psychoanalyse me. I know this sounds absurd. The Germans at the end of the war were developing this Box for the examination of prisoners. The Russians have perfected it. They don't need any of the old physical means of persuasion. They can see into the minds of the most obdurate. The Existentialists in Paris first started using it for psycho-analysing people who would not voluntarily submit to treatment. They first break the patient's nerve by acting all sorts of violent scenes which he thinks are really happening. They confuse him until he doesn't distinguish between natural sounds and those they induce. They make all kinds of preposterous accusations against him. Then when they get him in a receptive mood they start on their psycho-analysis. As you can imagine it's a hellish invention in the wrong hands. Angel's are very much the wrong hands. He's an amateur and a conceited ass. That young man who came to the hotel with my tickets was there to measure my 'life-waves'. I should have thought they could equally well have got them on board. Perhaps there is some particular gadget they have to get in London for each person. I don't know. There is still a good deal about the whole business I don't know. When I get back I will make enquiries. I'm not the first person they've tried it on. They drove an actor to suicide. I rather suspect they've been at work on poor Roger Stillingfleet. In fact I think we shall find a number of our friends who have behaved oddly lately have suffered from Angel.

Anyway they have had no success with me. I've seen through them. All they have done is to stop my working. So I am leaving them. I shall go straight to the Galleface in Colombo and look round from there for a quiet place in the hills. I'll telegraph when I arrive which should be about the time you get this letter.
All love.
G.

'Gilbert,' said Angel, 'you can't send that letter.'

'I am certainly going to – by air mail from Port Said.'

'It's going to make trouble.'

'I hope so.'

'You don't understand the importance of the work we're doing. Did you see the *Cocktail Party*? Do you remember the second act? We are like the people in that, a little band doing good, sworn to secrecy, working behind the scenes everywhere –'

'You're a pretentious busy-body.'

'Look here, Gilbert –'

'And who the devil said you might use my Christian name?'

'Gilbert.'

'Mr Pinfold to you.'

'Mr Pinfold, I admit we've not handled your case properly. We'll leave you in peace if you'll destroy that letter.'

'*I* am leaving *you*, my good Angel. The question does not arise.'

Goneril cut in: 'We'll give you hell for this, Gilbert. We'll get you and you know it. We'll never let you go. We've got you.'

'Oh, shut up,' said Mr Pinfold.

He felt himself master of the field: caught unawares, with unfamiliar barbarous weapons, treacherously ambushed when, as it were, he was under the cover of the Red Cross, he had rallied and routed the enemy. Their grand strategy had been utterly frustrated. All they could do now was snipe.

This they did continuously during the last twenty-four hours of the voyage. Mr Pinfold went about his business in a babble of jeering, threatening, cajoling voices. He gave notice to the purser of his intention of leaving the ship and sent a message by wireless engaging an air passage to Colombo.

'You can't go, Gilbert. They won't let you off the ship. The doctor has you under observation. He'll keep you in a home because you're mad, Gilbert . . . You haven't the money. You can't hire a car . . . Your passport expired last week . . . They won't take traveller's cheques in Egypt . . .' 'He's got dollars, the beast.' 'Well, that's criminal. He ought to have declared them. They'll get him for that.' 'They won't let you through the military zone, Gilbert' (this was in 1954). 'The army will turn you back. Egyptian terrorists are bombing private cars on the canal road.'

Mr Pinfold fought back with the enemy's weapons. He was obliged to hear all they said. They were obliged to hear him. They could not measure his emotions, but every thought which took verbal shape in his mind, was audible in Angel's headquarters and they were unable, it seemed, to disconnect their box. Mr Pinfold set out to wear them down with sheer boredom. He took a copy of *Westward Ho!* from the ship's library and read it very slowly hour by hour. At first Goneril attempted to correct his pronunciation. At first Angel pretended to find psychological significance in the varying emphasis he gave to different words. But after an hour or so they gave up these pretences and cried in frank despair: 'Gilbert, for God's sake stop.'

Then Mr Pinfold tormented them in his turn by making gibberish of the text, reading alternate lines, alternate words, reading backwards, until they pleaded for a respite. Hour after hour Mr Pinfold remorselessly read on.

On his last evening he felt magnanimous towards all except Angel and Goneril. Word had got round the passengers that he was leaving them and as he sauntered among them he noted genuine regret in the scraps of talk he overheard.

'Is it really because of that game of Mr Angel's?' he heard Mrs Benson ask.

'He's very much annoyed with all of us.'

'You can hardly blame him. I'm sorry now I took any part in it.'

'It wasn't really very funny. I never saw the point really.'

'What's more we've cost him a lot of money. He may be able to afford it, but it's unfair, all the same.'

'I never believed half they said about him.'

'I wish I'd got to know him. I believe he's really very nice.'

'He's a very distinguished man and we've behaved like a lot of badly brought up children.'

There was no hatred or ridicule now in any of their conversations. That evening before dinner, he joined the Scarfields.

'In a couple of days it will be getting hot,' she said.

'I shan't be here.'

'Not here? I thought you were going to Colombo?'

He explained the change of plan.

'Oh, what a pity,' she said with an unmistakable innocence. 'It's only after Port Said that one ever really gets to know people.'

'I think I'll dine at your table tonight.'

'Do. We've missed you.'

So Mr Pinfold returned to the Captain's table and ordered champagne for them all. None except the Captain knew of his imminent departure. Throughout all the tumult of the journey this little group had remained isolated and unaware of what was afoot. Mr Pinfold was still not sure of the Captain. That quiet sea-dog had turned a Nelson eye on proceedings far beyond the scope of his imagination.

'I'm sorry we shan't have you with us, particularly now you are feeling so much better,' he said, raising his glass. 'I hope you have a comfortable flight.'

'Urgent business, I suppose?' said Glover.

'Just impatience,' said Mr Pinfold.

He remained with the group. Glover gave him advice about tailors in Colombo and cool hotels in the hills suitable for literary work. When they broke up, Mr Pinfold said goodbye, for the *Caliban* was due in harbour early and all would be busy next morning.

On his way to his cabin he met the dark figure of Mr Murdoch, who stopped and spoke to him. His manner was genial and his voice richly redolent of the industrial North.

'Purser tells me you're landing tomorrow,' he said. 'So am I. How do you reckon to get to Cairo?'

'I haven't really thought. Train, I suppose.'

'Ever been in a Wog train? Filthy dirty and slow. I tell you what, my firm's sending a car for me. I'd be glad of your company.'

So it was arranged they should travel together.

The night still belonged to Angel and Goneril. 'Don't trust Murdoch,' they whispered. 'Murdoch is your enemy.' There was no peace in the cabin and Mr Pinfold remained on deck watching for the poor little pharos of Port Said, recognized its beam, saw the pilot come aboard with a launchful of officials in tarbooshes, saw the water-front come clear in view, populous even at that hour with touts and scarab-sellers.

In the hubbub of early morning and the successive interviews with port officials Mr Pinfold was intermittently aware that Goneril and Angel were still jabbering, still impotently trying to obstruct. Only when at last he went down the gangway, did they fall silent. Mr Pinfold had been to Port Said often before. He had never expected to feel affection for the place. That day he did. He watched patiently while unshaven, smoking officials examined him, his passport and his baggage. He cheerfully paid a number of absurd impositions. An English agent of Mr Murdoch's company warned them:

'. . . Pretty tricky drive at the moment. Only last week there was a chap hired a car to go to Cairo. The Wog drove off the road just after Ismailia into a village. He was set on, all his luggage pinched. They even took his clothes. Not a stitch on when the police picked him up. And all they said was he ought to consider himself lucky they hadn't cut his throat.'

Mr Pinfold did not care. He posted his letter to his wife. He and Murdoch drank a bottle of beer at a café and suffered their boots to be cleaned two or three times. The funnels of the *Caliban* were plainly to be seen from where he sat, but no voices came from her. Then he and Murdoch drove away out of sight of the unhappy ship.

The road to Cairo was more warlike than he had known it ten years back when Rommel was at the gates. They passed through lanes of barbed wire, halted and showed his passport at numerous barriers, crept in dust behind convoys of army trucks, each with a sentry crouched on the tail-board with a tommy-gun at the ready. There came a longer halt and closer scrutiny at the turning out of the Canal Zone, where swarthy, sullen English soldiers gave place to swarthy, sullen Egyptians in almost identical uniforms. Murdoch was a man of few words and Mr Pinfold sat enveloped in his own impervious peace.

Once during the war he had gone on a parachute course which had ended ignominiously with his breaking a leg in his first drop, but he treasured as the most serene and exalted experience of his life the moment of liberation when he regained consciousness after the shock of the slipstream. A quarter of a minute before he had crouched over the open man-hole in the floor of the machine, in dusk and deafening noise, trussed in harness, crowded by apprehensive fellow-tyros. Then the despatching officer had signalled; down he had plunged into a moment of night, to come to himself in a silent, sunlit heaven, gently supported by what had seemed irksome bonds, absolutely isolated. There were other parachutes all round him holding other swaying bodies; there was an instructor on the ground bawling advice through a loudspeaker; but Mr Pinfold felt himself free of all human communication, the sole inhabitant of a private, delicious universe. The rapture was brief. Almost at once he knew he was not floating but falling; the field leaped up at him; a few seconds later he was lying on grass entangled in cords, being shouted at, breathless, bruised, with a sharp pain in the shin. But in that moment of solitude prosaic, earthbound Mr Pinfold had been one with hashish-eaters and Corybantes and Californian gurus, high on the back-stairs of mysticism. His mood on the road to Cairo was barely less ecstatic.

Cairo was still pocked and gutted by the recent riots. It was thronged with stamp-dealers who had come for the sale of the royal collection. Mr Pinfold had difficulty in finding a room. Murdoch obtained one for him. There was difficulty with his air passage and there too Murdoch helped. Finally on the second day when Mr Pinfold was provided by the concierge of his hotel with all the requisite documents – including a medical certificate and a sworn statement necessary for a halt in Arabia, that he was a Christian – and his departure was fixed for midnight, Murdoch invited him to dine with his business associates in Ghezira.

'They'll be delighted. They don't see many people from home these days. And to tell you the truth I'm glad to have a companion myself. I don't much like driving about alone after dark.'

So they went to dinner in a block of expensive, modern flats. The lift was out of order. As they climbed the stairs they passed an Egyptian soldier squatting in a flat doorway, chewing nuts, with his rifle propped behind him.

'One of the old princesses,' said Murdoch, 'under house-arrest.'

Host and hostess greeted them kindly. Mr Pinfold looked about him. The drawing-room was furnished with the trophies of long residence in the East. On the chimney-piece was the framed photograph of a peer in coronation-robes. Mr Pinfold studied it.

'Surely that's Simon Dumbleton?'

'Yes, he's a great friend of ours. Do you know him?'

Before he could answer another voice broke in on that cosy scene.

'No, you don't, Gilbert,' said Goneril. 'Liar. Snob. You only pretend to know him because he's a lord.'

Chapter Eight

PINFOLD REGAINED

Mr Pinfold landed at Colombo three days later. He had spent one almost sleepless night in the aeroplane where a pallid Parsee sprawled and grunted and heaved beside him; and a second equally wakeful alone in a huge, teetotal hotel in Bombay. Night and day Angel, Goneril and Magaret chattered to him in their several idioms. He was becoming like the mother of fractious children who has learned to go about her business with a mind closed to their utterances; except that he had no business. He could only sit hour after hour waiting in one place or another for meals he did not want. Sometimes from sheer boredom he spoke to Margaret and learned from her further details of the conspiracy.

'Are you still in the ship?'

'No. We got off at Aden.'

'All of you?'

'All three.'

'But the others?'

'There never were any others, Gilbert. Just my brother and sister-in-law and me. You saw our names in the passenger list, Mr and Mrs and Miss Angel. I thought you understood all that.'

'But your mother and father?'

'They're in England, at home – quite near Lychpole.'

'Never in the ship?'

'Darling, you are slow in the uptake. What you heard was my brother. He's really awfully good at imitations. That's how he first got taken on by the BBC.'

'And Goneril is married to your brother? There was never anything between her and the Captain?'

'No, of course not. She's beastly but not like that. All *that* was part of the Plan.'

'I think I'm beginning to understand. You must see it's all rather confusing.' Mr Pinfold puzzled his weary head over the matter; then gave it up and asked: 'What are you doing in Aden?'

'Me? Nothing. The others have their work. It's awfully dull for me. May I talk to you sometimes? I know I'm not a bit clever but I'll try not to be a bore. I do so want company.'

'Why don't you go and see the mermaid?'

'I don't understand.'

'There used to be a mermaid at Aden in a box in one of the hotels – stuffed.'

'Don't tease, Gilbert.'

'I'm not teasing. And anyway that comes pretty badly from a member of your family. *Tease* indeed.'

'Oh, Gilbert, you don't understand. We were only trying to help you.'

'Who the devil said I needed help?'

'Don't be cross, Gilbert; not with me anyway. And you did need help you know. Often their plans work beautifully.'

'Well, you must realize by now that it hasn't worked with me.'

'Oh, no,' said Margaret sadly. 'It hasn't worked at all.'

'Then why not leave me alone?'

'They never will now, because they hate you. And I never will, never. You see I love you so. Try not to hate me, darling.'

From Cairo to Colombo he talked intermittently to Margaret. To the Angels, husband and wife, he made no answer.

Ceylon was a new country to Mr Pinfold but he had no sense of exhilaration on arrival. He was tired and sweaty. He was wearing the wrong clothes. His first act after leaving his luggage at the hotel was to seek the tailor Glover had recommended. The man promised to work all night and have three suits ready for him to try on next morning.

'You're too fat. You'll look ridiculous in them. They won't fit . . . You can't afford them . . . The tailor's lying. He won't make clothes for you,' Goneril monotonously interpolated.

Mr Pinfold returned to his hotel and wrote to his wife: '*I have arrived safe and well. There does not seem to be much to see or do in Colombo. I will move as soon as I have some clothes. I rather doubt whether I shall get any work done, I had a disappointment leaving the ship. I thought I should get out of range of those psycho-analysts and their infernal Box. But not at all. They still annoy me with the whole length of India between us. As I write this letter they keep interrupting. It will be quite impossible to do any of my book. There must be some way of cutting the "vital waves". I think it might be worth consulting Father Westmacott when I get back. He knows all about existentialism and psychology and ghosts and diabolic possession. Sometimes I wonder whether it is not literally the Devil who is molesting me.'*

He posted this by air mail. Then he sat on the terrace watching the new cheap cars drive up and away. Here, unlike Bombay, one could drink. He drank bottled English beer. The sky darkened. A thunderstorm broke. He moved from the terrace into the lofty hall. To a man at Mr Pinfold's time of life few throngs comprise only strangers. In the busy hall he was greeted by an acquaintance from New York, a collector for one of the art galleries, on his way to visit a ruined city on the other side of the island. He asked Mr Pinfold to join him.

At that moment a gentle servant appeared at his side: 'Mr Peenfold, sir, cable.'

It came from his wife and read: '*Implore you return immediately.*'

It was not like Mrs Pinfold to issue a summons of this kind. Could she be ill? Or one of the children? Had the house burned down? She would, surely? have given some explanation. It occurred to Mr Pinfold that she must be concerned on his account. That letter he had sent from Port Said, had it said anything to cause alarm? He answered: '*All well. Returning soon. Have written today. Off to the ruins,*' and rejoined his new companion. They dined together cheerfully, having many tastes and friends and memories in common. All that evening, though there was an undertone in his ears, Mr Pinfold was oblivious of the Angels. Not till late, when he was alone in his room, did the voices break through. 'We heard you, Gilbert. You were lying to that American. You've never stayed at Rhinebeck. You've never heard of Magnasco. You don't know Osbert Sitwell.'

'Oh God,' said Mr Pinfold, 'how you bore me!'

It was cooler among the ruins. There was refreshment in the leafy roads, in the spectacle of grey elephants and orange-robed, shaven-pated monks ambling meditatively in the dust. They stopped at rest-houses where they were greeted and zealously served by old servants of the British Raj. Mr Pinfold enjoyed himself. On the way back they stopped at the shrine of Kandy and saw the Buddha's tooth ceremoniously exposed. This seemed to exhaust the artistic resources of the island. The American was on his way farther east. They parted company four days later at the hotel in Colombo where they had met. Mr Pinfold was alone once more and at a loose end. He found waiting for him a pile of clothes from the tailor and another cable from his wife: '*Both your letters received. Am coming to join you.*'

It had been handed in at Lychpole that morning.

'He hates his wife,' said Goneril. 'She bores you, doesn't she, Gilbert? You don't want to go home, do you? You dread seeing her again.'

That decided him. He cabled: '*Returning at once*' and set about his preparations.

The three suits were pale, pinkish buff ('How smart you look,' cried Margaret); they were not entirely useless. He wore them on successive days; first in Colombo.

It was Sunday and he went to Mass for the first time since he had been struck ill. The voices followed him. The taxi took him first to the Anglican church. '. . . What's the difference, Gilbert? It's all nonsense anyway. You don't believe in God. There's no one here to show off to. No one will listen to your prayers – except us. *We* shall hear them. You're going to pray to be left alone, aren't you, Gilbert? Aren't you? But only we will hear and we won't let you alone. Never, Gilbert, never . . .' But when he reached the little Catholic church which, ironically enough, he found to be dedicated to St Michael and the Angels, only Margaret followed him into the dusky, crowded interior. She knew the Mass and made the Latin responses in clear, gentle tones. Epistle and Gospel were read in the vernacular. There was a short sermon, during which Mr Pinfold asked: 'Margaret, are you a Catholic?'

'In a way.'

'In what way?'

'That's something you mustn't ask.'

Then she rose with him to recite the creed and later, at the sacring-bell, she urged: 'Pray for *them*, Gilbert. They need prayers.' But Mr Pinfold could not pray for Angel and Goneril.

On Monday he arranged his passage. On Tuesday he spent another ineffably tedious night at Bombay. On Wednesday night at Karachi he changed back into winter clothes. Somewhere on the sea they may have passed the *Caliban*. They steered far clear of Aden. Across the Moslem world the voices of hate pursued Mr Pinfold. It was when they reached Christendom that Angel changed his tune. At breakfast at Rome Mr Pinfold addressed the waiter, who spoke rather good English, in rather bad Italian. It was an affectation which Goneril was quick to exploit.

'No spikka da Eenglish,' she jeered. 'Kissa da monk. Dolce far niente.'

'Shut up,' said Angel sharply. 'We've had enough of that. I've got to talk to Gilbert seriously. Listen, Gilbert, I've got a proposition to make.'

But Mr Pinfold would not answer.

Intermittently throughout the flight to Paris Angel attempted to open a discussion.

'Gilbert, do listen to me. We've got to come to some arrangement. Time's getting short. Gilbert, old boy, do be reasonable.'

His tone changed from friendliness to cajolery, at length to a whine; the voice which had been so well-bred, was now the underdog's voice which Mr Pinfold remembered from their brief meeting at Lychpole.

'Do speak to him, Gilbert,' Margaret pleaded. 'He's really very worried.'

'So he should be. If your miserable brother wants me to reply he can address me properly, as "Mr Pinfold", or "Sir".'

'Very well, Mr Pinfold, sir,' said Angel.

'That's better. Now what have you to say?'

'I want to apologize. I've made a mess of the whole Plan.'

'You certainly have.'

'It was a serious scientific experiment. Then I let personal malice interfere. I'm sorry, Mr Pinfold.'

'Well, keep quiet then.'

'That's just what I was going to suggest. Look here, Gil – Mr Pinfold, sir – let's do a deal. I'll switch off the apparatus. I promise on my honour we'll none of us ever worry you again. All we ask in return is that you don't say anything to anyone in England about us. It could ruin our whole work if it got talked about. Just say nothing, and you'll never hear from us again. Tell your wife you had noises in the head through taking those grey pills. Tell her anything you like but tell her it's all over. She'll believe you. She'll be delighted to hear it.'

'I'll think it over,' said Mr Pinfold.

He thought it over. There were strong attractions in the bargain. Could Angel be trusted? He was in a panic now at the prospect of getting into trouble with the BBC –

'Not the BBC, darling,' said Margaret. 'It isn't them that worry him. They know all about his experiments. It's Reggie Graves-Upton. *He* must never know. He's a sort of cousin, you see, and he would tell our aunt and father and mother and everyone. It would cause the most frightful complications. Gilbert, you must never tell *anyone*, promise, especially not cousin Reggie.'

'And you, Meg,' said Mr Pinfold in bantering but fond tones, 'are you going to leave me alone too?'

'Oh, Gilbert dearest, it's not a thing to joke about. I've so loved being with you. I shall miss you more than anyone I've ever known in my life. I shall never forget you. If my brother switches off it will be a kind of death for me. But I know I have to suffer. I'll be brave. You *must* accept the offer, Gilbert.'

'I'll let you know before I reach London,' said Mr Pinfold.

Presently they were over England.

'Well,' said Angel, 'what's your answer?'

'I said "London".'

Later they were over London airport. 'Fasten your belts, please. No smoking.'

'Here we are,' said Angel. 'Speak up. Is it a deal?'

'I don't call this London,' said Mr Pinfold.

He had cabled to his wife from Rome that he would go straight to the hotel they always used. He did not wait for the other passengers to board the bus. Instead he hired a car. Not until they were in the borough of Acton did he reply to Angel. Then he said:

'The answer is: no.'

'You can't mean it.' Angel was unaffectedly aghast. 'Why, Mr Pinfold, sir? Why?'

'First, because I don't accept your word of honour. You don't know what honour is. Secondly, I thoroughly dislike you and your revolting wife. You have been extremely offensive to me and I intend to make you suffer for it. Thirdly, I think your plans, your work as you call it, highly dangerous. You've driven one man to suicide, perhaps others, too, that I don't know about. You tried to drive me. Heaven knows what you've done to Roger Stillingfleet. Heaven knows who you may attack next. Apart from any private resentment I feel, I regard you as a public menace that has got to be silenced.'

'All right, Gilbert, if that's the way you want it –'

'Don't call me "Gilbert" and don't talk like a film gangster.'

'All right, Gilbert. You'll pay for this.'

But there was no confidence to his threats. Angel was a beaten man and knew it.

'Mrs Pinfold arrived an hour ago,' the concierge told him. 'She is waiting for you in your room.'

Mr Pinfold took the lift, walked down the corridor and opened the door, with Goneril and Angel raucous on either side. He was shy of his wife, when they met.

'You *look* all right,' she said.

'I *am* all right. I have this trouble I wrote to you about, but I hope I can get it cleared up. I'm sorry not to be more affectionate, but it's a little embarrassing having three people listening to everything one says.'

'Yes,' said Mrs Pinfold. 'It must be. I can see that. Have you had luncheon?'

'Hours ago, in Paris. Of course there's the difference of an hour.'

'I've had none. I'll order something now.'

'How you hate her, Gilbert! How she bores you!' said Goneril.

'Don't believe a word she says,' said Angel.

'She's very pretty,' Margaret conceded, 'and very kind. But she is not good enough for you. I suppose you think I'm jealous. Well, I am.'

'I'm sorry to be so uncommunicative,' said Mr Pinfold. 'You see these abominable people keep talking to me.'

'Most distracting,' said Mrs Pinfold.

'Most.'

The waiter brought a tray. When he had gone Mrs Pinfold said: 'You know you've got it all wrong about this Mr Angel. As soon as I got your letter I telephoned to Arthur at the BBC and enquired. Angel has been in England all the time.'

'*Don't listen to her. She's lying.*'

Mr Pinfold was dumbfounded.

'Are you absolutely sure?'

'Ask them yourself.'

Mr Pinfold went to the telephone. He had a friend named Arthur high in the talks department.

'Arthur, that fellow who came down to interview me last summer, Angel – haven't you sent him to Aden . . . you haven't? He's in England now? . . . No, I don't want to speak to him . . . It's just that I ran across someone rather like him on board ship . . . Goodbye . . . Well,' he said to his wife, 'I simply don't know what to make of this.'

'I may as well tell you the truth,' said Angel. 'We never were in that ship. We worked the whole thing from the studio in England.'

'They must be working the whole thing from a studio in England,' said Mr Pinfold.

'My poor darling,' said Mrs Pinfold, 'no one's "worked" anything. You're imagining it all. Just to make sure I asked Father Westmacott as you suggested. He says the whole thing's utterly impossible. There just isn't any sort of invention by the Gestapo or the BBC or the Existentialists or the psychoanalysts – nothing at all, the least like what you think.'

'No Box?'

'No Box.'

'Don't believe her. She's lying. She's lying,' said Goneril but with every word her voice dwindled as though a great distance was being put between them. Her last word was little more than the thin grating of a slate-pencil.

'You mean that everything I've heard said, I've been saying to myself? It's hardly conceivable.'

'It's perfectly true, darling,' said Margaret. 'I never had a brother or a sister-in-law, no father, no mother, nothing . . . I don't exist, Gilbert. There isn't any me, anywhere at all . . . but I do love you, Gilbert. I don't exist but I do love . . . Goodbye . . . Love . . .' and her voice too trailed away, sank to a whisper, a sigh, the rustle of a pillow; then was silent.

Mr Pinfold sat in the silence. There had been other occasions of seeming release which had proved illusory. This he knew was the final truth. He was alone with his wife.

'They've gone,' he said at length. 'In that minute. Gone for good.'

'I hope that's true. What are we going to do now? I couldn't make any plans till I knew what sort of state I'd find you in. Father Westmacott gave me the name of a man he says we can trust.'

'A looney doctor?'

'A psychologist – but a Catholic so he must be all right.'

'No,' said Mr Pinfold. 'I've had enough of psychology. How about taking the tea train home?'

Mrs Pinfold hesitated. She had come to London prepared to see her husband into a nursing-home. She said: 'Are you sure you oughtn't to see somebody?'

'I might see Drake,' said Mr Pinfold.

So they went to Paddington and took their seats in the restaurant car. It was full of neighbours returning from a day's shopping. They ate toasted buns and the familiar landscape rolled past invisible in the dark and misted window-panes.

'We heard you'd gone to the tropics, Gilbert.'

'Just back.'

'You didn't stay long. Was it boring?'

'No,' said Mr Pinfold, 'not the least boring. It was most exciting. But I had enough.'

Their neighbours always had thought Mr Pinfold rather odd.

'But it *was* exciting,' said Mr Pinfold when he and his wife were alone in the car driving home. 'It was the most exciting thing, really, that ever happened to me,' and during the days which followed he recounted every detail of his long ordeal.

The hard frost had given place to fog and intermittent sleet. The house was as cold as ever but Mr Pinfold was content to sit over the fire and, like a warrior returned from a hard fought victory, relive his trials, endurances and achievements. No sound troubled him from that other half-world into which he had stumbled but there was nothing dreamlike about his memories. They remained undiminished and unobscured, as sharp and hard as any event of his waking life. 'What I can't understand is this,' he said: 'If I was supplying all the information to the Angels, why did I tell them such a lot of rot? I mean to say, if I wanted to draw up an indictment of myself, I could make a far blacker and more plausible case than they did. I can't understand.'

Mr Pinfold never has understood this; nor has anyone been able to suggest a satisfactory explanation.

'You know,' he said, some evenings later. 'I was very near accepting Angel's offer. Supposing I had, and the voices had stopped just as they have done now, I should have believed that that infernal Box existed. All my life I should have lived in the fear that at any moment the whole thing might start up again. Or for all I knew they might just have been listening all the time and not saying anything. It would have been an awful situation.'

'It was very brave of you to turn down the offer,' said Mrs Pinfold.

'It was sheer bad temper,' said Mr Pinfold quite truthfully.

'All the same, I think you ought to see a doctor. There must have been something the matter with you.'

'Just those pills,' said Mr Pinfold.

They were his last illusion. When finally Dr Drake came Mr Pinfold said: 'Those grey pills you gave me. They were pretty strong.'

'They seem to have worked,' said Dr Drake.

'Could they have made me hear voices?'

'Good heavens, no.'

'Not if they were mixed with bromide and chloral?'

'There wasn't any chloral in the mixture I gave you.'

'No. But to tell you the truth I had a bottle of my own.'

Dr Drake did not seem shocked by the revelation. 'That is always a trouble with patients,' he said. 'One never knows what else they're taking on the quiet. I've known people make themselves thoroughly ill.'

'I *was* thoroughly ill. I heard voices for nearly a fortnight.'

'And they've stopped now?'

'Yes.'

'And you've stopped the bromide and chloral?'

'Yes.'

'Then I don't think we have far to look. I should keep off that mixture if I were you. It can't be the right thing for you. I'll send something else. Those voices were pretty offensive, I suppose?'

'Abominably. How did you know?'

'They always are. Lots of people hear voices from time to time – nearly always offensive.'

'You don't think he ought to see a psychologist?' asked Mrs Pinfold.

'He can if he likes, of course, but it sounds like a perfectly simple case of poisoning to me.'

'That's a relief,' said Mrs Pinfold, but Mr Pinfold accepted this diagnosis less eagerly. He knew, and the others did not know, – not even his wife, least of all his medical adviser, – that he had endured a great ordeal and, unaided, had emerged the victor.

There was a triumph to be celebrated, even if a mocking slave stood always beside him in his chariot, reminding him of mortality.

Next day was Sunday. After Mass Mr Pinfold said:

'You know I can't face the Bruiser. It's going to be several weeks before I can talk to him about his Box. Have a fire lighted in the library. I'm going to do some writing.'

As the wood crackled and a barely perceptible warmth began to spread among the chilly shelves, Mr Pinfold sat down to work for the first time since his fiftieth birthday. He took the pile of manuscript, his unfinished novel, from the drawer and glanced through it. The story was still clear in his mind. He knew what had to be done. But there was more urgent business first, a hamper to be unpacked of fresh, rich experiences – perishable goods.

He returned the manuscript to the drawer, spread a new quire of foolscap before him and wrote in his neat, steady hand:

The Ordeal of Gilbert Pinfold
A Conversation Piece
Chapter One
Portrait of the Artist in Middle-age

APPENDIX

The extended Appendix which follows will, it is hoped, serve two related functions. Firstly, to substantiate the case made in the Introduction, that *The Ordeal of Gilbert Pinfold* is a distinguished and brilliant post-war novel, deserving the kind of supporting apparatus printed here; and secondly, to provide a variety of contextual evidence as to the particular and peculiar ways in which the novel and Waugh's biography are entangled. Though fully capable of standing on its own (as Waugh intended), the novel gains in resonance and pointedness when seen in the light of the evolving social and critical contexts in which it found itself and to which (as Waugh also intended) it was a form of response.

For reasons of space all seven items (which are arranged in chronological order of context; thus Frances Donaldson's evidence is placed where its story chronologically corresponds) have been abridged; the three interviews with Waugh are merely excerpted.

Rather than attempting to represent the two radio interviews (items 1 and 2) by a properly weighted sampling of all their material (both go over the familiar family narrative; both have inconsequential passages), the decision was made to excerpt them in such a way as to give at least some plausibility to Waugh's conviction (crucial to the onset of his madness) that they, the first particularly, could be read as antagonistic interrogations.

The extracts from the Stephen Black interview (item 1) appear here for, I believe, the first time. Black was one of three interviewers involved in *Frankly Speaking* (item 2). This exchange, I think, has heretofore only been available as brief quotations in Martin Stannard's biography. As the origin of Pinfold's Angel, Black has the best claim to head a collection of *Pinfold* documents.

CONTENTS

These are arranged chronologically by context. For reasons of space items 3–6 have been lightly abridged. In the case of all 7 items [. . .] indicates editorial excisions.

I

Excerpt from Personal Call

The BBC Overseas Service interview between Waugh and Stephen Black, from which these extracts are excerpted, was the encounter which, according to Auberon Waugh, 'drove my father mad'. The interview took place in Waugh's home. It corresponds with the Angel interview in Pinfold.

BLACK: I'm wondering if you can tell us why you – where you derive this sense of satire, this bitterness about the current events – the world in which we live today.

WAUGH: Well you've said two rather different things there. Bitterness about the world we live in is surely common to the whole of mankind. No one doubts that the whole of civilization is very rapidly moving into chaos. Whether one's bitter about that or resigned is just according to whether one's good tempered or bad tempered.

BLACK: And there are people who believe that civilization is going on and on and up and up as was once said.

WAUGH: I think they must be locked up in lunatic asylums by now.

BLACK: And you're convinced that it is going down?

WAUGH: Well of course.

BLACK: And have you any great mission in telling the world that through your books, or is it just that when you write you express what you feel yourself?

WAUGH: That is the material provided for me to do my work with. If I am given a mahogany plank that's what I have to work with. And a decadent world is the material I'm given.

BLACK: So that you see all aspects of the modern world as decadent?

WAUGH: Some are more decadent than others. Certain things like the Roman Catholic Church can never be decadent by their nature. Though they can decrease in numbers or give a superficial appearance in certain places as decadence.

BLACK: You are a Roman Catholic, Mɪ Waugh?

WAUGH: I am, yes.

BLACK: Have you always been a Roman Catholic?

WAUGH: No, for the last 25 or 30 years.

BLACK: You became converted to the Roman Catholic faith?

WAUGH: Yes.

BLACK: Would you like to tell me something about the reasons for your conversion?

WAUGH: Well you know, I don't think I would. Because they aren't interesting. There's no human story in it. It was simply a fact of recognizing a plausible rational system, of following the arguments with proof of the historic truth of Christianity.

[. . .]

BLACK: Mr Waugh can we [. . .] have your views on some of the modern movements that are greatly influencing man's thoughts today – we'll leave Communism, on which we're probably all agreed, but I would like to ask you what are your views on the ideas of the psychologist Freud?

WAUGH: I'm afraid I've never read him. Not a word he's written.

BLACK: So in fact you would say that you really know nothing about the work of Freud.

WAUGH: Nothing whatever.

BLACK: And that, I may say, leaves me rather in the air as to how you arrive at this extremely satirical approach to the world, in which these ideas of Freud are continually playing a part in men's lives and men's attitudes today, and –

WAUGH: Not in the characters I write about. They've never heard of Freud, my people. Except the purely comic clowns.

[. . .]

BLACK: What did you read at Oxford?

WAUGH: The subject I was supposed to read was history.

BLACK: Didn't you really read history?

WAUGH: Not with any marked success; I took a bad third.

BLACK: And when you came down from Oxford what did you do then?

WAUGH: Oh then I went straight to an art school, where I was rather idle, and anyway realized I didn't draw well enough, and hadn't enough application ever to become a serious painter.

BLACK: You were living at home then, and going to the art school in London.

WAUGH: That's right.

BLACK: And what were your activities if you were not busy with your art during that time?

WAUGH: Drinking mostly.

BLACK: And were you interested in women at all at that time?

WAUGH: Not particularly – drink I preferred.

BLACK: And you were writing, of course?

WAUGH: No, not a word.

BLACK: How old were you when you started to earn your own living then?

WAUGH: I'll have to think about that – 25.

BLACK: And your first real success came when?

WAUGH: My second novel was the first popular success – a book called *Vile Bodies*.

[. . .]

BLACK: Where were you when the book was published?

WAUGH: I'm awfully sorry, I don't know.

BLACK: In France? Or Italy?

WAUGH: I think France. I'm pretty sure Paris, but I couldn't go closer than that.

BLACK: And you've no clear picture in your mind of this moment of success, because that was your real moment of success.

WAUGH: I've never been particularly ambitious about that sort of thing.

BLACK: You didn't really care then whether you had a success or not?

WAUGH: Well, it's clearly more convenient to have money than not to have money.

[. . .]

BLACK: Tell me, Mr Waugh, where did you go after you came back from abroad and you'd had this success with *Vile Bodies* at the age of – how old were you?

WAUGH: 25–26–28, I must have been, I think.

BLACK: You were 28, and you were abroad and you'd had a great success as a writer. What did you do next?

WAUGH: Then I went abroad again.

BLACK: And where did you live? Did you settle down anywhere?

WAUGH: No. I went to Abyssinia for the first time, for the Coronation – that must have been 1930 when I was 27.

[. . .]

BLACK: You say for the first time. Did you go to Abyssinia again then?

WAUGH: Oh yes, twice afterwards.

BLACK: When was the second time?

WAUGH: The second time was when the war was brewing. And then I went as a fully-fledged correspondent, and I was a great failure at it.

BLACK: The war? You mean the Abyssinian war between Abyssinia and Italy?

WAUGH: Yes.

[. . .]

BLACK: And when the Second World War started what were you doing, were you living here at the time?

WAUGH: I was writing a book.

BLACK: Which book, Mr Waugh?

WAUGH: Well it was never finished and – because of the war. It would have been rather good, I think. It's been published as a short story called 'Work Suspended'. The first two Chapters of it that is.

[. . .]

BLACK: Tell me Mr Waugh, when the war ended and you came out of the Army had you only one idea – to come back to this very lovely house and settle down again as a writer, or had it in any way disturbed your vision of the world as you wanted it for yourself?

WAUGH: Oh not in the least. I just wanted to come back here.

2

Excerpt from Frankly Speaking

Two separate encounters in London were edited together to make the interview broadcast on the Home Service, excerpted here. Waugh requested the second out of dissatisfaction with the first. There were three interviewers on each occasion, Stephen Black was one of them.

INTERVIEWER: Do you find that writing comes easily to you or is it a hard labour?

WAUGH: Gets harder as I get older. It's disagreeable work.

INTERVIEWER: It's disagreeable work?

WAUGH: I find it so, yes.

INTERVIEWER: In what way disagreeable – the actual physical writing?

WAUGH: Well, that doesn't give you any release in a muscular way, that most forms of work do. And it's a cramping sort of position to be in and so on. But of course the real disagreeable part is the thinking so hard.

INTERVIEWER: Are you a fairly facile writer? I mean, do you work quickly and you don't have to keep crossing out your ideas and rewriting them?

WAUGH: I write everything about twice I suppose.

INTERVIEWER: Do you write it twice on the same bit of paper?

WAUGH: No, I tear up the bad effort and start again. And there are a great many changes all the time. If I'm at work on a book, the words are running in my head all the time, and I'll get up in the middle of a meal, to run off to change a word, and – like that.

INTERVIEWER: And when you are writing a book, do you work a great many hours a day on it?

WAUGH: Well, really all the time. Not in the sense that I'm sitting at the desk all the time, but it's in my mind whatever I'm doing.

INTERVIEWER: How long do you sit at the desk?

WAUGH: I should think on an average about four hours.

INTERVIEWER: How long does it take you to write a book?

WAUGH: Longer and longer as I get older. I used to be able to write a full length book in about two months, and now it takes me something like a year.

INTERVIEWER: Apart from earning a living by writing, Mr Waugh, why do you write?

WAUGH: As distinct from earning a living in some other way do you mean?

INTERVIEWER: Yes, or even that way – I mean, do you wish to express some novel thoughts, or do you wish to convey a message or what do you –

WAUGH: No, I wish to make a pleasant object. I think any work of art is something exterior to oneself, it's the making of something whether it's a bed-table or a book.

INTERVIEWER: And are you much affected while you're working, by your environment?

WAUGH: Well, all I ask is quiet, and solitude, not being disturbed.

[. . .]

INTERVIEWER: And have you many leisure interests which you pursue steadily?

WAUGH: Well [. . .] you've caught me at a notoriously dangerous age, because at fifty one's got bored with the pleasures of youth, and one hasn't yet quite acquired the pleasures of age. So at the moment you find me rather bored.

INTERVIEWER: What would you call the pleasures of youth?

WAUGH: The pleasures of youth are meeting new people, going to new places, having new experiences, being surprised and shocked and amused. And after fifty it's harder to find these things.

INTERVIEWER: I just wondered what your interests were, I mean the interests which you would pursue more whole-heartedly if you had more time.

WAUGH: If I had more time and more money, I'd certainly collect a great deal more. I'm a very keen collector and have been from earliest infancy.

INTERVIEWER: A collector of what?

WAUGH: Primarily paintings, but also furniture and any works of art.

INTERVIEWER: Contemporary paintings.

WAUGH: Oh no, no. Oh no, no, no. I mean real paintings.

INTERVIEWER: What period?

WAUGH: Anything up to about 1870.

INTERVIEWER: What painters do you admire most?

WAUGH: Augustus Egg I'd put among the highest.

INTERVIEWER: You think real painting stopped about 1850?

WAUGH: In England, certainly.

[. . .]

INTERVIEWER: Well now, can you give us any reasons in your mind, of this decay, general decay in the arts? As a whole.

WAUGH: Pure sloth chiefly, sloth.

[...]

INTERVIEWER: Do you find it easy to get on with the man in the street?

WAUGH: I've never met such a person.

INTERVIEWER: Do you like people generally when you meet them in trains or buses? Or on a ship.

WAUGH: I never travel in a bus, and I never address a stranger in a train.

INTERVIEWER: Well you meet people on board ship, for example, when travelling.

WAUGH: I've never introduced myself or been introduced to anybody on board a ship. If I find friends on board, then I'm delighted.

INTERVIEWER: But you can't go about in a sort of Trappist condition – you must meet people. Do you enjoy meeting people?

WAUGH: By the time one's fifty, one has met a great number of people and it's always agreeable if one has a sense of curiosity to meet them again if they turn up on board ship, for example, as you suggest. It's very amusing suddenly to find someone you haven't seen for twenty years, and to inquire what's happened to him in the mean time. The prospect of just being introduced to somebody as just a person, a man, as you might say, in the street, is entirely repugnant.

[...]

INTERVIEWER: Could I ask you what failings in individuals, in others, you could most readily excuse?

WAUGH: Drunkenness.

INTERVIEWER: Any others? Or are you so severe?

WAUGH: Anger. Lust. Dishonouring their father and mother. Coveting their neighbour's ox, ass, wife. Killing. I think there is almost nothing I can't excuse except perhaps worshipping graven images. That seems to me idiotic.

INTERVIEWER: That you put as the – oh, what do you think are the most serious crimes in the calendar?

WAUGH: Well, that's really not for me to decide.

[...]

INTERVIEWER: You are in favour of capital punishment?

WAUGH: For an enormous number of offences.

INTERVIEWER: Yes. And you yourself would be prepared to carry it out?

WAUGH: Do you mean actually do the hanging as well?

INTERVIEWER: Yes.

WAUGH: I should think it's very odd to choose a novelist for such tasks.

INTERVIEWER: Supposing they were prepared to train you for the job, would you take it on?

WAUGH: Well certainly.

INTERVIEWER: You would.

WAUGH: Certainly.

INTERVIEWER: Would you like such a job Mr Waugh?

WAUGH: Not the least.

INTERVIEWER: Have you – you have, of course, Mr Waugh, travelled a great deal.

WAUGH: A fair amount.

INTERVIEWER: A fair amount, yes. You – how do you find people of various countries, various nationalities, various parts of the world – are they all much about the same as you were now saying, or are they all individuals? What I mean is, have they desires, aspirations in common, or are they –

WAUGH: I clearly can't make myself understood. I was saying that people weren't ever anywhere alike at all. There is no such thing as a man in the street, there is no ordinary run of mankind; there are only individuals who are totally different, and whether a man is naked and black and stands on one foot in the Sudan, or is clothed in some kind of costume in the bus in England, they are still individuals and entirely different characters.

INTERVIEWER: Then you think that travel is not useful to a novelist, for example. You might as well stay at home in Gloucestershire.

WAUGH: Well, a novelist again; you see you're always trying to use these meaningless phrases – there's no such thing as a novelist: there are a great variety of novelists. Certain novelists can indeed stay at home, like Jane Austen, and produce admirable novels out of just what they see within five miles of their own rectory. Other people, like Conrad, have to go to the Seven Seas in order to find stories.

INTERVIEWER: I think you said earlier that you weren't interested in people in groups but when you travel you meet people in groups. You rarely have time when travelling really to meet individuals. Or do you find that you do?

WAUGH: Well, of course, the truth is that one doesn't look on them as individuals when you're travelling. You know they are individuals, but if you're just in a town, say, in Morocco watching a religious festival, you're simply enjoying a spectacle as someone might like going to the theatre.

INTERVIEWER: You're enjoying a spectacle, apart from the festival itself, of crowds, and yet crowds you don't like.

WAUGH: Well, I shouldn't really wish to be mixed up in the crowd of people slashing themselves with daggers and going into ecstatic frenzies, you know. I'd sooner be in an upper window looking down on them.

INTERVIEWER: You like, in fact, generally speaking to be in an upper window looking down?

WAUGH: If it's a matter of crowds, I like the spectacle of a strange crowd, not the contact of a familiar one.

[. . .]

INTERVIEWER: Can you tell me this? Are you yourself as an individual conscious of any particular failing of yourself?

WAUGH: I mean, are you asking me to confess to some moral lapse, or to inadequacy in talent?

INTERVIEWER: Well I should like to ask you to confess to some particular moral lapse, but what I really mean is what – in what respect do you as a human being feel that you have primarily failed?

WAUGH: I've never learned French well, and I've never learned any other language at all. I've forgotten most of my classics; I can't often remember people's faces in the streets, and I don't like music. Those are very grave failings.

INTERVIEWER: But no others – you're not conscious of?

WAUGH: Those are the ones that worry me most.

3
'The Real Mr Pinfold'

Frances Donaldson and her husband Jack were friends and neighbours of the Waugh family. This account of the 'real Mr Pinfold' arose from their close involvement in the Pinfold story on Waugh's return to England.

We were present on the periphery of the events on which Evelyn founded *The Ordeal of Gilbert Pinfold*. When I first read this novel I noticed that it differed in many respects from what I cannot help regarding as the real story. Since the major events took place in Evelyn's mind there is for that part of it no real story, but there was, nevertheless, a sequence of actual events leading up to and away from the period of mental disturbance which he described in the book, and secondly there was the version he told himself at the time. There were also some details of his recovery recounted by Laura in his presence, with which he did not argue. When I read *Pinfold* I was disappointed because in my view the version he gave there was less interesting and less amusing than the story as we knew it. From that day until after I had written this account I had not re-read the novel and, although I could remember what he left out of the book, I could not be sure what he put in. I propose here, in the interests of an eye-witness account, to describe the events as I remember them regardless of the fact that some parts of my story have been wonderfully better told by Evelyn himself.

[. . .]

Evelyn suffered permanently and terribly from insomnia. He strove against this affliction in many ways. At one time for quite a long period he used to get up in the early hours and shave. He said that his smooth face on the smooth pillow induced sleep. But in the main he had to rely on drugs, and, since in matters that concerned himself he was completely reckless, as he acquired resistance he increased the dose.

He employed in those days – it would not be accurate to say he was attended by, because he seldom saw him – a doctor whose practice was in a neighbouring town, and whom he referred to as 'My Medical Adviser', conversationally the 'MA'. The MA was a nervous man who at that time had great troubles of his own. He was terrified of Evelyn as was another local doctor who attended the children and who had once been reproved for entering the house by opening the door and walking in when he had failed to get an immediate answer to the bell. These things may or may not account for the fact that Evelyn was able to acquire unlimited quantities of a sleeping draught containing bromide and chloral. I am almost sure he had more than one source of supply.

In the winter of 1953 he suffered from pain, diagnosed, I believe, as rheumatism, and he was unusually ill and melancholy. He resorted to the bromide and chloral as a pain-killer by day as well as a sleep-inducer by night, and over a period of about six weeks he absorbed poisonously large quantities. Then after Christmas he departed, as he invariably did at this time of year, on his travels. On this occasion he took ship for Colombo. It throws a light on subsequent events and on Evelyn's character that he left the bromide and chloral behind him.

A week or so after he left, Laura came to our house and told us she was horribly worried about him. She asked for our word that what she was about to say would go no further, and then for Jack's help. She said that Evelyn had seemed very ill and melancholy when he left, but that, since with every day he spent at home he became worse, she had let him go, believing that nothing but the change would cure him. She then read to us selected parts of several letters she had received from him. In these letters he said that travelling on the ship with him there was a party of 'existentialists' who had perfected a form of long-range telepathy. For some reason of which he was not aware, he had incurred their hostility and they were using their unusual gift to persecute him. It had begun by his being plagued by the sound of his name in the air and, at night when he went to bed, by half-heard conversations in which his name constantly occurred and which seemed at first to come from the next door cabin. Soon he was allowed no respite from these voices by day or night and he was quite unable to sleep. The last of the letters was written from a hotel in Cairo and said that he had left the ship and intended to continue his journey over land in order to escape from his enemies. It was this letter which brought Laura to see us. Evelyn said that he had had twenty-four hours peace in the hotel in Cairo but on the second day the voices had mockingly resumed their continuous conversation and their extraordinary power seemed in no way diminished through separation by miles of ocean. He referred to a neighbour who believed in the ministration of 'the Box' – a matter which had earned his amusement and scorn – and said that he now believed he had been wrong in dismissing so easily the possibility of this kind of long-distance control. Then he apologized for the incoherence of his expression. It was not very easy, he said, to write coherently when every sentence you wrote was immediately repeated by a bodiless voice.

This is all I remember of his letters, and I think it was all that at that time he said. But it was enough. Not merely the matter but the manner of these letters was so totally unlike Evelyn – the sadly apologetic air, the defeated spirit. Only the handwriting convinced one they were written by him.

Laura said she felt someone must go and fetch him back. She had thought it over and believed it must be a man, partly in case Evelyn was getting into trouble, but chiefly because – in spite of the dispirited letters – he might be belligerently unwilling to accept this kind of interference. She asked Jack if he would go.

It was immediately arranged that she should give him a cheque for a sufficient sum of money and that he would take the first aeroplane. But when he came to make the arrangements he found that he could not enter Colombo without a certificate of inoculation against typhoid – a paper which takes ten days to obtain. We considered whether he should nevertheless go and either bribe or force his way in, a thing Laura said Evelyn had often done in the past in other countries. Finally it was decided that both he and Laura should have the first of the injections and go together before the second only if it seemed absolutely necessary. Before the period was up Evelyn solved the difficulty by announcing by cable that he was on his way home.

When Laura asked Jack to go she warned us that she thought it possible that, when Evelyn recovered his mind, he might be so angry that she had confided in us that it would spoil our friendship forever. Consequently, when she went to London to meet him we did not expect to hear, unless privately from her, any news of either of them for several weeks. When she discussed with me what she was going to say and do when she met him, I felt very much frightened, because she proposed to behave as one would to a person who is sane, whereas it seemed to me that Evelyn was quite clearly insane. I thought her approach should be more tentative and more subtle. However, she was immovable in her opinion.

Two, or possibly three, days later, to our intense surprise we received a message saying that the Waughs were on their way back to Piers Court and Evelyn wished us to go to dinner.

When we walked into the room there he was, looking extremely thin, which suited him, but otherwise apparently perfectly normal and in the highest good spirits. He greeted Jack with some words showing that he knew of the typhoid inoculation.

'A thing,' he said, 'I would do for no man.'

Then between them they told us this story.

As Laura walked up the stairs of the Hyde Park Hotel she heard a voice ask in a high, unrecognizable squeak whether she had yet arrived. She looked up and to her surprise saw Evelyn. She said that his voice was distorted by disuse, because for weeks he had spoken to no one. I have no idea whether this is a likely effect.

As soon as they reached their bedroom Evelyn began to tell Laura what had happened to him. He said that on board ship there had been a family named Black. The father of this family was someone they knew. He was the man who had interrogated him in a broadcast interview he had recently given. This man had a wife, a son and a daughter and the whole family used the infernal powers he had told her about to persecute him. Only the daughter showed any mercy, and she at times seemed to pity him. This girl he told Laura they also knew. She was engaged to a young man – he mentioned the name – who lived in Wotton-under-Edge and who had brought her to luncheon at Piers Court.

'But Evelyn,' Laura objected, 'that girl's name wasn't Black, it was So-and-So, and she had nothing to do with the BBC man.'

Laura said that when she said this Evelyn saw almost at once it was true. He reacted to this startling piece of information in the manner of the sane. They discussed the details for some time and Laura tried to persuade him that he had been ill and must see a doctor. Very well, he replied, but before doing so they would test other links in his story. He took command of the situation, devised a plan and told Laura how to carry it out. On his instructions she telephoned to the BBC and asked to speak to Mr Black. To her horror the answering voice said that Mr Black was at present away. She asked where he was and when he was expected to return, and then she was told that he had been in hospital for some weeks and, although he was recovering from his illness, it was not yet known when he would return.

So much for Mr and Miss Black. Yet Evelyn could still hear their voices. They decided at this point to ask Father Caraman to come round to advise them and, when he arrived, they told him the whole of this story. Father Caraman sent at once for the late E. B. Strauss, a psycho-analyst who was also a Roman Catholic. Strauss said, and later other doctors confirmed this view, that Evelyn was suffering from the quantities of chloral he had absorbed in the weeks before he went away. He said that if he had eaten and slept properly he would have quickly recovered. But in all these weeks Evelyn had been unable either to eat or sleep. Strauss proceeded to ensure him a night's rest by administering a different drug – paraldehyde – and he persuaded him to eat. Now here he was still, he said, occasionally and faintly hearing the voices but otherwise entirely recovered.

Up to this point the story had been told, with interruptions, by Laura. Now Evelyn took it over.

His behaviour seemed to us extraordinary and as usual completely unexpected. Laura, who in my opinion is the only person who has ever had the slightest idea of how Evelyn really thought and felt, had believed that he might be irreconcilably put against us by the knowledge that we had been told of his misfortunes. But on the contrary he seemed not merely in the highest good humour, but apparently extremely pleased with himself. He had the air of someone who has brought off an unexpected coup or discovered in himself some unsuspected gift. I, who have what I believe to be a normal horror of madness, was much relieved that chloral and not inherent weakness had caused the mental aberration through which he had passed. But Evelyn, then and ever after, chose to behave as though he had had a true mental breakdown. Either immediately before we saw him or soon afterwards he met a woman friend in London who said:

'Oh, Evelyn, I hear you've been ill. I hope you are better.'

Evelyn burst into laughter and replied: 'I know that Laura has been putting it about that I've been ill. But it isn't true. I've been off my head.'

[. . .]

Evelyn was always tremendously diverted by the spectacle of someone making an ass of himself. On this evening his illness was so close to him that it was still slightly upon him, and, if proof were needed for the genuineness of his suffering, we had it in his letters and on his thin face. Yet he told the story with a detachment and a mockery that if he had been speaking of some other person would have seemed, as he often did seem, inhumanly cruel and insensitive. It was not merely that the element of self-pity was entirely missing; although he had recovered his senses only two or three days before, he quite clearly regarded his misadventures as outrageously funny.

[. . .]

He began as he had in his letters and as I think he also did in *Pinfold* by saying that he had at first believed that there were some people in the next cabin who were deliberately trying to annoy him. He could not completely hear their conversation but he could hear that his name again and again recurred. During the night this continued and he was unable to sleep. He had resolved to ignore this – very unlike him – until he recognized some words of his own and he realized that copies of some cables he had sent to England were being read out loud. Then he went to the Captain.

He told the Captain that in the cabin next to his there was a family who interfered with his peace. He would not have complained about this but he felt that one ought to be able to put complete trust in the discretion of the radio operator. He was sorry to have to say it, but copies of cables he had sent to England had been passed to this family.

The Captain replied to this with complete gravity and courtesy. He said there was only one family on board ship and they were not in a cabin anywhere near Evelyn's. He suggested that they go together to interview the radio operator. This they did and the Captain asked the operator for copies of the cables Evelyn had sent to England. The operator replied that he had sent only one, on the first day out. He produced a copy of this cable which was addressed to Laura and merely said that he was well.

Evelyn believed the Captain and the operator, but, as he had to account for the voices which grew louder and more persistent, he then evolved the theory of long-range telepathy. He also went to the bar in an effort to meet the one mysterious family. Here he met 'Mr Black' whom he recognized immediately as an enemy, his wife, his son and his daughter, whom only later when she began to take pity on him did he recognize as the girl who had come to luncheon. While he was with them they talked normally in their own voices and telepathically in their persecuting voices, and he realized he was up against a fiendish combination.

This conversation took place more than ten years ago and I cannot remember it in detail. There were, however, three set pieces.

In the first Evelyn had become convinced from words overheard that a serious attempt to harm him was to be made at night in his cabin. Dressed in his pyjamas and a coat with a stick in his hand – I think with a bowler hat on his head but Jack cannot remember this – he waited throughout the night outside his cabin door, lonely, and brave, to repel the expected attack. Nothing happened.

In the second, unable to sleep, he wandered alone on the deck again at night. He became aware that in the silence a group of people were taking part in some great activity. Lurking, preposterous in his pyjamas, in the background, he watched a ship draw alongside and he saw the Captain of his own ship in command of a small party of men transfer to the other ship a stretcher which held a dead body. The following morning he congratulated the Captain on the efficiency of the operation.

The third concerned his partial triumph over the voices. He believed by the time he flew home and before he met Laura that he was already beginning to recover, and with the first strength he could command he began the counter-attack. The weapon he chose and the success which attended his efforts provided the most grotesque incident of all. In or near Stinchcombe there lived at that time a beautiful and charming old maiden lady. On Sunday mornings, after she had attended matins in the Anglican church and the Waughs' mass in the Roman Catholic one she used often to call at Piers Court for a glass of sherry. Evelyn now discovered that the family Black were in some way related to this old lady and he threatened them with exposure of their persecution to her. Soon he had them cowering in fear and begging him not to proceed to this horrible reprisal. Evelyn acted these scenes of their fear and his dominating use of this powerful name, and the humour of the situation lay in the fact that, in the sense that they had appeared to him, these things were true. Evelyn, the merciless, thrice-armed, self-reliant terror of the sane world had, in his insanity, adopted for his shield this gentle, ineffectual old lady.

I asked him whether the Captain of the ship had seemed glad to be rid of him, and he replied that, if so, he had been unaware of it. He had been treated with kindness and courtesy. Only one incident had struck him as odd. While in Ceylon he had run into a young man who had been on the ship. This young man had looked at him sorrowfully and asked him if he was feeling better. Evelyn who was not aware of having been ill could not understand his concern.

Since writing the preceding words I have re-read *Pinfold*. It is tempting to correct the mistakes of memory, but there is the consideration that, to anyone who has knowledge of such things, a memory completely accurate over a period of twelve years is even more suspect than one that is normally fallible.

So first of all, here is a small point: the MA was the Medical Attendant not the Medical Adviser. Secondly, I incline to think there was no bowler hat. But, far more difficult to explain away, Evelyn in *Pinfold* gives not merely an accurate but a lovingly lavish description of the intake of bromide and chloral. Having explained to the chemist that it is a waste of bottle space for him to dilute the mixture with water when this can so easily be done at home, Mr Pinfold mixes it neat with Crème de Menthe and sloshes it down whenever the inclination takes him; whereas I had believed that he went off his head without the aid of any outside agency. However, I seem not to be alone in this mistake. Evelyn's son says, 'When my father was eventually driven mad by the jackals snarling and whining around his ankles . . . All the malicious sneers . . . directed at him in his lifetime came home to roost until, by an iron effort of the will, he sent them back to Fleet Street and the obituary columns.'

But Evelyn made no iron effort of will – although by nature he was entirely capable of it – he simply ceased to overdose himself with chloral and recovered when the effects of it had left his body. I think the misapprehension is due to two things. The first is that, although he wrote accurately of what had happened, conversationally he always preferred to treat his experience as a short period of madness. Secondly, it may be that most people are not aware of the effect of strong doses of chloral. Evelyn himself knew all about it because in his youth he wrote a life of Rossetti.

In all other respects my memory is pedestrianly accurate.

[. . .]

The wash-hand stand designed by William Burges with panels painted by Sir Edward Poynton was given him by John Betjeman and when it was delivered he did go through all these motions of trying to recover a tap which existed only in his imagination. However, at the time, although we were very much amused by the story of his aberration, it did not occur to us – at any rate not to Jack and me – that it was sufficiently abnormal to suggest mental disturbance. It often happens that people remember things wrongly, even things they have liked very much and examined very closely. It is more usual to forget details than to invent them but we were accustomed to the ceaseless working of Evelyn's imagination. For instance, on one occasion, years before this time, he had been very anxious that we should all go together to see the film of *Monsieur Verdoux* in Dursley because he had enjoyed it so much in London. As we came out of the cinema at the end of the film, Laura, Jack and I spoke of it with pleasure, saying how amusing we had found it. Evelyn was deeply disappointed. He said that so many of the funniest scenes he remembered had, on this occasion, not been there.

Nevertheless, on the second reading I still find *Pinfold* a disappointing book. It starts admittedly with some of the most brilliant pages he ever wrote – astonishing both for the extent of the revelations and the quality of the writing – but from the moment Mr Pinfold arrives on the boat I find his story, though similar in detail, infinitely less moving than the one that Evelyn told to us. The figure that he described on his return home, baffled and lonely but bravely battling against unknown and uncontrollable forces, had a true affinity with all the best tragi-comic creations in history – Charlie Chaplin at once springs to mind. Then too the Captain in this story was throughout a grave and courteous person, accepting politely Evelyn's revelations about his radio operator and his mysterious congratulations on the efficiency of some unaccomplished naval operation, while the daughter of the persecuting family was an innocent maiden moved by pity for the sufferings of a stranger. In *Pinfold* the Captain is at one moment a torturer with a female accomplice whose counterpart can be found in most thrillers from Sapper's *Bulldog Drummond* to Ian Fleming's *From Russia With Love*, while the daughter's interest in Pinfold is of a sexual and, to me, embarrassing kind.

It is clearly possible that the second is the 'true' story and that there were details of his experience which Evelyn did not care to describe to us. Equally there are indications in the book that the novelist is practising his art which support my view that the real happenings differed from those related there. Here is an example. Evelyn invariably and rather maliciously referred to people whose English name might have been derived from some German or Jewish equivalent by what he conceived to have been the original. Anyone whose name ended in 'don' or 'ston' or 'den' always received a rich and lingering 'stein', while Waterman, for instance, might become Wasserman. In one of the scenes of the persecution of Mr Pinfold the bullying voices insist that his real name is Peinfeld and that he is a German and a Jew. It is difficult to see how this can be anything but a later invention when one remembers that the real sufferer from these unreal assailants had a good Scottish name impossible to distort in this way.

Probably his experiences were too blurred and too diffuse to do more than inspire *The Ordeal of Gilbert Pinfold* and Evelyn naturally used his gifts to improve the theme he had so painfully acquired. It would not have disturbed him in the least to know that I thought he had failed.

4

'Awake My Soul! It is a Lord'

This article was written in response to an attempted invasion of Waugh's country privacy by Nancy Spain, a Beaverbrook journalist, and Lord Noel-Buxton. Waugh perceived the Beaverbrook press to be engaged in a conspiracy to belittle him.

'*I'm not on business. I'm a member of the House of Lords.*' These moving and rather mysterious words were uttered on my doorstep the other evening and recorded by the leading literary critic of the Beaverbrook press. They have haunted me, waking and sleeping, ever since. I am sometimes accused of a partiality for lords; whatever touches them, it is hinted, vicariously touches me. Certainly the nobleman who tried to insinuate himself into my house half an hour before dinner that evening, has become a nine days' obsession.

[. . .]

But to explain his presence. The popular papers, I conceive, are fitfully and uneasily aware that there are spheres of English life in which they hold a negligible influence. The fifty or sixty thousand people in this country who alone support the Arts, do not go to Lord Beaverbrook's critics for guidance. So it is that artists of all kinds form part of the battle-training of green reporters. 'Don't lounge about the office, lad,' the editors say, 'sit up and insult an artist.' Rather frequently writers, among others, are troubled by the telephone asking for interviews. When these are refused, the journalist goes to what in a newspaper office is lightly called 'the library', takes the file of his predecessors' mis-statements, copies it out, adds a few of his own, and no one suffers except the readers of the popular press, who must, I should think, be getting bored with the recitation of old, false anecdotes. That is the normal routine – unless there is a lord handy, who is not subject to the conventions of the trade.

On the morning of the visit my wife said: 'An *Express* reporter and a lord wanted to come and see you this afternoon.'

'You told them not to?'

'Of course.'

'What lord?'

'Noel someone.'

'Has Noël Coward got a peerage? I'd like to see him.'

'No, it wasn't anyone I had heard of.'

There, I supposed, the matter ended. But that evening, just as I was going to prepare myself for dinner, I heard an altercation at the front door. My poor wife, weary from the hay-field, was being kept from her bath by a forbidding pair.

The lady of the party, Miss Spain, has recorded in two columns their day's doings. They were on what she called a 'pilgrimage'. This took them, uninvited, to tea with the Poet Laureate. 'Lord Noel-Buxton just walked into the house,' she writes, while she trampled the hay. The poet was 'silent, dreaming back in the past', thinking, no doubt, that in all his years before the mast he had never met such tough customers. He gave them oat-cake. Then he brightened, 'his blue eyes danced'. The old 'darling' had thought of a way out. He urged them on to me. ' "See you? Of course he'll see you." ' On they came to the village where I live which, curiously, they found to be a 'straggly collection of prefabricated houses' (there is not one in the place), and entered the pub, where they got into talk with its rustic patrons. I have since made inquiries and learn that they somehow gave the impression that they were touts for television. Members of the village band sought to interest them in their music, and the cordiality, thus mistakenly engendered, emboldened the two pilgrims. They attempted to effect an entry into my house and wrangled until I dismissed them in terms intelligible even to them.

Lord Noel-Buxton seems to have been unaware of having done anything odd. 'Oh, Nancy, do stop!' he is said to have cried, when I went out to see that they were not slipping round to suck up to the cook. 'He's coming to apologize.'

A faulty appreciation.

What, I have been asking myself ever since, was Lord Noel-Buxton's part in the escapade? He is not, I have established, on the pay-roll of the *Daily Express*. All he seems to have got out of it is a jaunt in a motorcar, an oat-cake and a novel he can hardly hope to understand. Who, in the popular phrase, does he think he is?

Well, I looked him up and find that he is the second generation of one of Ramsay MacDonald's creation. To the student of social stratification this is significant. Is there, in our midst, unregarded, a new social sub-class? The men who bought peerages from Lloyd George believed they were founding aristocratic houses, and there was, indeed, then a reasonable supposition that a generation or two of inherited wealth might refine the descendants of the gross originators. But the men who were put into ermine by MacDonald believed that the order they were entering was doomed. That statesman's bizarre appointments in the Church of England are eliminated by time, but the Upper House stands and the peerages he created survive. Are there, I wonder, many such orphans of the storm which blew itself out? Here, at any rate, was one specimen in full plumage on my doorstep.

I asked a secretarial agency, who sometimes helps me, to find out something about him. All they could say was that he is not strong, poor fellow, and was invalided out of the Territorial Army at the beginning of the war. Now, when he is not on a literary pilgrimage, he appears to spend much time paddling in rivers.

He clearly cannot have met many other lords. Students of *Punch* know that from the Eighties of the past century until the Thirties of this there was a standing joke about the distressed descendants of Crusaders who were reduced to retail trade. Now the thing is commonplace; not perhaps at the Co-operative Stores where, presumably, Lord Noel-Buxton does his shopping; but it is hard to believe that nowhere in the purlieus of the Upper House has he ever been approached with an advantageous offer of wine or clothing. But we must believe it. 'I'm not on business. I'm a member of the House of Lords.' The two ideas, in the mind of this naive nobleman, are axiomatically irreconcilable.

We have many sorts of lord in our country: lords haughty, who think that commoners all seek their acquaintance and must be kept at a distance; lords affable, who like mixing with their fellow-men of all degrees and know the conventions of good society by which introductions are effected; lords lavish and leisurely and dead-broke lords eager to earn an honest living. In Lord Noel-Buxton we see the lord predatory. He appears to think that his barony gives him the right to a seat at the dinner-table in any private house in the kingdom.

Fear of this lord is clearly the beginning of wisdom.

5
'What Was Wrong With Pinfold'

J. B. Priestley's celebrated review of Pinfold *has been largely derided, most notably by Waugh (in the Appendix item that follows). But it contains enough woundingly pertinent material to have elicited Waugh's unusual response in the first place.*

Mr Evelyn Waugh's semi-autobiographical novel, *The Ordeal of Gilbert Pinfold*, has been both sharply attacked and enthusiastically praised. Literary criticism is not our concern here, but perhaps I ought to add that I liked the beginning of the story, was prepared to admire the general plan of it, but found the hallucination scenes aboard ship rather crude and tedious, quite without the nightmare quality I had expected to find in them. This surprised me in a writer I have long admired – and indeed I was one of the very first to shout his praises – a novelist of originality, great technical skill, and personal distinction. I came to the conclusion that in these scenes he had got himself bogged down somewhere between reality and invention: reality, because he was describing more or less what had happened to himself; invention, because he had decided, perhaps hastily at the last moment, to substitute imaginary imaginary voices for the imaginary voices he himself seemed to hear; and that this would explain why, being hasty substitutions, they seem far below his usual level of creation and invention. But all this is guesswork. And it is not Mr Waugh but Gilbert Pinfold who is the subject of this essay.

Pinfold, we are told, is a middle-aged novelist of some distinction. He is well known abroad, where foreign students write theses on his work. He lives in an old house in the country, where his wife, who is younger than he is, farms their property. He has a large young family. He no longer travels widely as he used to do, and now pays only infrequent visits to London, though he is still a member of 'Bellamy's Club'.

[. . .]

His wife is a born Catholic and he is a convert. His days, we are told, are passed in writing, reading and managing his own small affairs. He lives as he wants to live and, unlike most people nowadays, is perfectly contented with his lot.

Nevertheless, he drinks a good deal, indeed rather too much. And because he sleeps badly he finds himself taking larger and larger doses of an opiate or sedative that he keeps mixed with Crème de Menthe, a remedy based on an old prescription. So it is a boozy and half-doped Pinfold who finds his way, not without difficulty, to the cabin he has booked for a three-week voyage to the East. It is in this cabin that he begins to hear the voices that torment him, belonging to persecutors who have no existence, who are creations of his own unconscious. For the benefit of Jungians, it may be added that both the Shadow and the Anima are busily engaged in these spectral intrigues. Poor Pinfold finds himself in a kind of waking nightmare, out of which he does not emerge until he returns home. The local doctor tells him he has been the victim of the bromide and chloral he has been swigging so heartily. We leave him, safe and cosy again in his study, ready to start work, but preferring to his unfinished novel a more urgent piece: *The Ordeal of Gilbert Pinfold*.

But if Pinfold imagines his troubles are over, he is a fool. He has been warned. Because the voices talked a lot of rubbish, making the most ridiculous accusations, he is ignoring the underlying truth uniting them all, the idea that he is not what he thinks he is, that he is busy deceiving both himself and other people. Consciously he has rejected this idea for some time; he has drowned it in alcohol, bromide and chloral; and now it can only batter its way through to him by staging a crude drama of lunatic voices. And though they are a long way from the truth in their detailed charges, they are right, these voices, when they tell him that he is a fake. It is of course Pinfold remonstrating with Pinfold; the fundamental self telling the ego not to be a mountebank. What is on trial here is the Pinfold *persona*. This *persona* is inadequate: the drink hinted at it; the dope more than suggested it; the voices proved it.

The style of life deliberately adopted by Pinfold is that of those old Catholic landed families, whose women live for the children and the home farm and whose men, except in wartime when, like Pinfold, they are ready to defend their country, detach themselves from the national life, behaving from choice as their ancestors were compelled to do from necessity, because of their religion. Everything we learn about Pinfold fits this style of life – with one supremely important exception, the fact, the obstinate fact, that he is by profession a writer, an artist. And this is the central truth about Pinfold, who could never have achieved any distinction as a novelist if he had not been essentially an artist. He is not a Catholic landed gentleman pretending to be an author. He is an author pretending to be a Catholic landed gentleman. But why, you may ask, should he not be both? Because they are not compatible. And this is not merely my opinion. It is really Pinfold's opinion too.

Though Pinfold may imagine he has achieved a style of life that suits him perfectly, his behaviour shows that he is wrong. Take the heavy drinking. Some men drink a lot because their work demands that they should appear to be easy and affable with persons they rather dislike; other men do it because they are natually gregarious and like to lap it up with the boys; others again, like some politicians, journalists, actors, take to booze because their days and nights are a difficult mixture of boring waits and sudden crises. But Pinfold belongs to none of these groups. He is a solitary soaker, hoping to deaden his mind against reality. This explains too his reckless traffic with opiates and sedatives. Anything is better than lying awake at three in the morning, when the *persona* is transparent and brittle. So in the end the voices arrive. Their accusations are absurd, monstrous; he is an alien who has changed his name, a homosexual, a traitor, a would-be-murderer; always they miss the mark, perhaps deliberately overshooting at it, as if there could be a deception even in these attempts to end deception; nevertheless, they are telling him he is not what he pretends to be. And if they stopped clowning and, perhaps with his consent, spoke plainly, they would say: 'Pinfold, you are a professional writer, a novelist, an artist, so stop pretending you represent some obscure but arrogant landed family that never had an idea in its head'.

Pinfold has to do some writing, from time to time, otherwise he could not earn a living. And when he is in the middle of a book he behaves like an artist, breaking the country gentleman pattern; but such times

> were a small part of his year. On most nights he was neither fretful nor apprehensive. He was merely bored. After even the idlest day he demanded six or seven hours of insensibility. With them behind him, with them to look forward to, he could face another idle day with something approaching jauntiness; and these his doses unfailingly provided . . .

This is very revealing. When he is not working, Pinfold is bored because his *persona* is inadequate, because the role he has condemned himself to play is too sketchy and empty, because the intellectual and artist in him feel frustrated and starved. An author is not an author only when he is writing. Genuine authorship, to which Pinfold, who is no hack, is committed, is just as much a way of life as farming or soldiering. It is one of the vocations. This is why, at a time when most people are demanding more and more for their goods and services, the author can safely be offered less, for it is an open secret, no matter what he may say, that he is in love with his trade. If the worst came to the worst, he would take a clerkship at the gasworks and pay out of his savings to be printed.

What we may call *Pinfolding* – the artist elaborately pretending not to be an artist – is an old trick here in England, thanks to our aristocratic tradition and our public suspicion of intellect and the arts. [. . .] It saves us from the solemn posturing we have observed among our foreign colleagues, who are more portentous about a short review than we could be about an epic creation. We avoid the *Cher Maître* touch. Yet I think the Continental attitude, for all its pomposity, extravagance, incitement to charlatanry, is saner, healthier, better for both the arts and the nation, than ours is. If authors and artists in this country are not only officially regarded without favour but even singled out for unjust treatment – as I for one believe – then the Pinfolds are partly to blame. They not only do not support their profession: they go over to the enemy. Congreve may have shrugged away his reputation as a poet and dramatist, but at least he identified himself with a class from which were drawn the chief patrons of poetry and the drama, whereas the Pinfolds are hiding themselves among fox-hunters, pheasant slaughterers, horse and cattle breeders.

Let Pinfold take warning. He will break down again, and next time may never find a way back to his study. The central self he is trying to deny, that self which grew up among books and authors and not among partridges and hunters, that self which even now desperately seeks expression in ideas and words, will crack if it is walled up again within a false style of life. Whatever Mrs Pinfold and the family and the neighbours may think and say, Pinfold must step out of his role as the Cotswold gentleman quietly regretting the Reform Bill of 1832, and if he cannot discover an accepted role as English man of letters – and I admit this is not easy – he must create one, hoping it will be recognizable. He must be at all times the man of ideas, the intellectual, the artist, even if he is asked to resign from Bellamy's Club. If not; if he settles down again to sulk and soak behind that inadequate *persona*, waiting for a message from Bonnie Prince Charlie; then not poppy, nor mandragora, nor all the drowsy syrups of the world, shall ever medicine him.

6

'Anything Wrong with Priestley?'

This is Waugh's response (in the right-of-centre Spectator*) to Priestley's review (in the left-of-centre* New Statesman*). Readers can judge for themselves who, if anyone, comes best out of the exchange.*

In the *New Statesman* of August 31 Mr J. B. Priestley published an article entitled 'What was wrong with Pinfold?' 'Pinfold', I should explain, is the name I gave to the leading character of my last book, a confessedly autobiographical novel which had already been reviewed (very civilly) in the literary columns of that curiously two-faced magazine. The contrast is notorious between the Jekyll of culture, wit and ingenious competitions and the Hyde of querulous atheism and economics which prefaces it. Mr Priestley's article appeared in Hyde's section. He is not concerned to help me with my writing, as he is so well qualified to do, but to admonish me about the state of my soul, a subject on which I cannot allow him complete mastership. With 'Let Pinfold take warning' he proclaims in prophetic tones, and with the added authority of some tags from Jung, that I shall soon go permanently off my rocker. The symptoms are that I try to combine two incompatible roles, those of the artist and the Catholic country gentleman.

Which of those dangers to the artistic life, I wonder, does he regard as the more deadly. Not living in the country, surely? Unless I am misinformed Mr Priestley was at my age a landed proprietor on a scale by which my own modest holding is a peasant's patch.

Catholicism? It is true that my Church imposes certain restrictions which Mr Priestley might find irksome, but he must have observed that a very large number of his fellow writers profess a creed and attempt to follow a moral law which are either Roman Catholic or, from a Jungian point of view, are almost identical. Mr T. S. Eliot, Dame Edith Sitwell, Mr Betjeman, Mr Graham Greene, Miss Rose Macaulay – the list is illustrious and long. Are they all heading for the bin?

No, what gets Mr Priestley's goat (supposing he allows such a deleterious animal in his lush pastures) is my attempt to behave like a gentleman. Mr Priestley has often hinted at a distaste for the upper classes but, having early adopted the *persona* of a generous-hearted, genial fellow, he has only once, I think, attempted to portray them. On that occasion, of which more later, he showed a rather remote acquaintance, like Dickens in creating Sir Mulberry Hawke. It is the strain of minding his manners that is driving poor Pinfold cuckoo. 'He must,' writes Mr Priestley, 'be at all times the man of ideas, the intellectual, the artist, even if he is asked to resign from Bellamy's Club' (a fictitious institution that occurs in some of my books). Mr Priestley's clubs must be much stricter than mine. Where I belong I never heard of the committee inquiring into the members' 'ideas'. It is true that we are forbidden to cheat at cards or strike the servants, but for the life of me I can't see anything particularly artistic in either of those activities.

Naturally I hunger for Mr Priestley's good opinion and would like to keep my sanity for a few more years. I am an old dog to learn new tricks but I dare say I could be taught an accent at a school of elocution. I should not find it beyond me to behave like a cad on occasions – there are several shining examples in the literary world. My hair grows strongly still; I could wear it long. I could hire a Teddyboy suit and lark about the dance halls with a bicycle chain. But would this satisfy Mr Priestley? Would he not be quick to detect and denounce this new *persona*? 'There was Waugh,' he would say, 'a man of humane education and accustomed to polite society. Tried to pass as Redbrick. No wonder he's in the padded cell.'

I do not flatter myself that Mr Priestley's solicitude springs solely from love of me. What, I think, really troubles him is that by my manner of life I am letting down the side, all eleven of them whoever they are whom Mr Priestley captains. 'If authors and artists in this country,' he writes, 'are not only officially regarded without favour but even singled out for unjust treatment – as I for one believe – then the Pinfolds are partly to blame. They not only do not support their profession; they go over to the enemy.'

I say, Priestley old man, are you sure you are feeling all right? Any voices? I mean to say! No narcotics or brandy in your case, I know, but when a chap starts talking about 'the enemy' and believing, for one, that he is singled out for unjust treatment, isn't it time he consulted his Jungian about his *anima*? Who is persecuting poor Mr Priestley? Mr Macmillan does not ask him to breakfast as Gladstone might have done. His income, like everyone else's, is confiscated and 'redistributed' in the Welfare State. Tennyson's life was made hideous by importunate admirers; Mr Priestley can walk down Piccadilly with a poppy or a lily, but he will be unmolested by the mob who pursue television performers. Is this what Mr Priestley means by unjust treatment? Pinfold, he says, is vainly waiting for a message from Bonnie Prince Charlie. Is it possible that Mr Priestley is awaiting a summons to Windsor from Queen Victoria?

Mr Priestley is an older, richer, more popular man than I, but I cannot forbear saying: 'Let him take warning.' He has had some sharp disappointments in the last twelve years; perhaps he would call them 'traumas'. The voices he hears, like Pinfold's, may be those of a wildly distorted conscience. There was, indeed, a *trahison des clercs* some twenty years back which has left the literary world much discredited. It was then that the astute foresaw the social revolution and knew who would emerge top dog. They went to great lengths to suck up to the lower classes or, as they called it, to 'identify themselves with the workers'. Few excelled Mr Priestley in his zeal for social justice. It is instructive to re-read his powerful novel *Blackout in Gretley*, which was written at a very dark time in the war when national unity was of vital importance. Its simple theme is that the English upper classes were in conspiracy to keep the workers in subjection even at the cost of national defeat. The villain, Tarlington, is everything deplorable, a man of good family and of smart appearance, a Conservative, the director of an engineering works, a courageous officer in 1914 – and, of course, a German spy.

[. . .]

'This country has the choice during the next two years,' a virtuous character says, 'of coming fully to life and beginning all over again or of rapidly decaying and dying on the same old feet. It can only accomplish the first by taking a firm grip on about fifty thousand important, influential gentlemanly persons and telling them firmly to shut up and do nothing if they don't want to be put to doing some most unpleasant work.'

Came the dawn. Mr Priestley was disappointed. No concentration camp was made for the upper classes. Nor have the triumphant workers shown themselves generous or discerning patrons of the arts. Gratitude, perhaps, is not one of their salient virtues. When they feel the need for a little aesthetic pleasure they do not queue at the experimental theatre; they pile into charabancs and tramp round the nearest collection of heirlooms and family portraits; quite enough to inflame the naked artist with an itch of persecution mania.

7

Excerpt from 'Face to Face'

John Freeman's television interviews were famous for reducing their subjects to tears. Waugh was well-prepared for the encounter. These excerpts from the 1960 interview centre on the Pinfold *story.*

FREEMAN: Could I ask you some questions now about *Pinfold*? The question that everybody broadly wants to ask you is how far *Pinfold* is an account of your own brief illness?

WAUGH: Almost exact. In fact, it had to be cut down a lot. It would be infinitely tedious to have recorded everything. It's the account of three weeks hallucinations going on absolutely continuously.

FREEMAN: And you heard voices?

WAUGH: I heard all these voices. If I'd written down everything the voices said, it would have been immensely boring. One had to be selective.

FREEMAN: But did they say the same thing to you that they said to Pinfold?

WAUGH: Oh yes, rather. Again and again and again, day and night.

FREEMAN: And there were three different kinds of voices really who talked to Pinfold; there was the beautiful girl who made appointments with him . . .

WAUGH: They gradually thinned down, if you remember the book. At first I conceived that everyone was involved – I was rationalizing it all the time, it was not in the least like losing one's reason, it was simply one's reason working hard on the wrong premises.

FREEMAN: Yes. But I wonder why the voices said what they did? I mean, have you any notion . . .

WAUGH: I always wondered that.

FREEMAN: . . . why you should conjure up this lovely girl who made appointments, and you never kept the appointment?

WAUGH: Half did – if you remember the story – went out to look for her and she wasn't there.

FREEMAN: And then the other, the most odious voice said that Pinfold was a homosexual, a communist Jew, parvenu and so on. Were these the kind of hallucinations that you yourself felt?

WAUGH: Oh yes, those were the voices exactly.

FREEMAN: And in your own life was it the neighbours who were making these remarks, because if you remember in *Pinfold* his neighbours were involved in this persecution.

WAUGH: I've no idea what my neighbours said about me!

FREEMAN: But did you feel that your neighbours were . . .

WAUGH: No. The whole thing was so puzzling I had to, if you remember, invent the theory that the Broadcasting Society – your own people – were involved.

FREEMAN: Well, I was going to ask you. Have you in fact a particular deep feeling about the BBC? (NO) Because it comes again into a number of your books, which is why I asked, always in a slightly pejorative context.

WAUGH: Well, everyone thinks ill of the BBC, but I don't think I'm more violent than anybody else.

FREEMAN: In the life that you've chosen to lead now – you lead the life of a country gentleman, almost a squirarchic life – do you get on happily with your neighbours?

WAUGH: Well, it's not really accurate to say I lead a squirarchic life. I mean, a squirarchic life means sitting on the bench of magistrates and going round cattle shows and that kind of thing. I lead a life of absolute solitude.

FREEMAN: You don't, in fact take part in the activities of your . . .

WAUGH: No. I live in the country because I like to be alone.

FREEMAN: Well now, you have made a very noticeable rejection of life, because this is not true – at one time you lived in the town, you mixed in society, you wrote books about society and now you've withdrawn completely. Were you conscious of a sudden decision to do that?

WAUGH: It happened about eight years ago, not suddenly but I suddenly got bored with – not suddenly, I gradually got bored with society, largely I think through deafness – and I can hear you perfectly, and I can hear one person perfectly, but if there's a crowd I get dazed: but I think it's probably psychosomatic because I don't hear because I'm bored, not I'm bored because I can't hear.

FREEMAN: Do you ever reflect on the difference between the sort of life you've chosen now and your own family background?

WAUGH: There's very little difference.

FREEMAN: Well, do you have people to stay with you constantly, do you still mix in the literary world?

WAUGH: I'm not as hospitable as my father was. He was always having people to stay.

FREEMAN: And do you miss that or not?

WAUGH: No.

FREEMAN: One wonders – this may sound rude but it genuinely arises out of the things you've said and the things you've written – one wonders whether this is in some curious way a kind of charade that you've decided to assume the attitude of country life, which in your books doesn't seem as if it's entirely natural to you.

WAUGH: It's quite true I haven't the smallest interest in country life, in the agricultural sense or the local government sense. The country to me is a place where I can be silent.

FREEMAN: Are you very sensitive to the criticisms of others – unkind reviews of your books?

WAUGH: I don't think so.

FREEMAN: I've often wondered, for instance, at the time in the middle of the thirties when you were assailed by – well, by Rose Macaulay and one or two others for being a fascist, because you reported the Abyssinian war from the Italian side – did that upset you or prey on your mind at all?

WAUGH: I wasn't even aware she assailed me.

FREEMAN: Well then, that's a very effective answer. Have you ever brooded on what appears to you to be unjust or adverse criticism?

WAUGH: No, I'm afraid if someone praises me I think what an ass and if they abuse me I think what an ass.

FREEMAN: And if they say nothing about you at all and take no notice of you?

WAUGH: That's the best I can hope for.

FREEMAN: You like that when it happens, do you? (YES) Why are you appearing in this programme?

WAUGH: Poverty. We've both been hired to talk in this deliriously happy way.

[. . .]

FREEMAN: I'd like now to ask you a last question and I want to go back to *Pinfold*. Looking back on that mental breakdown that you had then, and then your life as you see it – can you see that there's any permanent conflict or instability perhaps between the way of life in which you were brought up and the way of life in which you've chosen to live now?

WAUGH: Oh, I know what you're getting at, that ass Priestley said that in an article. I think I dealt with it in the *Spectator* – that's what you're thinking of. He wrote it in the *New Statesman* and I answered in the *Spectator*.

FREEMAN: Well, I was not particularly thinking of this but I was asking you whether you ever had any fear that that sort of thing may happen to you again?

WAUGH: No, no. That's poor old Priestley thought that.